To C...

Dedication

Janet Mullany

Enjoy!

Janet Mullany

A SIGNET BOOK

SIGNET
Published by New American Library, a division of
Penguin Group (USA) Inc., 375 Hudson Street,
New York, New York 10014, USA
Penguin Group (Canada), 90 Eglinton Avenue East, Suite 700, Toronto,
Ontario M4P 2Y3, Canada (a division of Pearson Penguin Canada Inc.)
Penguin Books Ltd., 80 Strand, London WC2R 0RL, England
Penguin Ireland, 25 St. Stephen's Green, Dublin 2,
Ireland (a division of Penguin Books Ltd.)
Penguin Group (Australia), 250 Camberwell Road, Camberwell, Victoria 3124,
Australia (a division of Pearson Australia Group Pty. Ltd.)
Penguin Books India Pvt. Ltd., 11 Community Centre, Panchsheel Park,
New Delhi - 110 017, India
Penguin Group (NZ), cnr Airborne and Rosedale Roads, Albany,
Auckland 1310, New Zealand (a division of Pearson New Zealand Ltd.)
Penguin Books (South Africa) (Pty.) Ltd., 24 Sturdee Avenue,
Rosebank, Johannesburg 2196, South Africa

Penguin Books Ltd., Registered Offices:
80 Strand, London WC2R 0RL, England

First published by Signet, an imprint of New American Library,
a division of Penguin Group (USA) Inc.

First Printing, September 2005
10 9 8 7 6 5 4 3 2 1

Copyright © Janet Mullany, 2005
All rights reserved

 REGISTERED TRADEMARK—MARCA REGISTRADA

Printed in the United States of America

*This book is dedicated to the memory
of my mother, Bea Dowling (1917–2003).*

ACKNOWLEDGMENTS

Big hugs and thanks to my fantastic critique group, the Tarts—Kathy Affeldt, Lisa Cochrane, Kate Dolan, Kathy Love, and Chris Zampi—who don't let me get away with anything. Additional thanks to *Dedication*'s first cheerleader, Bobbi Smith; both the Beau Monde (and the judges of the 2004 Royal Ascot Contest) and Maryland Romance Writers; the Wet Noodle Posse, otherwise known as the 2003 Golden Heart Finalists; Serena Jones, my editor at NAL; Gail Orgelfinger, who reads my stuff and helps me keep my life on track; the Romanticcritwits, especially Adrienne Regard, who asks the awkward questions and serves as resident horse expert; my online writing friends Sammi Hoard, Brenda Lewis, and Linda Easley; my long-lost but recently found friend Maureen Sarson; the Mullanys, in particular Rosie, for her enthusiasm and faith in my abilities; and my husband, Steve, for leaving me alone to write; and my daughter, Alison Hill, for providing me with solitude, nice cups of tea, and hot dinners during revisions.

Chapter One

As the rosy fingers of dawn touched the gloom of a sullen sky, a stranger might have been observed making his weary way toward the forbidding crags, loud with the cry of wolves and ravens, from which the tower of our story looms. Reader, tremble for Ludovico, the last of a mighty line of princes, for his troubles are hardly begun, and his adventures are to be horrid beyond all comprehension.
— *The Ruined Tower* by Mrs. Ravenwood.

London, 1813

*I*t was a devil of a way to celebrate his forty-third birthday. Adam Ashworth stood in the smoke-flecked dampness of early morning on the doorstep of Viscount Tillotson's London house and crashed the knocker again.

The door opened to reveal the viscount's butler, a leather apron over his uniform and a polishing cloth in one hand.

"His Lordship is not home, sir. If you would care to leave your card—"

"Balderdash," Adam said as he pushed past the man. "Tell him his guardian, Mr. Adam Ashworth, is here."

"Very well, sir." The butler, lips in a tight line of disapproval, took Adam's hat and gloves.

"And please tell him I am here on urgent business."

"It's all right, Simpson."

At the sound of his ward's voice, Adam breathed a sigh of relief.

Luke, wearing a gaudy dressing gown, bounded barefoot down the stairs. He flung his arms around Adam. "Sir, it is so good to see you. But why did you not tell me you were coming? You'll have some breakfast, won't you? And how are . . . ?" His voice trailed away and he gulped. "There is not bad news, is there, Uncle? Is everyone at home well?"

"Where is she?" Adam muttered as the butler edged slowly away.

"She? Who?"

"Damn it, Luke! You know well what I mean. You are scarce in town a month before you get yourself in a scrape. My sister writes to me—" He produced the creased letter from his pocket. Luke's butler regarded them with open interest. "I suggest we go somewhere more private for this conversation."

"Very well." Luke nodded to a footman, who opened the door of the drawing room. When they were inside and the door closed, he said, "Sir, I can only think that you have serious business, to arrive so early in the day. What's the matter?"

"The matter, sir, as you know very well, is this. My sister writes that you blatantly keep a mistress in this house for the best part of a fortnight, during which time you shun polite society. Luke, what has possessed you to act so imprudently?"

Luke stared at him. "A mistress? That is what she says?"

Adam gripped his ward's arm. "I was hoping it was not true. Luke, if you have an itch, then satisfy it, but in a way that society will accept. It is one thing to take a mistress and keep her in a discreet sort of way, but to have her openly in your own house—" He broke off and paced away from the young man. "You are not yet one-and-twenty. You are supposed to be in town to find a wife. This is not a good start. Obviously I failed as your guardian in not explaining the etiquette of such matters—why are you laughing?"

Luke shook his head. "Aunt Priscilla wrote you this?"

"I am gratified it amuses you. Now tell me the truth of the matter. You have a young woman in this house?"

"I do, sir. But it is quite respectable, I assure you. She is a lady, and has a companion, an older lady, with her—"

"A lady? No lady would allow herself to be in such a compromising situation. Doubtless her companion is her bawd. Oh, good God." Adam sank into a chair. He should never have let Luke come to town alone, a handsome innocent about to inherit a great deal of money. "Tell me, I beg you, that you have not made an offer of marriage to her."

Luke's gaze dropped. "I did, sir."

"What?" Adam sprang to his feet.

"She refused me. She said I did not know my own mind."

"Thank God. Get her out of the house, now, before she changes hers."

"I don't think she will, sir." Luke sat in a chair opposite Adam. "Uncle, I assure you my aunt has it all wrong."

"I suggest to you she does not. Why would any decent woman risk her own reputation, to live in your house, and after she has refused you?"

"She does not live here."

"It's nine in the morning," Adam said. "You are in your dressing gown, just risen from your bed. And you admit she's here now."

"Yes, sir, she is. But she's not my mistress. She's here for the light. Come, Uncle, I'll explain everything."

"The light? What are you babbling about? Have you lost your wits?" He allowed Luke to lead him up the stairs. Doubtless he could bribe the girl into silence, the bawd too, and with any luck, society might laugh this off as a youthful indiscretion.

"Sir," said Luke, flinging open the library door, "this is Miss Elaine Twyford. Miss Twyford, this is Mr. Adam Ashford, my guardian."

A young woman turned from an easel as Adam and

Luke entered the room. She dropped a curtsy, graceful despite the shapeless, paint-spattered smock she wore. "Good morning, sir. The viscount has spoken often of you. I am very glad to meet you."

Adam ignored her outstretched hand. "I regret that I cannot say the same, Miss Twyford. I only learned of your existence yesterday, from one concerned for my ward's well-being."

He saw her blink in surprise, and a flush stain her high cheekbones. "I see, sir." She turned away from him and spoke to Luke. "We shall resume when you are ready, sir, unless you would like me to leave so you can speak with Mr. Ashworth."

"No, we should not waste this light, and my guardian is most anxious to see what we are up to here. Uncle, do have some coffee." Luke pushed him into a chair and handed him a cup. "There, you will feel better, now. Shall I order you some breakfast?"

"No, thank you, and don't treat me like a senile idiot, Luke," Adam muttered. The pale sunlight of an early-summer morning poured through the large windows, illuminating Miss Twyford at her easel, intent on mixing paint. Chairs and tables were pushed against the book-shelves to make space for a dais in the center of the room.

With a rustle of silk, Luke discarded his dressing gown and stepped onto the dais. Adam nearly choked on his coffee. *Thank God,* he thought, after his initial shock. Luke was wearing a pair of linen underdrawers. The young man lay down, and draped a piece of fabric over his hips, pinching the material into folds.

"Your left leg bent a little more, if you please." Miss Twyford had the dispassionate tone of a tailor measuring a customer for a coat. She glanced at Adam. "I had the greatest trouble in persuading the viscount to pose for me. For such a beautiful man, he is extraordinarily modest."

Beautiful? Adam, unaccustomed to thinking of his god-son in such terms, tried to compare Luke to one of the wonders of antiquity he had viewed on the Grand Tour. Certainly, he was inoffensive in appearance, well-proportioned and muscular, with fair hair tumbled into a carelessly fashionable style and bright blue eyes. But what sort of woman would refer to a man's beauty?

A lightskirt, out to flatter a client, certainly.

Except Miss Twyford had little of the lightskirt about her. If anything, she looked almost nunlike—brown hair scraped back into a Grecian knot, but lacking the artfully loosened curls to soften and ornament the style's simplicity. Her gown, beneath the voluminous smock, appeared to be of a drab dun color, and if it were not for the deft grace with which she wielded her brush, and the vivacity of expression in her gray eyes, Adam would have dismissed her as a plain woman.

Yet Luke, God bless his innocent soul, seemed besotted with her. And who was she? She didn't speak like a woman of education or birth, although her voice was pleasing enough—but then Adam himself still retained traces of his Sussex accent. So she wasn't a bored lady of the *ton* enjoying a lighthearted hobby—but how the devil had a common woman taken up the profession of painter?

"Who is the viscount supposed to represent?" Adam said.

"Narcissus, Mr. Ashworth. The edge of the dais represents the bank of the pond." She hesitated. "You may look at some of my work in the portfolio on the table, there, if you wish."

"In a moment, Miss Twyford. What I really want to know is why you are so eager to compromise yourself. My ward will be thought of as wicked or dashing, no bad things for a man. But you, madam, if you have any reputation whatsoever, are lost in the eyes of society."

A voice came from behind him. "Fortunately, sir, we have little credibility in the eyes of polite society to begin with."

Adam's cup rattled on its saucer. He turned in disbelief to the new speaker, his mouth gone suddenly dry.

Miss Twyford gave another of her startling smiles. "Mrs. Craigmont, we wondered where you were. This is Viscount Tillotson's guardian, Mr. Adam Ashworth."

"Mr. Ashworth, I regret I was not here when you arrived. I have been exchanging recipes with the viscount's cook." She still had the same smile, damn her, that same velvety growl to her voice. Once he had found it enticing that she had not known her power; now, he was fairly sure she did—and knew how to wield it.

"You look very well, Fab—Mrs. Craigmont."

"So do you," she said. "How strange that we should meet again after all this time."

"Good Lord, I had quite forgotten," Luke said. "It is Uncle Adam's birthday. He is forty-three," he added. "Many happy returns, sir."

I'll kill you, you little bastard, Adam thought, and forced a smile on his face.

Miss Twyford returned to her easel. "Please keep still, sir."

On the pretext of rising to examine Miss Twyford's sketches, Adam moved to where he could get a better look at Fabienne. She still had the profile of a goddess on an ancient coin, the same arrogant tilt of her head. She wore her simple gown of soft green wool with the assurance of a woman who knew she looked well, and a paisley shawl thrown over her shoulders added rich accents that complemented her dark hair and olive skin.

"You should put your spectacles on," Luke commented.

I'll kill you very slowly, you little bastard. Adam put his spectacles on. He leafed through the portfolio with rising interest and astonishment. "Miss Twyford, forgive me if I have seemed less than courteous. I know nothing of you, but you are clearly an artist."

Miss Twyford appeared to be biting back a laugh. "Thank you, sir."

"It is a pity you are not a man," Adam blundered on.

"It is not a pity at all," Luke commented.

Miss Twyford blushed.

"I must agree with your ward, sir. I quite like my

protégée as she is." Fabienne stepped forward. "I assure you, you need have no concerns about the propriety of this venture. The viscount is a gentleman, and Miss Twyford, as you noted, is an artist."

"You are her patroness?"

"Yes. I have a salon, and several artists and writers I try to help. You should come while you are in town, Mr. Ashworth. We meet every Wednesday afternoon."

"A salon—how charmingly old-fashioned. I regret I shall not be available."

Fabienne shrugged, apparently oblivious to his sarcasm. She had lost virtually all of that pretty accent, but she still shrugged like a Frenchwoman. "A pity. The viscount always enjoys our discussions."

"Indeed. He tells me, Mrs. Craigmont, that he made an offer for Miss Twyford's hand. He is under age. Although I am not a blood relative, I am his guardian. He cannot marry without my permission, and I certainly do not intend to give it."

Both women looked amused.

"But I refused him," Miss Twyford said.

"So you did. It is one of the few things in your favor, Miss Twyford."

"Uncle!" Luke sat up and his improvised loincloth fell off.

"Please resume your position, sir." Miss Twyford stuck her paintbrush behind her ear.

Luke lay motionless, Miss Twyford continued to paint, and Fabienne Craigmont, although silent and out of sight, continued to make her presence known. Adam heard the sound of a page turning, and wondered what she was reading.

The clock ticked and Miss Twyford's brush made faint hissing sounds on the canvas.

Adam stifled a yawn.

Despite the unsettling presence of Fabienne, and several cups of his ward's excellent coffee, he found himself feeling the effects of a lost night's sleep.

"I see I've been sent here on a fool's errand," he said eventually, and stood. "I'm not saying I approve of this,

Luke, but it seems a harmless enough occupation. I hope you don't catch cold. I'll go to visit my sister."

He bowed over Fabienne's hand, warm and small in his own, and felt an undeniable sizzle, a shock of recognition that alarmed him. She was still beautiful—she was, what, seven and thirty now?—although fine lines appeared around her dark, almond-shaped eyes when she smiled at him.

"How delightful that we should meet again, Adam," she murmured. "I can scarcely believe it."

He pressed his lips briefly to her hand. "Good-bye, Mrs. Craigmont, Miss Twyford. Luke, we should dine together this evening at my club."

"Excellent, Uncle." Luke flung his arms around him. "You must tell me all the news, how the babies are."

"Your babies, sir?" Miss Twyford asked.

"No, no, they are his daughter, Barbara Sanders', children," Luke explained before Adam could say a word. "She is widowed and lives with him in the country."

Fabienne raised her fine eyebrows. "So you are a grandfather?"

And thanks to Luke's efforts, also a country bumpkin approaching his dotage. "I am. Good day, madam."

"You are a silly ninny," Adam remarked. A shave, a change of clothes, and the company of his sister, Priscilla, had revived his energy and good spirits.

The Countess of Eglinton smiled and poured tea. "So you've always said, dear brother. Well, it is delightful to have you visit, now you are recovered from the shock of your advanced age. That has never been a problem for me, as you know."

He eyed her bright chestnut hair, the same color as his, but without a trace of gray. "Yes, it quite defies mathematical law that you are three years my senior but have never achieved your fortieth birthday."

"I doubt I ever shall," Priscilla replied. "Are you sure you cannot stay longer than one night? Eglinton and I should so like to have more of your company."

"I have had quite enough of my birthday already, thank you. But tell me what you know about this Mrs. Craigmont."

"Well." Priscilla pursed her lips. "She is most elegant. You should have seen her gown at the theater the other night—"

"Prissy, I did not travel all night from Sussex to hear you blather of gowns. Who is she? Is she respectable?"

"She is not of the *ton,* of course, but I have seen her at some very select gatherings. She is a widow, I believe. Her younger brother, the Count of Argonac, is a very charming man. I wonder he is not married, although of course he has only his title and looks to recommend him. But he is French and in exile, so what can you expect? He has a fencing academy, which Luke and some of the other young men attend—it is quite fashionable. I believe she is sponsor to several artists and writers, and many people from society attend her soirees. But you must understand my concern. I would not write to you unless I were truly worried."

"Hmm." Adam sipped his tea, and regarded Priscilla with affection. "I do appreciate your concern, sister, I assure you. What is this you're reading?" He picked up a book from the sofa and fumbled for his spectacles.

"Nothing that would interest so learned a person as you. It is Mrs. Ravenwood's latest novel, *The Ruined Tower.*" She snatched it back from him. "It is delightfully horrid. All London is mad over it and I am not yet finished with it, so do not even think to borrow it. Tell me, how are all your brood?"

Adam smiled. "We are all well. I have Jonathan's latest letter home to show you, and Barbara and the little ones send you their love and kisses. The children are into all sorts of mischief, and they chatter incessantly— they must take after their great-aunt. Julia speaks her own baby language still, but with Will you can almost have a sensible conversation."

"Adam." His sister stared into her teacup. "I do wish you would marry again."

"What?" He laughed. "Why should I? I do very well as I am. I look after my land and my pigs, I play with my grandchildren, and I write my treatise—"

"Oh, your treatise. Pooh. I trust you will not talk of it. Sometimes I think you make things up to confuse me."

Adam crossed to the window, looking at the bustle of the street outside, and tapped his fingers on the windowsill.

"Pray, brother, do not do that. It is most annoying."

He grinned. "Yes, it used to drive Mags to distraction."

"And you really don't wish to remarry? I know some quite charming eligible women who would probably tolerate you. Why don't you stay in town and let me introduce you to them?"

"No, Prissy. Thank you, but I'm content. And I couldn't find anyone to match Mags."

"Oh, Adam." She sighed. "You have been alone so long now, buried in the country, and I wish—"

"Let me show you the letter from Jonathan," he said. "I think he wrote it aboard ship during a storm, but you can make it out. Of course it is from some weeks ago, but he seems well and cheerful."

Her face brightened as she unfolded the letter from his thirteen-year-old midshipman son. Dear Prissy, still ready to play the protective elder sister and affectionate aunt.

Twenty years ago, smarting from an unexpected rejection and conscious of his family duty, Adam committed the unfashionable and unplanned act of falling in love with his own wife. Now he suffered painful guilt as the memory of her beloved face and voice faded. Mags had been his center, his refuge. She had rescued him from madness.

And today, a reminder of that madness, of the man he had been, had come back into his life.

Chapter Two

Elvira removed the letter from the secret panel with
trembling fingers. She read it, amazed at its contents—
a letter from one unknown to her, but which expressed
nobility and delicacy with every word.
            —The Ruined Tower by Mrs. Ravenwood.

The greatest living poet in England, if not the universe, according to his own frequently expressed
opinion, kissed the palm of Fabienne's hand. He was
handsome if slightly overweight, with one black curl that
tumbled over his forehead. Fabienne suspected he spent
many hours in front of his mirror, taming that curl into
careless abandon, and perfecting his wicked smile. She
was exactly three inches taller than him.

"Fabienne, Mrs. Craigmont, you are cruel to me," he
whispered over the hubbub of her drawing room. "Why
do you deny me so?"

"Certainly you may have some more tea," she said.

"Have pity on me. I ache for you."

She laughed. "One part of you may ache for me, but
I do not think it is your heart."

"Ah, you wrong me. You wound me deeply. You
would find me the most tender, the most reverent, the
most ardent of lovers."

She poured milk into his cup. "How cruel, sir, to leave
me thereafter languishing for that I can no longer have."

"Oh, Fabienne. You injure me. You know I would
cleave only to you."

"As you do to so many others."

The poet sighed and flashed his dark, deep-set eyes at Elaine as she bent to pour tea. "Thank you, my dear Miss Twyford. You are very kind, but our patroness breaks my heart."

"Perhaps you'd better write a poem about it, sir."

He gazed after Elaine as she moved away through the crowded drawing room. "What a lovely child she is, so fresh and virginal."

"You told me just the other day virgins bore you."

He kissed her hand. "Well, this is promising. Do I detect jealousy?"

She withdrew her hand from his. "No, sir, it is a warning that my protégée has only one lover, and a jealous one—her muse."

"Indeed? I suspect your relationship with Miss Twyford is far more intimate than I can imagine." He smiled dreamily. "It is a wonderful thought, the sacred and the profane, the innocent and the experienced, together with the greatest poet of our age."

Fabienne wanted to applaud him. He tried so hard to be wicked, and occasionally managed to hit his target. "You certainly have a remarkable mind. I believe it is time for you to read to us, sir."

"Very well." His breath warmed her ear. "And how many of the men in this room have been your lover?"

"Why, sir, all of them, of course, except you and my brother." She smiled sweetly, and gestured to the front of the room.

At the conclusion of the reading, the poet bowed low in Fabienne's direction. She moved around the room, chatting with her guests, until a familar name caught her attention.

"Well, I say that Mrs. Ravenwood is a poet," the greatest poet in England declared. "By God, if she were a man, she would be my brother."

"But my dear sir," the Earl of Greenmore drawled, "pray listen to this." He opened Fabienne's copy of *The Ruined Tower,* and read aloud, " '*Elvira heaved many a heavy sigh, her soul troubled. As she gazed from the battlements, she marveled at the many watchfires burning in front of the grim fortress where she was held, and at the sound of pipes and flutes from the shepherds who watched their flocks below . . .'* Well, gentlemen, need I be more plain? This is based on the opening of Book Ten, I believe, of the *Iliad*. Mrs. Ravenwood *is* a man, a gentleman of some education. Mrs. Craigmont, what do you think of my theory?"

"I think it is rubbish, my lord. I have written to Mrs. Ravenwood and she has responded. I believe her to be a female."

"Well, who is she?" Greenmore said.

"She lives quietly in a small village—Shercross, in Sussex—and she said very little about herself."

"Shercross?" Elaine, at Fabienne's side, blushed as she usually did when speaking to gentlemen. "Luke's godfather, Mr. Ashworth, whom you met last week, Fabienne, lives but a mile outside the village. Luke says it is a pretty spot."

Adam again. "How extraordinary. Do you think he knows her?"

"Mrs. Craigmont?"

Fabienne turned to the man who addressed her. A handsome man around her own age, he wore a military uniform that hugged his broad shoulders, and his fair hair was arranged in a fashionable disarray that rivaled the poet's.

"Pardon me for my forwardness. I was brought here by Greenmore, and wished to meet my hostess. Captain George Sanders, at your service, madam."

"You are indeed welcome, Captain." There was something about the man that repelled her, a knowing gleam in his eye that made her step away from him.

He took her hand and murmured, "I should like to call on you, Mrs. Craigmont, at a time when you have fewer admirers in your house. I think you and I should become better acquainted."

"I should be happy to receive you at my future salons since you enjoyed this one so much." She loosened her hand before he could raise it to his lips, and decided to shift the conversation on to more general topics. "We were talking of the village of Shercross. I believe you may have a relative there."

"Indeed?" His blue eyes were cold and appraising now. "A relative?"

"Yes, a widowed lady, a Mrs. Sanders. She lives there with her father, Mr. Ashworth, and her two children, I believe."

"A widowed lady." His smile was cool. "I must visit her. I am sure she would enjoy the attentions of a family member." He caught her hand again. "I am most indebted to you, Mrs. Craigmont. I hope to see you when I am in London next."

She gave an indifferent nod and turned away, not in the mood for flirting, and her suspicion confirmed that there was something unpleasant about George Sanders despite his good looks.

After her guests were gone, she sat at her desk and picked up the letter from the mysterious Mrs. Ravenwood. She smoothed out its folds, and considered this new twist—Mrs. Ravenwood was a neighbor, and almost certainly an acquaintance, of Adam Ashworth. She wondered Luke had not mentioned it, but Luke was hardly an arbiter of the literary arts. He attended her salons only to see Elaine, and today he had been tempted away by something more interesting—a trip to help a friend buy a new horse. Elaine had not been pleased.

Poor Elaine. For all her good intentions of not entrapping Luke, she was drawn to him, and he to her, and Fabienne knew, with a heavy heart, that it was an unsuitable match. Had Luke been more sophisticated, and Elaine less rigid in her moral beliefs, Fabienne would have feared for the young woman's virtue. *Thank God Luke's not like his godfather,* she thought. *He'd have been up her skirts in a minute, and whispering sweet words in her ear to make her melt.*

When Fabienne first met Adam Ashworth, London was still new and strange, the twittering English accents and the pursuits of polite society baffling to her. All she knew was that she must marry soon, and well, and so she and her mother dressed in their best and braved the intricacies of lust, rivalry, and ambition of London society.

When a young man, elegantly dressed in blue-gray satin that matched his eyes, bowed and addressed her in perfect French, she almost fell into his arms with relief. Far too easily, he lured her outside, away from the dancing and gambling and gossip. The chill of frost in the garden almost disguised the scents of London—waste and smoke, a gust of fetid river air. The moon was obscured by a haze of dirty cloud.

He kissed her hand, gazed into her eyes, and told her she was as beautiful as Venus—in English. And his name was Adam Ashworth, with no "sir" or title attached.

She giggled despite her disappointment.

"Flattery is wasted on you, I see, Miss Argonac. Let us try jealousy. I am an engaged man and can never be yours."

"My felicitations."

"My father has arranged that I should marry a pudding of a girl in the country," he told her. "She'll do well enough as a broodmare for me. If her wit were as great as her bosom, I might feel more tenderly inclined toward her. I suggest you don't think of her. I think of her as little as possible."

"That is all too obvious," Fabienne told him.

"And you? Does not your *maman* wish you to find a rich English lord to marry as soon as possible? I wonder she lets you alone with a man of bad reputation."

"She doesn't know I'm with you."

She knew her mother was at the gaming table, eyes bright and frantic.

"So tell me your story." He took the fringe of her shawl and brushed it against her cheek. "You escaped from Paris under a load of turnips, I suppose."

"The revolution was betrayed," she said. "And no, I did not escape under a load of—what is that word? Our land is in Normandy, by the coast. My mother, brother, and I came on a fishing boat with all our jewelry sewn into our clothes. I wish I had stayed with Papa."

"You do not." He ran a long, elegant finger around the narrow ribbon at her neck. "I am very glad you are here, Miss Argonac. I intend to make you mad for me. You will beg me to commit shameless and depraved acts on your person, and I shall be happy to oblige you. Naturally, since I am an accomplished libertine, once I have had my way with you I shall cast you aside and seek my next conquest. I trust this is acceptable?"

She had laughed. God help her, she had laughed.

She sighed and turned her attention once more to the letter from Mrs. Ravenwood. In a bold, graceful hand, the authoress thanked Mrs. Craigmont for her invitation, but regretted that she never visited London.

Fabienne sharpened her pen, dipped it into the ink and wrote.

> My dear Mrs. Ravenwood,
>   Many I know join with me in expressing how your writing, although of a popular nature, reveals that you are more than . . .

No, that sounded patronizing. Maybe Mrs. Ravenwood lived in reduced circumstances and could not afford to mix in London society—although surely she had made a good living with her three wildly popular novels.

Fabienne crumpled up her first effort and began to write. She stated quite simply that she would like to meet Mrs. Ravenwood; that she, Fabienne, had means at her disposal if travel or circumstances were difficult for the writer, and she was able to offer several artists introductions and support.

Ippolite wandered into the room as Fabienne dropped sealing wax on the folded letter. "Are you writing to a lover, sister?"

She smiled at him. "Mind your own business, you little monkey. Will you dine out tonight?"

"I think so." He sat on a chair and tipped it back on its legs. "You had a nightmare again last night."

"Did I?" Fabienne tapped the letter on the polished surface of her desk. "I don't remember," she lied.

"Hmm." Ippolite dropped the chair back on to all four legs. "You were mightily distressed. I wish you would tell me what it is that causes you such unrest."

"You think to serve as confessor?" She hesitated, wondering if she could break the silence of nearly two decades. "Do you remember coming to England all those years ago?"

He grinned. "I vomited on your gown on the fishing boat and you slapped me and threatened to throw me overboard."

"I am sure I did no such thing. No, later, when we were in London."

"I remember that room we lived in, and how crowded and strange London was," he said. "One time some men tried to get money from our mother. They threatened her, and said we should all rot in Newgate. And the silk flowers, my God. Even now I could make silk flowers in my sleep."

Fabienne nodded. "Do you remember what happened after we moved out of the room?"

"After Mr. Rowe's visit, when you became betrothed? You and *Maman* cried a lot. I remember that. I thought it strange, since *Maman* had only laughed at our misfortune before. And then I was sent to school—to become an English gentleman." He gave an ironic smile. "And you and our mother went to the country so that her cough could become better. I never saw her again, or Papa—or you, until you returned to England."

She was both relieved and disappointed that he could not make the way easier for her.

"Is there something that troubles you still from your first marriage?" Ippolite asked. "It must have been lonely, going to a strange land to marry a man you had met but once."

"It was no better or worse than many other marriages, I suppose." Fabienne turned the letter over in her hands. "I am sorry I woke you last night."

"You didn't. It was six in the morning, and I had just returned home."

She gave a sigh of exasperation. "You are a shameless rake. You are five and twenty—why do you not marry?"

"Bah," he replied. "I've no interest in some silly miss out of the schoolroom, in love with a glamorous French title and the idea of impoverished nobility. I'd sooner marry Miss Twyford."

"Ippolite!" She grasped his arm. "Absolutely, no. I do not jest, brother. Please let her alone."

"Certainly, if that is what you wish. I assure you, I think of her as another sister, a sweet girl, and that is all."

Fabienne breathed a sigh of relief and smiled at him, her brother, her little monkey. "Go, then, and keep out of trouble."

"You have a letter," Elaine announced. "It is from Sussex."

"Thank you." Fabienne tossed it onto her desk, heart pounding.

"Do you not wish to open it?"

"No, it is nothing important. I shall read it this afternoon when we return from Viscount Tillotson's house."

"The painting is nearly finished," Elaine said, eyes downcast. "I shall not see him for much longer."

"Oh, sweetheart," Fabienne said, "don't be sad. I have an idea to cheer us both up. I think we should go on a journey and stay at some pretty place for a few days. Would you like that?"

Elaine shook her head. "I can't. I have Miss Fannon's portrait to start next week."

Fabienne nodded and put her arm around her protégée's shoulders. "You are right, of course. Come, smile for me."

Elaine gave a brief, gallant smile and wiped her eyes on her sleeve.

"Where is your handkerchief?"

"I think I used it for my brushes."

Fabienne sighed and handed Elaine hers. "Blow. Good."

My dear Mrs. Craigmont,

I am greatly honored that you should choose to make me such a generous offer, but I cannot accept. My circumstances are somewhat unusual; forgive me if I do not explain further.

Suffice it to say that I never expected my poor scribblings to receive the adulation they have, and am amazed that so many wish to read them. My own life is totally devoid of the sinister and horrid events of which I write; in fact, if I were to write of my own experiences, I should deal only with the small absurdities of the lives I and my neighbors lead.

Shercross is a small place on the Brighton Road. The most exciting event of the day, if a neighbor does not kill a pig or dig a root of potatoes with a monstrous amount of young, is to watch for the arrival of the stagecoach at the inn. We have also a shop that sells everything except what you most need—heaven forbid you should lose a glove, or need some mother of pearl buttons. But if you need an ounce of peppers, an African mask, or an ivory carving from the frozen north, the shopkeeper, Mr. Pettigrew, who retired from the sea, can well oblige you.

It is a pretty enough village, and it suits me very well. I do exceedingly well in this trivial universe, and have no desire to change anything in my life. I thank you again for your kind words, and remain your devoted servant,

Sybil Ravenwood.

Fabienne laid the letter down, disappointed. She had spun a fantasy in her head the past few days, imagining Mrs. Ravenwood as anxious for a female confidante and friend as herself, and anticipating a gradual deep intimacy. Maybe Mrs. Ravenwood only thought she offered patronage, not friendship. Whatever the circumstances,

even if she wrote surrounded by a dozen children and
an adoring husband, or was a lonely widow, Fabienne
could be her friend.

> *My dear Mrs. Ravenwood,*
>   *May I dare suggest a correspondence, and a possible
> friendship, may be beneficial to us both? I know little
> of your circumstances, but understand from other art-
> ists that it is all too easy to feel isolated and set apart
> from society by nature of your calling. I too, as an
> unmarried woman on the fringes of the* ton, *do not fit
> easily into society. Although I am surrounded by
> many, there are few with whom I dare be intimate.*
>   *I am by birth French, have lived abroad in India
> for more than a dozen years, and finding myself wid-
> owed for the second time, decided to return to En-
> gland, where my brother lives. I have ties of affection
> here, chiefly amongst the artists I support, and in par-
> ticular for Elaine Twyford, a most gifted young painter
> whom I discovered living in obscurity and who now
> lives in my house.*
>   *I need a friend. I suspect you do, too; you observe
> acutely, but do you feel, do you have anyone in whom
> you can confide without fear?*

She signed the letter, quickly, with only her first name,
before she could read it over and change her mind.
   Mrs. Ravenwood's answer, when it came, was brief.

> *Dear madam,*
>   *Once again, I am most sensible of the honor you do
> me. I must ask you not to write again.*
>
>   *Yours faithfully,*
>   *Sybil Ravenwood.*

Fabienne crushed the letter in her hand, flung it across
the room, and burst into tears of rage and disappointment. After a while, she stopped and blew her nose.
   She was in dire need of fresh country air.

Chapter Three

"What a delightful prospect your castle has, indeed, Lord Molfitain," Alicia cried. *"But tell me, sir, who is it who lives in the ancient wing yonder? For last night, I swore I saw a light there."*

"I assure you, madam, you are mistaken. That wing has been deserted for nigh two centuries." The forbidding visage of her host struck fear into Alicia's heart.
—The Curse of the Molfitains by Mrs. Ravenwood.

The housekeeper stared at Fabienne, confusion on her pleasant face.

"Why, no, ma'am, Mrs. Ravenwood is not here. 'Tis such a pity, you coming all the way from London to see her."

Fabienne's heart sank. "But this is most strange. She told me she rarely travels. How long ago did she leave?"

The woman looked over Fabienne's shoulder, and a smile broke out on her face. "Ah, ma'am, here's Mr. Ashworth. He'll explain it better to you."

Explain what? Fabienne turned with a shock to see Adam Ashworth strolling down the street toward Rose Cottage. He was accompanied by a couple of dogs, a small boy who dragged a stick in the dust, and a young woman leading a goat cart, in which sat a baby chewing on a silver rattle.

"Good afternoon, Mrs. Piper—" Adam broke off. Fabienne tried to stifle a giggle at his expression of consternation. "Mrs. Craigmont, this is a surprise indeed."

"I was telling the lady, sir," Mrs. Piper said, "that Mrs. Ravenwood is not here."

"Ah. Yes. I believe she has gone to Bath."

"To Bath? I hope she is not unwell." So that explained Mrs. Ravenwood's reticence and isolation; she must be an invalid.

"No, no. Quite well, I believe. I really know little of it."

Mrs. Piper nodded vigorously. "Yes, sir, that must be the matter of it. Good afternoon to you, Mrs. Sanders," she added as the young woman with the goat cart approached.

"Papa, will you not introduce us?" The young woman, apparently Mrs. Sanders, smiled at Fabienne, and caught the small boy by the arm. "Will, please bow to the ladies."

"Master Will, I declare, you wear breeches," Mrs. Piper said. "What a great boy you have become."

"Yes, it's his first day out as a man," Adam said. "But I almost forgot why we are come here. We killed a pig, Mrs. Piper, and have a joint for you." He produced a cheesecloth-wrapped bundle from under his arm. The dogs sniffed and jostled around him, tails waving, and he pushed them away. They flopped into a miniature patch of shade, tongues lolling.

"Why, sir, this is most kind. I shall have my girl prepare it directly, with some of those apples from your orchard that I bottled. There is nothing I like better than roast pork, and everyone knows your pigs produce the sweetest-tasting meat."

"Well, of course you know I have a scientific method of feeding my pigs. I . . ."

Mrs. Piper nodded and smiled as he discoursed on what was obviously a favorite subject.

"We must introduce ourselves, since Papa has begun to talk of pigs." Mrs. Sanders turned to Fabienne, and held out a hand. She was a tall woman, but bore little resemblance otherwise to her father, with a heart-shaped face beneath a mass of dark curls. "I am Barbara Sanders, and these two, my children, Will and Julia."

"I am Fabienne Craigmont. It is a pleasure to meet you. What pretty children you have."

"Thank you. I—"

"Well, Babs," Adam turned to his daughter. "It's time we returned home. Mrs. Craigmont, it was a pleasant surprise to see you again. You stay with acquaintances in the neighborhood, I presume."

"No, indeed, I intend to stay at the inn and return to London tomorrow. Good afternoon, Mrs. Sanders, Mrs. Piper."

"At the inn?" Barbara looked shocked. "Oh, you cannot stay there. It has fleas and lice, I am sure. It is a very low place. Papa, we should invite Mrs. Craigmont to stay with us."

"Ah. Yes, of course. We should be honored, Mrs. Craigmont."

"That is most kind," Fabienne said. She felt a momentary pang, seeing the disappointment in Barbara's face. The inn had seemed a reasonable enough sort of place; she had certainly stayed in worse. But the look of horror in Adam's eyes stirred a devil within her. "Thank you. I accept with pleasure."

"The house is a mile or so away. I trust walking there will not be a problem? And you like pork, I hope. We have a quantity of pig to eat at dinner." He whistled to the dogs.

"If your maid and luggage are at the inn we can send for them," Barbara suggested.

"Thank you, that is most kind. I have a small bag there. My maid did not accompany me."

"You travel alone? That is an adventure. Come, let us catch up with Papa before he starts to walk fast, thinking he is alone." She grasped the goat's beard to urge it forward, and the procession set off down the dusty street of the village.

"This is a very charming village, just as Mrs. Ravenwood described it. I wonder at her going away so suddenly," Fabienne said to Barbara.

"I regret I have never met her. You have visited Sussex before, Mrs. Craigmont?"

"No, never. Please, let us use each other's Christian names. There is no need to be so stiff and formal. I am Fabienne."

Barbara smiled. "Thank you. Oh, Papa, Fabienne, please wait. I have to stop at Mr. Pettigrew's shop." She produced a scrap of embroidery silk from her reticule. "Would you be so kind as to stay with Julia?"

As her mother left, Julia opened her mouth in a howl of distress.

"Oh, there, hush now." Fabienne picked the baby up as Adam stepped forward. "Your mama will be back in a moment."

She jiggled Julia, who gulped, stared at her with wide blue-gray eyes—she had inherited her grandfather's eyes, Fabienne noticed—and then beamed, revealing four white teeth.

"You have children, Mrs. Craigmont?" Adam asked.

"No. But I like babies. And great boys too." She smiled at Will, who ducked his head against his grandfather's coat.

Barbara emerged from the shop, a frown on her pretty face. "Mr. Pettigrew is too annoying. Of course he has no embroidery thread, but he sold me some spice. He said it would be delicious with our pork. How is it that everyone knows we killed a pig?"

She took Julia from Fabienne's arms with a smile and placed the baby back in the goat cart.

Adam grinned. "What did he sell you this time?"

"I don't know." Barbara passed a paper cone to Fabienne. "Do you recognize this?"

Fabienne picked out a small black pod. "It is cardamom, and it would go well with pork, although probably not the way your cook prepares it. I lived in India for some years, and my cook there used it extensively."

"India?" Will's eyes were wide. "Grandpapa and I read a book about India. Did you see elephants?"

"Yes, many times. And snake charmers, and once a tiger on a tiger hunt. I shall tell you about them later, if you like."

Will nodded his head with enthusiasm, and ran to

catch up with his grandfather, who strode ahead, hands in pockets, the dogs weaving and circling around them. Adam led them off the dusty road onto a grassy path, flanked by thickets of brambles and nodding heads of Queen Anne's lace.

"It's a pity my brothers are not home," Barbara said. "Jonathan is in the Navy and Luke— Well, he is not really my brother. He is Papa's godson. Viscount Tillotson is in London. But I am glad of female company. We have not entertained much since Mama died ten years ago."

"Forgive me for saying this, but you seem very young to be a widow with two small children."

"I married when I was fifteen," Barbara said. "Papa was much against the match, but—oh." She raised her hand to her mouth. "Papa said I was not to tell anyone of this. I hope you are not shocked."

"Not at all," Fabienne said. "If you were in society, it would be a different matter, but I am not easy to shock. So you never had a season, or visited London?"

"No, never." Barbara shook her head.

"Do you not wish to marry again? You might have a better chance of finding a husband in London than here."

"I don't know. I—" Her words were interrupted by a raucous squawk.

"What is that?" Fabienne asked. "Is it a bird?"

Ahead of the two women, Adam and his grandson stood facing each other on the path.

"No," Adam said. "See, like this." He dropped to one knee and folded Will's hands together. "Now blow hard."

Will raised his joined hands to his mouth, and puffed his cheeks out. A faint squeak emerged.

"Good," Adam said. "Your mama is most accomplished at this, if she will allow herself to do something so vulgar."

"What are you doing?" Fabienne asked.

Barbara stuffed her gloves into her pocket, plucked a piece of grass and placed it between her thumbs. "This is one of the accomplishments of country living, like talking to your neighbors of how you feed your pigs." She produced a loud squawk of her own.

"I believe it is on the principle of playing an oboe, although less musical," Adam said. "The grass is the equivalent of the reed. Would you care to try, Mrs. Craigmont?"

"Certainly."

He handed her a blade of grass with a bow. "If I may make a suggestion, I believe removing your gloves will greatly aid the process."

"Of course." She unbuttoned her gloves and slid them from her fingers, slowly and with great care, as his eyes widened.

"Ah." Adam swallowed. "Yes. Now place your thumbs together, with the grass between."

His warm hands cupped hers. She remembered those long, clever fingers too well. She raised their joined hands to her mouth. "So now I blow hard?"

He nodded, face-to-face with her, leaning slightly toward her. He had aged well. There were a few lines around the blue-gray eyes in that angular face with a long, bumpy nose that just missed being handsome; gray was scattered among the rich brown hair at his temples. The last vestiges of the slenderness of youth had gone; in maturity, he was broad-shouldered and strong, a well-made man.

"Grandpapa." Will tugged at his grandfather's coat with one hand, the other clutched at his own breeches.

"Excuse us, ladies." Adam dropped her hands, and hauled his grandson aside and slightly behind the two women. The two males stood side by side at the edge of the path, backs turned, their posture unmistakable.

Barbara frowned. "I do beg your pardon. It is always the way with them. When he and my brothers walk with me, it is like taking out a pack of dogs—they unbutton and water the bushes before they are scarcely out of view of the house."

Fabienne smiled. "My brother is much the same. It is such a convenience of their anatomy, I have always thought."

Will ran up to them, and caught his mother's hand. "Mama, Mrs. Craigmont, Grandpapa's doodle is much bigger than mine."

Fabienne raised her hands to her lips, gave an experimental puff, and produced a sound worthy of a deranged crow.

"This is your special wine, Papa," Barbara said.

"I thought it worth drinking. It is not often that we have company, and we also celebrate my grandson's first day as a man." Adam raised his glass toward Fabienne. "I put this wine down when my son, Jonathan, was born."

"I am honored, sir," she replied. "It is very fine."

"If you will excuse me, I must see to the children," Barbara said. "Will was busy drawing pictures of tigers and elephants, and it is high time I put him to bed."

"Give them a kiss from me, Babs." As the door closed behind her, Adam turned to Fabienne. "We have eaten a truly prodigious amount of pork. Would you care to take a turn on the terrace?"

Outside the air was heavy with the scent of honeysuckle as the shadows lengthened, and a sliver of new moon rode in the indigo sky. Adam pointed at the horizon. "The evening star, there," he said. "See how the bats fly out. Can you hear them still?"

She concentrated and heard the faint piping. "Can you?"

He shook his head. "No, I lost that ability some fifteen years ago, I think. I did not notice it had gone for the longest time."

"I like the country," Fabienne said as he fell silent. "My brother and I visited the Earl of Greenmore's house in Hertfordshire a few weeks ago. I was surprised that Mrs. Ravenwood was not there, for you know she dedicated her last book to him."

"Yes, well, she is little in society. Or so I have been told." He picked at a lump of moss on the balustrade of the terrace. "I never thought to see you again."

"I must admit it was a surprise to me too."

"Well then," he said. "I shall speak plainly. I suppose my indiscreet daughter has blabbed all of our family secrets to you already."

"You mean her marriage?"

"I love her," he said. "I love my grandchildren. And I should warn you, Mrs. Craigmont, that I will tolerate no breath of scandal from any source to hurt my daughter, or my son's career. Or the reputation of my ward."

"So you warned us at Tillotson's house," she said. "How well you play the moralist these days, Adam."

He flushed. "I think you know what I mean."

"Ah, but you forget one thing." She laughed at his discomfort. "You ruined me, Adam. It gives you little credibility, however respectable you claim to be now."

"Excuse me, madam. You hardly fit any definition of a ruined woman. You do not parade yourself on the Strand with a painted face. You have wealth, independence, and status. There are probably a great many women who would grit their teeth and allow themselves to be ruined to attain what you have now. Consider my daughter—" He stopped.

"By your standards, she is entirely respectable," Fabienne said. "A widow who has returned to her father's house."

"It is of no matter." He fell silent, drumming his fingers on the balustrade.

Barbara joined them on the terrace. "What a beautiful night."

Adam nodded. He seemed distracted. "I should go to work on my treatise, if you will excuse me."

"Your treatise?"

"A mathematical treatise, Mrs. Craigmont."

She remembered now. He had been a rising mathematician at Cambridge when he was a very young man.

"Do not let Papa talk of it," Barbara said. "It is even worse than the pigs. No one understands a word he says. I suppose you will be in the library for hours, Papa, so I shall bid you good night." She kissed his cheek.

"Good night, Babs, Mrs. Craigmont." He bowed and left them.

*   *   *

That bloody woman.

Both of them.

He had been a fool to leave them alone together.

He was fairly sure, from the conversation at dinner, that their time together had been spent in innocuous pursuits and conversation, playing with the children, viewing the house and garden, and gossiping about bonnets, sleeves, childbirth, and other such uncontroversial feminine topics.

Adam had planned a long afternoon and evening in the study, with a short break to bolt down some pig, and then get back to work. He hadn't wanted a polite, leisurely dinner—which to be honest, he'd quite enjoyed—in the company of two pleasant women, even if he did not trust one as far as he could throw her. She looked particularly handsome that evening by the glow of the candles, and in the early-evening light.

And earlier, the way she'd looked him in the eye and removed her gloves, creating an intimate act in the baring of her fingers—good God.

What on earth was she up to?

It was his own fault. It was the letter, that damned letter, where words had spilled out, his heart unlocked. He'd rambled on pointlessly about the village, and had wanted to tell her more. He wanted to tell her that he understood her loneliness, that he had been on his own for years, and that his life was unsettled and unsatisfactory since that meeting at Luke's. And now . . . He didn't know what he wanted. Not her. Certainly not her. Nor could he possibly repair the damage he had done her.

Whatever fine-sounding political ideals on the freedom of man and woman they had both believed in then, by the standards of society and decency, he had used her with the intention of discarding her. It didn't even matter that she had chosen to end the liaison. He had reacted at first to her rejection with anger and injured pride; later, he had mourned the loss, and punished himself with a self-imposed burden of secrecy.

He shrugged off his coat and tossed it onto a chair,

unbuttoned his waistcoat, and loosened his neckcloth. It would not do to brood on the past. Pressing matters were at hand—that damned Cecilia, the stupid girl.

Cecilia. Where was she, the little ninny? . . . Oh, yes. Captured and locked into a room remarkably similar to this one—stone-flagged and with high, arched windows. Of course for his purposes the walls would be draped by sinister spiderwebs. And instead of a carved motif of leaves and flowers, Cecilia would realize, with the obligatory thrill of horror, that the stonework in her prison was of grinning skulls.

When moonlight revealed an asymmetry in the paneling she would naturally rise and fiddle around with it. A secret door would swing back with an ominous—of course—creak, revealing—what? A secret passage? No, too easy, too overdone, too obvious. A skeleton? No, the stupid girl would scream and faint.

Adam glanced at the picture of his mother that hung opposite. There was something he'd never noticed before in her oval face and wide smile, something that came and went out of his mind with a frustrating rapidity.

A portrait.

Yes, that was it.

A portrait of a woman, dressed in the fashion of a century ago, who looked exactly like Cecilia.

He began to write.

Chapter Four

*Who would think that on such a morn as this, after
the sun rose amidst the innocent songs of birds, and
all seemed well in dewy splendor, that the fresh new
day would bring only betrayal and sadness?*
         —*The Castle Perilous* by Mrs. Ravenwood.

"*I* beg your pardon. I really must go to bed." Barbara
yawned. "Julia wakes me at first light."

"I did not mean to keep you from your rest," Fabienne
said. "I've so enjoyed talking to you."

"Oh, I too. Are you sure you will not stay a few days
longer? If it would not bore you, that is. You could borrow some dresses from me."

"You're a whole head taller than me," Fabienne said.
"Thank you, but I must return to London. Elaine will
miss me."

"I should so like to meet her." Barbara hesitated at
the doorway of Fabienne's room. "Do you need a maid
tonight? I can send mine in to help you undress."

"Thank you, no. I can manage. Do you think you will
come to London?"

"I don't know. It is up to Papa—he means well, but
sometimes I feel like a prisoner here in his house, and . . .
I beg your pardon. I should not talk of these matters."
Barbara turned to Fabienne and gave her a quick kiss
on the cheek. "Good night."

As the bedchamber door closed behind Barbara, the
porcelain clock on the mantelpiece struck ten. The room

was old-fashioned, paneled with dark oak, and with an elaborate plaster ceiling. A tapestry of a hunting scene, faded with age, hung on one wall. The bed was high, with bedposts carved with flowers and foliage, and a faded silk cover. There was little other furniture except a massive wooden armchair, and a chest, bound in bands of iron and with the date 1577 carved on it. A blue-and-white china bowl filled with dried rose petals stood on the chest. Altogether the room resembled a setting in one of Mrs. Ravenwood's novels.

Mrs. Ravenwood.

Fabienne grinned with delight. Now she knew Adam's secret.

The respectable Mr. Ashworth kept a mistress in the village, much to the embarrassment of his daughter, who was forced to become a conspirator. Fabienne very much doubted Mrs. Ravenwood was at Bath; probably she had been hiding in the parlor, her ear to the door, as the unwelcome visitor was disposed of. And as for Adam's treatise—Fabienne suspected his treatise was composed in Mrs. Ravenwood's bed.

She crossed to the window and opened it, breathing in the fragrant night air. Despite the earliness of the hour—in London, the evening's entertainment would scarcely be under way—she was tired from her early start this morning, the events of the day, and the large amount of delicious roast pork she had consumed. She should go to bed.

"No!" Fabienne sat bolt upright, gasping for breath, heart pounding. Of course she would dream here, under the same roof as Adam. Thank God she had not screamed aloud.

The dream was always so vivid—the slow advance of the two masked men, shrouded in long cloaks.

Who has he brought with him? And why?

Neither of them was Adam.

She darted toward the door, and one of the men laughed and stepped into her path. His companion locked the door, the click of the key loud and harsh in her ears.

I wish to go. Please, let me go.

She was glad she had woken at that point.

As she crossed to the fireplace to light a candle, from somewhere in the depths of the house a deep-voiced clock struck the half hour, echoed seconds later by the silvery tone of the clock in her room. It was half past two. A couple of books stood on the mantelpiece, and she resolved to read herself to sleep until she discovered her choices were a Greek text or a book of sermons.

She picked up her candlestick again and threw a shawl around her shoulders. No one would be about at this hour. She could safely raid Adam's library and see if anyone in the house read anything other than Greek, mathematics, or sermons.

She crept down the wide oak staircase, casting a shadow that flickered over the portraits of long-dead, bumpy-nosed Ashworths, and turned toward the library. Barbara had shown her around the house, many rooms of which reminded her of Mrs. Ravenwood's settings— the oldest parts of it had once been a monastery. Now she knew the way—through this pointed archway festooned with stylized stone grapevines, with a fox hidden amongst the leaves. The library was straight ahead, the door slightly ajar, and a glimmer of light came from within.

Inside, she paused and looked around. A candle burned on a desk heaped with papers, and now she saw a coat and waistcoat tossed onto a nearby chair. Their owner could not be far away. She hesitated, looking into the darkness of the far end of the room. Nothing stirred. Well, there were plenty of books close by. She raised her candle to view the titles on the nearest shelf.

A sinister growl came from the shadows. "What are you doing here, Mrs. Craigmont?"

She stifled a shriek and dropped her candle. It fell to the floor and rolled away, the flame extinguished. "What are *you* doing here?"

"I beg your pardon. This is my house, my library, madam. Why are you here?" He moved toward her.

"I am looking for a book. I wish to read something." Her words sounded inadequate and foolish.

"I see." He took his spectacles off and tossed them onto his desk. Now he was only a foot or so away from her, tall and forbidding in shirt and breeches.

"Well, why do you lurk in the dark to frighten me so?"

He held up a book. "I was fetching this when I heard you make your not particularly discreet entrance, Mrs. Craigmont. I snuffed my candle to see what you were about."

"Oh, do not be ridiculous. Why else would I be here?"

"I wonder." He paused in front of her, a little too close.

"What do you mean—" Oh, God. She was here, alone, wearing only a nightgown and shawl. Did he think she had come here to seduce him? "I think I had best leave. I see this is not a convenient time for you."

"Oh, please, Mrs. Craigmont. It is not at all inconvenient. On the contrary, I think we both know what you seek." His smile was taunting and predatory.

Fabienne stared back at him, determined not to show any fear. She was no longer a terrified girl who would beg for mercy, a victim of casual lust, Adam's or any other man's.

His easy, sarcastic smile and arrogant stance angered her. "Good night, Mr. Ashworth." She stepped back and her heel touched the base of a bookshelf, her shoulders brushing against the uneven ridges of books. He followed her that one step back, adept as a dancer or fencer, and placed one hand on the shelf at her shoulder, half entrapping her, daring her to move.

"One moment, Mrs. Craigmont." He trailed his fingers along her jawbone and splayed his fingers into her loosened hair, drawing her face to his.

"Stop—"

The word had hardly left her lips before his mouth blocked further speech in a kiss that was surprisingly gentle, despite his threatening aspect. There was strength there, certainly in the force of his embrace, and the press of his hips, but it was as though he knew that sweetness would disarm her more than any show of force. His lips withdrew, then brushed hers, posing a hesitant question, a promise of passion withheld—for the moment.

Damn him.

Her body arched into his, returning that implicit message as her mouth opened, and years, and pain, and her common sense faded away.

"Damn you!" She wrenched away from him.

He raised his eyebrows and fingered a lock of hair that fell on her neck, his touch as potent as it had been at Tillotson's house, as it had always been. "Well?"

"Damn you, Adam Ashworth." Rage made her breath fast and shallow. She hoped it was only rage. "Damn you. So you still know how to kiss a woman. And you're still a bastard."

He stepped back and bowed. "Your servant, madam."

She swung her hand back and slapped his face as hard as she could. "Good night, Mr. Ashworth."

"Good night, Mrs. Craigmont." He crossed to the library door and opened it, a mocking smile on his face.

Head high, she walked past him, willing herself not to hurry. Out of the library, she ran through the dark stone passage, blundered into something that stood in the way, and hurried up the staircase, longing for the safety of her room. Bedclothes pulled over her head, she waited for her pulse to return to normal. The thunder of her heartbeat, she assured herself, was only attributable to her flight upstairs.

It was nothing to do with Adam, damn him.

Nothing at all.

Damn him, she thought. *Damn him. God rot him.* She lay awake for what seemed like hours before falling into a restless sleep.

Fabienne awoke to bright sunlight and birdsong, the distant lowing of cows, and the scents of the countryside, hay and manure, floating in through the open window. A maidservant entered bearing a tray of tea and toast.

"Good morning, mistress, and a fine one it is, too."

She set down the tray and shut the window. " 'Tis dangerous, mistress. You'll catch a fever with the window open so. I beg pardon for the lateness, but we're all at sixes and sevens with the captain come from London to claim Mrs. Sanders, and the master's in a rare state about it."

"But I thought—"

"Oh." The woman looked taken aback. "Beg your pardon, mistress. I thought you would have known. Mr. Ashworth put it about that she was a widow since she lived separate from her husband and he thought to save her reputation. But whatever tiff they've had, now they're billing and cooing, though Master William is shy of his father, and the baby doesn't know him."

"*Captain* Sanders, you said?" Fabienne got out of bed and splashed water over her face. She felt muzzy-headed and stupid. Was this the Captain Sanders she had met in London and whom she had told of a female relative in Sussex?

"Why, yes, such a handsome gentleman."

Fabienne dressed and made her way downstairs to the parlor, uneasiness weighing her down.

Yesterday the room had represented happy domesticity, with its battered, comfortable furniture, Will's toys scattered on the floor, and a tangle of embroidery thread on the sofa. Now Adam stood rigid in the center of the room, fists clenched, facing another man, who turned and bowed low as she entered.

"Why, Fabienne, how delightful to see you again." Sanders' low, caressing voice suggested a great degree of intimacy. He crossed to her and kissed her hand before she could stop him. "Mr. Ashworth, it is the charming Mrs. Craigmont who has acted as Cupid, and restored my beloved wife and children to me." As Fabienne drew her hand away, he added, "Can you believe that she and her dear papa concocted a preposterous story of her flight to an elderly aunt in the wilds of Scotland, sending me on the wildest of goose chases? But thanks to you, she is restored to me."

"But I—" Fabienne was shocked into silence by the

smirk on Sanders' face and the sudden, hostile expression in Adam's eyes.

Adam addressed Sanders. "You are not welcome, here, sir, and I suggest you leave. Good day to you."

"Why, Barbara, my dear," Sanders said as the door opened. "Why are your eyes so red? I trust you have not been weeping at the thought of leaving your papa's house."

Barbara shook her head. She gave Fabienne a weak smile.

"Come, bid your papa farewell." Sanders took Barbara's hand and tucked it into the crook of one arm. "Are the children ready to leave?"

"Papa," Barbara said, her voice unsteady.

Adam glared at her, his fingers tapping the back of a chair.

"Papa, please do not be angry with me."

Fabienne took the opportunity of moving toward the door.

Adam spoke as her hand closed on the door handle. "Wait, Mrs. Craigmont. I should prefer you stay."

"I would rather not, sir. This is a family matter."

"Of course. You are merely the instigator of this happy reunion. You may as well know what your meddling has caused."

"My meddling?" Fabienne took a step toward him, itching to slap him again. "Spread lies about your daughter's marital state, sir, and you may be assured trouble will come your way."

"Touché, Mrs. Craigmont." He gave a faint smile.

"Mrs. Craigmont has nothing with which to reproach herself." Sanders' words had an unpleasantly intimate twinge.

"Indeed." Adam's lips tightened. He gave Fabienne a contemptuous glance.

"Enough!" Fabienne said. "Mr. Ashworth, I have met Captain Sanders once before. I do not possibly see how he can construe that as any sort of understanding between us. I can only say that I regret I unwittingly betrayed a confidence."

Adam ignored her. "Sanders, you and I had an agreement. You have broken it."

"Surely you do not suggest that agreement supersedes a wedding vow your daughter made before God?"

"I . . ." Barbara gazed at her father. "Papa, please speak to me."

"I am disappointed in you, my dear," Sanders said. He released her. "You had best come and say farewell to your children, Barbara, and I'll be on my way."

"No!" Barbara ran to her father and tugged at his sleeve. "Papa, tell him he cannot take the children. He must not!"

Sanders' smile was triumphant. "You forget, my dear wife, both you and your children belong to me. I'll leave behind a disobedient wife, but the children I can, and will, take."

Adam laid his hand on his daughter's shoulder. When he spoke, his expression was still grim, but his voice gentle. "Babs, you know to what you return, but what he says is true. The children are his."

"Exactly. And I have run out of patience." Sanders turned to Fabienne. "My dear Mrs. Craigmont, if you please, tell whichever servant lurks outside with his ear to the door that I am ready to leave."

"I will not," Fabienne said. "I will not be your ally in this sorry affair."

"And you shall not play fast and loose with my daughter's feelings anymore." Adam advanced on Sanders, fists clenched. "Leave my house. I care not a jot for your legal rights, nor your person. Go, or I'll throw you out myself!"

"Go to the devil!" Sanders backed away. "You should have a care, at your age, sir. I'll take what is mine, and damn you."

"You whoreson!" Adam's fist shot out, catching Sanders on the jaw. Sanders staggered back, clutching at a chair to regain his balance.

"Papa!" Barbara darted forward between the two men and reached a hand to Sanders' swelling jaw. "My dear, are you much hurt? Oh, Papa, how could you?"

Sanders pushed her hand away. "Pray do not fuss. Fetch your bags and we'll leave directly."

"Babs, do you wish to go?" Adam spoke quietly to his daughter.

"Yes, sir, I must. It is as he says. I made a vow."

"As he did. To honor you, to cherish you. Babs, you know my protection is yours, against him, against society, as long as you need it."

"No. I cannot stay." Barbara hung her head.

"Babs, I beg of you." Adam held his hands out to her.

"No! I will not be a prisoner in your house. I will not lie to the world, and be neither wife nor daughter. And I will not be treated by you as though I were a wayward child!"

There was a long pause. Adam stuck his hands in his breeches pockets and raised his chin. "Very well. I regret I did not realize the extent of your suffering under my roof."

"Papa." Her voice quivered. "I did not mean—"

"Just remember, miss, I gave you shelter when many a father would have turned you from his door, and as I should have done. Go, then. I trust this time your husband honors his vows, for you'll not find refuge with me again. You've made your bed, and you'll lie on it."

Adam stalked out, the door slamming shut behind him.

"Barbara, stop your blubbering." There was a steely, unpleasant edge to Sanders' voice. He opened the door, muttering an oath. "You there, get the children ready to travel. We leave in ten minutes."

Fabienne took Barbara's hand. "Give your father time. I hope he will relent." She took a card from her reticule. "This is my address in London. Please call on me."

"Thank you. I shall, if George allows it." Barbara gave her husband a nervous glance.

"I am sure he shall," Fabienne said, loud enough for Sanders to hear.

"Mrs. Craigmont, I thank you again for your help in finding my wife, and wish you good day." Sanders held the parlor door open.

As Fabienne walked past Sanders, he whispered, "I

am not ungrateful, my dear Fabienne. I will call on you soon."

"I shall be delighted to receive Mrs. Sanders," Fabienne said, and walked out, sick at heart. Now all she had to do was retrieve her bag of belongings from her room and leave, but two figures at the foot of the staircase blocked her way. Neither of them saw her pause in the shadowy corner of the hall.

Will stood next to his grandfather, kicking the newel post. "But I wanted to ride with you today, Grandpapa."

"I looked forward to it too." Adam, seated on the bottom step of the staircase, rubbed the knuckles of one hand.

"I don't want to go away." Will's lower lip pushed out.

"You must go with your mama and papa," Adam said. "Come, be a brave boy and do as you're told. Give me a kiss good-bye."

"No." Will put his hands behind his back.

"Enough, boy." Adam stood, reaching his hand toward the bowed head of his grandson, as though to touch the child's hair one last time. He stepped away as a nursemaid with Julia in her arms, and another servant carrying their bags, descended the stairs. Adam nodded to them and walked away, toward the front door of the house and outside into the bright sunlight, his footsteps crunching on the gravel.

The nursemaid took Will's hand, and led him out, chattering to him. The small boy rubbed his eyes with his free hand, his head hanging.

Fabienne waited until they were outside, then ran upstairs and threw her few belongings into her traveling bag. When she came back down, the hall was deserted, apart from a boy who pushed a broom over the black-and-white marble tiles.

"The master wants to speak to you," the child said.

"Where is he?"

"In the wilderness. Follow the sound of the ax, mistress, and you'll find the master."

"The ax?" Now she heard it, a dull *thock-thock*.

"He likes to chop wood, mistress." The boy touched his forelock and applied himself to his sweeping.

"I see," said Fabienne, bemused, and a little apprehensive about meeting an angry and humiliated man armed with an ax. She walked out into the bright sunlight, the hem of her skirt darkening with dew as she crossed the lawn, past a knot garden, and toward a ruined stone arch. The sound of the ax grew louder.

His dogs lay on the grass nearby, and stood, stretching, tails waving, as she approached. Adam, ax in one hand, stepped back from a tree stump surrounded by pieces of kindling. Nearby, a large pile of roughly chopped pieces of timber indicated a sizable tree had been felled earlier. His coat, waistcoat, and neckcloth were tossed onto a nearby log.

"Mrs. Craigmont." He bent to lift another piece of wood onto the stump, and raised the ax. "Are you Sanders' mistress?"

"No, I am not! If you bade me meet you here to insult me, I shall leave. If you have anything civil to say to me, then please say it."

The ax fell and the wood split at its impact. "I beg your pardon." Adam wrenched the ax from the scored surface of the stump and pushed the severed wood onto its center. He indicated a large log. "Will you sit?"

"What do you wish to ask me?"

"Just this." He concentrated on the wood, splitting it into neat fragments. "If Barbara calls on you, I would be obliged if you let my sister, Lady Eglinton, know."

She shrugged. "After your discourtesy I owe you nothing."

He pushed the split wood from the block. "I apologize."

She bowed her head in acknowledgment. "Very well. I should possibly require a favor in return."

"I cannot imagine what I could possibly do for you, Mrs. Craigmont, but I am entirely at your service."

"Thank you." She changed the subject before he could question her further. "Why are you chopping wood?"

Adam raised the ax again, the muscles of his back clearly delineated against the damp linen of his shirt. "I sublimate my passions, madam. It is possibly a concept with which you are unfamiliar."

"I see you sublimate your manners, also. Good morning, Mr. Ashworth." She walked away from him. To hell with him if he wished to take out his anger and frustration on her.

"Fabienne, he beats her." The sadness and helplessness in his voice, as much as the shock of his use of her Christian name, made her turn back to him.

"Adam?" Fabienne looked at him, seeing again the fatigue on his face, gray shadows beneath his eyes, silvery stubble on his jaw. "She told you this?"

He swallowed. "She arrived unexpectedly here at the new year, her face bruised, and much shocked and saddened. She would not talk, just wept, for several days. She had other bruises, so her maid told me, and the marks of a belt on her back. Damn her!" He burst out. "Why did she go back to him?"

"He is the father of her children," Fabienne said. "And what he said is true, that he could take them."

"What could I have done? Cut him down like a dog in front of her? I almost wish to God I had." He gave a twisted smile. "I bought his commission as captain after I found he had got Babs with child and was almost bankrupt. He swore then he would forsake the gaming tables, a promise he did not keep. Maybe I should have defied society and decency then and let her raise his bastard under my roof. What could I do?"

"I don't know," Fabienne said. "What you did, you did for the best."

"I have done all I can," he said. "This is the end of it."

"But your grandchildren—"

"That, madam, is my business." He wrenched the ax from the tree stump.

"Then there is nothing more to say. You ask me for sympathy, or advice—I know not which—and then spurn it."

"Judge me if you will. Many a father would have

turned her away when she ran from her husband, not lied for her and offered her protection. Most men, I believe, would have long disowned a daughter who forced a father's consent to a marriage in such a way. I have had enough. I can do no more." He ran his thumb along the blade of the ax and watched the blood well. "She is dead to me now." Blood trickled down his hand, over the brand of a flame on his forearm, the mark he would carry for the rest of his life. She remembered that brand, remembered the hair and sinew of his arms, the texture and taste of his skin. Her tongue had once followed the path now traced by his blood. She shivered and drew her shawl more closely around herself.

One of the dogs whined, pushing its nose against Adam's thigh.

"It is your decision, sir," Fabienne said. "I am sorry for it. I would have expected more generosity, and less fear of society's wagging tongues from you."

"Would you?" He stanched the flow of blood with a handkerchief from his coat pocket. "Then you don't know me, Mrs. Craigmont, or the man I am now. It's easy enough to play the moralist, as you have pointed out to me, but you do not have children, madam, and it makes you a poor judge of this matter."

It was on the tip of her tongue to tell him what she had never told a soul, before she lashed out at him, close to tears herself now. "If I lack judgment, you lack delicacy. I lost a child, once, Mr. Ashworth. I'll bid you good day."

She turned and retraced her footsteps in the dew-darkened grass. She suspected he watched her leave, but did not turn to see.

Chapter Five

"These letters will tell you all," the hooded figure said,
pointing to a bundle of aged parchment, stained with
the decay of the grave, that lay beneath the yellowed
bones of the skeletal hand. "Yes, take them, and read
words no living being has seen, learn secrets so sacred
none dare speak of them. All save one thing that you
must discover yourself—if you have honor and daring enough."
    —The Curse of the Molfitains by Mrs. Ravenwood.

Forgive me.
    You asked me not to write, but I must.
    Much has happened in the past week. You know, of
course, that I came in search of you, and now I know
your reasons for concealment. If at any time you wish
to break free, please, I beg you, come to London,
where you have a friend—myself.
    As for me, I am lonely and troubled. As I told you,
my protégée, Elaine Twyford, lives with me, and is the
joy of my life. Yet I keep a secret from her which she
has every right to know, and which I should have told
her when first I discovered her and brought her to
London. I have never before told a soul of this.
    She is my natural daughter. I fear when I tell her
she will be angry and wounded, and I am weak enough
to postpone the revelation for my own protection.
    I do not dare to hope she will love me as my daugh-
ter, for Mrs. Twyford, who raised her, is her true

mother. Neither can I tell her who her father is. I wish only to make amends for my abandonment of her as an infant. I gave birth to her when I was very young, and betrothed to my first husband, Thomas Rowe. He was in India, preparing for his bride, never realizing I carried another's child. I was near crazy with fear that he would find out, and cut off support to my mother and brother, throwing us into penury amongst strangers. My mother was ill, dying of consumption, and advised me to abort the child as other women do. I could not.

Elaine knows, of course, that she is adopted, and accepts that she is illegitimate. Such children are taught to be content with their lot and I believe she thinks little about the truth of her parentage.

I saw her at her birth only briefly, yet I shall remember that moment all my life.

I cannot tell her the truth. It has been two years since she came to live with me, and I am struck dumb.

I justify it thus. Elaine is much troubled by London and by society, and fears her own corruption—and I am one of those she fears. I was shocked to discover she prays for me, fervently, every night, on her knees. She believes I am damned because I was raised as a Catholic, that there are rumors of my lovers, although I assure you I have been most discreet since she came to live in my house. I tell myself she is not ready to hear me yet, but I know the longer I leave it, the more she will hate me for my silence and deception.

Furthermore—and this also is my weak will speaking—she is in love with a man who probably will not marry her, though I am sure he will not act in any sort of ungentlemanly way toward her. I do not wish to make her suffer further—so I think to myself and despise myself for it.

I have also met recently with a man whom I once loved passionately, and it has awoken many memories of my past. I believed he loved me too—although I was young and foolish enough to believe anything— yet he betrayed me in the cruelest and most callous way. I have hated him for it, and now—well, I have not spent two decades planning revenge, like a character (I say it with all due respect) in one of your books, for I believe that way lies madness. I wish only for peace, for release from dreams that plague me, and I am at my wit's end.

How I wish we could meet and talk. I beg your pardon for writing only of myself, but believe me, you are much in my thoughts, and I hope I am not presumptuous in signing myself your most loyal friend,

Fabienne Craigmont.

My dearest Fabienne,

I was determined to write no more, as you know, but your letter moved me deeply. Although I had the best and noblest intentions as to why we should no longer correspond, I must reply.

I beg of you, tell your daughter the truth. You must. You know it, and maybe you will find that having spelled out your fears, they do not appear insurmountable. If she has any regard for you, she will forgive you. It may seem strange to advise a mother to throw herself upon her daughter's mercy, but that is what you must do. You mention she is devout, and surely she can forgive you, as her faith demands? Doubtless you have considered this yourself. You have lost your child once, but pray God you will not lose her again.

My heart too is lonely and sad. I have lost one dear to me, one who, despite many faults and much strife, is now gone, I believe forever. There can be no forgiveness here, I fear. I think much of the past, of mistakes I have made, of wrongs I cannot right. And you, of course, are quite correct. One cannot dedicate a lifetime to revenge or atonement for decades and remain sane. I am thankful that my work engages me and I am able to fill the hours and days as profitably as possible.

Although widowed now, I was fortunate enough to experience unexpected marital happiness for some ten years. We did not start well, for I was much enamored of another who had spurned me cruelly, and I fancied my heart broken for some time. Then I awoke one day

*and discovered myself to be in love, and the world
changed, and I counted myself the luckiest of beings.*

I never expect to have such happiness again.

*Fabienne, tell me of yourself, how you spend your
days. You are much in my thoughts. I slept last night
with your letter against my heart; is not that foolish?
We hardly know each other, but soul to soul, somehow, we can speak of intimate things. Now I sound
like a character from one of my own silly novels—one
of which awaits me, a stern mistress to whom I must
address myself ere long.*

*I could of course babble endlessly of village gossip,
and how Tom Blackhill grows a marrow of a monstrous size, and he claims it is such from pouring beer
on the roots to the toll of the church bell. It smacks of
witchcraft to me.*

*But I digress. Write again, and consider me indeed
your most devoted, and sympathetic, of friends,*

Sybil Ravenwood.

*   *   *

My dearest Sybil,
    How happy I was to receive your letter . . .

"Mrs. Craigmont, will you come to the kitchen,
ma'am?"

Fabienne frowned. "I told you I was not to be disturbed, Susan. What's wrong?"

"Beg your pardon. It's Miss Elaine. She's hurt."

"What?" Fabienne pushed her chair back. "How?"

"A sprained ankle, ma'am. Ma'am, do come down.
Monseer is in a foul mood, and there is egg all over
the floor."

Fabienne laid her pen down and proceeded to the
kitchen, where the cook mopped the floor, grumbling
and cursing in French. Elaine sat on a chair, her ankle
propped on one knee.

"She is a clumsy cow, madam!" The cook pointed at
Susan. "She broke a dozen eggs."

"I saw a mouse! I was frightened. I couldn't help it." Susan burst into tears.

"Ha! And the fire is out, and it is because there are too many women here!" The cook brandished his mop in emphasis, spattering the onlookers with dirty egg.

Fabienne sighed. "Enough, monsieur. Let me see your ankle, Elaine."

"I cannot walk on it. I slipped on the eggs."

Fabienne helped Elaine stand, and she and Susan assisted her upstairs, and settled her on the couch in Fabienne's parlor.

"I have to work," Elaine whined.

"Certainly not."

"But—"

"We shall send word to your clients. You must rest your ankle, as I am sure the doctor will tell you when he comes. Susan will bathe it for you."

"I will be so behind. I—"

"Oh, hush. You'll be up and about in a couple of days." Fabienne resisted the urge to stroke Elaine's hair, and turned back to her letter.

> . . . *Today I am plagued with domestic matters. My cook rages and roars like a demented beast, and* . . .

"Fabienne?"

"Go away, Ippolite."

Ippolite stood over Elaine, and scratched his head. "A sprain? Let me help. Susan, hand me that cloth."

"No!" Elaine pulled her skirts over her feet.

"Have some sense of decorum, brother. What is it you want?"

Ippolite thrust a piece of paper at Fabienne. "Look!"

"The laundry list?"

"Yes. It says ten shirts, but only eight came back."

"Talk to your manservant."

"But he's out. You sent him on some errand."

"Ippolite." Fabienne spoke firmly and clearly. "If you do not leave, I shall come and deal with your shirts myself. I shall bring a large pair of shears. Now leave."

He did so, muttering under his breath.

The front door bell jangled, and a few seconds later the footman announced the arrival of Viscount Tillotson. Although strongly tempted to tell him to come back another time, Fabienne relented when she saw how Elaine's face lit up.

. . . and I can scarcely believe it has taken me some twenty minutes, interrupted by household trivialities, to write this far.

My child is hurt, and sulks hideously on the sofa. She angers me so often, and then I feel guilty, but she can be difficult. She is kindest to Luke—the man with whom she is in love, and who visits now. He blushed most charmingly when she mentioned her sprained ankle, which made her blush in turn. I think he would like to bathe the injured limb, but I fear it might be too overwhelmingly amorous an act for them both.

And it rains—not like the steaming torrents of India, or the gentle showers of the countryside, but bad, dirty London rain that only makes worse the summer stink of the city. How I envy you in the country at such times! India, of course, had its share of filth and terrible afflictions. It was a vivid and shocking place, which I never came to understand; and always I felt myself a stranger there, even among the other Company people. My first marriage, to a Mr. Rowe, was not happy. I do not think he realized his bride was despoiled, but I am certain the marriage bed brought him little pleasure, and certainly not the child he hoped for. After his death I was in no hurry to marry again, but when Mr. Craigmont, a man I esteemed and respected, made me an offer, it seemed churlish to refuse.

He did not attempt to consummate the marriage. I had heard that such marriages exist, but I was still a young and tolerably beautiful woman. (This is not vanity. I know what I am.) And I wondered why he did not come to my bed.

He was a wise man. He knew I had delayed grieving for my losses, and suffered from hidden wounds. He possibly suspected my other, equally painful loss—my child, thoughts of whom stayed with me like a shadow. He knew that until I was beyond acknowledging my grief I could not enjoy the pleasures of my body, and it was true—only occasionally, alone, could I summon the ec- stasy of a skilled lover's hands and parts. (My dear friend, I trust I do not shock you with my frankness?)

So one day we rode out alone to a ruined temple where ancient people worshipped the body and the acts of love, in a hundred imaginative couplings on a stone frieze. I was shocked, aroused, and moved by their beauty. Emboldened by the heat and solitude, I raised my skirts and bid my husband have his way with me.

"No," he told me. "I would have you naked."

He asked of me what I did not think I could ever offer any man—absolute trust, a nakedness of body and soul. I was terrified. Among the ruined stones, I wept with mortification. He kindly straightened my clothing, and bid me tell him my sorrows. And words finally spilled out of me. I told of him of my father, who had gone nobly to his death, and of my mother, who until the day she died lived in a world of her own fantasy, believing my father to be alive and anticipating the restoration of our lands and fortunes. I told him everything—almost everything. I did not tell him of the child I had abandoned, although I know he saw the marks of childbearing on my belly. I told him only how I had loved unwisely when I was young, and of my betrayal.

After that, the removal of my clothing seemed not only trivial but natural, and for the first time in my life I achieved the highest ecstasy in a man's arms . . .

* * *

"Oh balderdash, Fabienne." Adam looked around to make sure no one was nearby. It was bad enough to be caught with a bulge in his breeches, but to be talking to himself too. . . . He rested the letter on the pigsty wall, adjusted his glasses, and read on.

. . . thus beginning the happiest time in my life. For although a man of advanced years, some twenty-five

*years my senior, Mr. Craigmont was a man of excep-
tional virility, well-versed in the arts of love, sympathetic to a woman's particular needs and desires. I
believe you will understand me. Not only did we mimic
the pagan immortals—I am blessed with great flexibil-
ity of the limbs—but we performed acts others might
call unnatural.*

Christ almighty. Adam looked around again, and tried
to adjust the tangle of shirt, underdrawers, and rigid flesh
inside his breeches. His pigs made rude grunting,
squelching sounds, their wet snouts twitching in a way
that suddenly seemed obscene.

> *Although I believe my first lover to have been com-
petent, I realize now he had rather too high an opinion
of his prowess. To his credit, though, since I held him
at arm's length for so long, delaying the act, it was no
wonder he could barely contain himself, leaving me
astonished and unsatisfied. I have found other young
men to be—*

"Devil take her!" Adam ripped the letter in half and
flung it into the pigsty. His pigs rushed forward with
enthusiastic slurps. Adam attempted to snatch the fragments of paper from their jaws, cursing heartily at both
the loss of the letter and at what he had read so far.

Damn her. And he had thought his identity was hidden! Why else would she throw out such barbs about his
amorous performance, hurl in his face casual admissions
about her other lovers? And he thought he had been so
careful in his correspondence to her, hedging between
the truth and his fictional identity.

Even though he had done his best to distract her in
the library, she must have seen his writing. But then she
had also hinted that he was Elaine's father—why had she
done so? He remembered the morning Barbara had left,
when Fabienne had mentioned she might call upon him
to return a favor. Did she wish him to acknowledge his
natural daughter? Somehow, he thought not.

Elaine. He thought again of the young woman, apparently his daughter. He had wept when first realizing the truth, his tears blurring Fabienne's words. Initial elation had faded to unease and sadness. He tried to recall Elaine's features, searching for a family resemblance.

Why had Fabienne not sent him word when she had found she was with child? And what would he have done? She might well have believed that Adam had tired of her, since he had told her it only a matter of time before he moved on to his next conquest. But the fact remained that she had written that devastating letter telling him their liaison was over. He had returned to the country, smarting at the indignity, the rake jilted, and married Mags to punish himself—to find someone else to punish. Poor Mags. She'd told him later how disappointed she was to have discovered her childhood sweetheart transformed into a wretch wallowing in self-pity.

Elaine, his daughter. One daughter lost, another found, and neither his to acknowledge. He remembered Babs' outburst in the library, the venom in her voice, the sweet daughter he thought he'd rescued, not imprisoned. There was still no word of her, and he had no idea what he would do if she begged for his pardon. She had rejected his protection and humiliated him in front of her blackhearted wretch of a husband and Fabienne—Fabienne, whom he had insisted stay in the room.

He was a fool. Mags would have told him so, he knew. *You may be cleverer than everyone else, Adam, but sometimes you're very stupid.*

Two daughters in London. He needed to see them. Or at least, to get another look at Elaine, maybe talk to her. And he'd probably see Fabienne too.

Of course he'd see Fabienne. He had to.

What in God's name was happening to him?

Chapter Six

Elvira moved among the gay throng, clad in the rich raiment that her captor insisted she don, although her heart was heavy in her breast. Soon the one she sought would reveal himself, by word or gesture, but meanwhile the revelry sickened her.

"Oh, why will you not come to me? Why must I suffer so?"

—The Ruined Tower by Mrs. Ravenwood.

"*I*t is so foolish of me." Barbara Sanders gestured at the bruise on her cheekbone. "I am very clumsy."

"And how are the children?" Fabienne enquired. "I should like to see them the next time you visit."

"Very well. Julia crawls now, and Will . . ." She paused to take a sip of tea and lapsed into silence again.

"I hope you have found pleasant lodgings."

"Oh, yes, they are quite comfortable. Only we are to move at the end of the week. There has been some misunderstanding with the lease, I believe." Her cup rattled on its saucer. She set it down quickly, not meeting Fabienne's eyes. It was the longest statement she had made since entering Fabienne's drawing room. After some desultory conversation about the weather and their respective states of health, Barbara had mentioned the fall—according to her—which had bruised her face.

"I hope you will send me word when you are settled," Fabienne said. "I should like you to meet Elaine. She is

at work today, finishing the classical piece—you know
Viscount Tillotson poses for her."

"Oh, yes." A flash of animation. "How is dear Luke?"

"Very well. Will you attend the ball next week to celebrate his coming of age?"

"I believe we are engaged that night." Barbara bit
her lip.

Fabienne could have kicked herself. Barbara, an out-
cast from her family, had obviously not been invited, and
might not even have known of it.

"Barbara, listen to me." Fabienne rose from her chair
and grasped the younger woman's hands. "I am not a
fool and you do not have to continue this masquerade
with me. Do not risk your health and life. Bring the
children here, or go to your aunt's. But please, I beg
you, do not stay with your husband."

Barbara pulled her hands away. "I—I assure you it is
not as it looks. It is just that he gets angry with me
sometimes, because I am—well, it is my way, I suppose.
I am quite well and most happy with my dearest George.
He cannot help that he is a passionate man."

"For God's sake, Barbara, think of your children."

A deep flush spread over Barbara's cheeks. She stood,
fumbling for her gloves and bonnet. "I love my children
and George is the most affectionate of fathers. I regret
I must leave now. Good afternoon."

"Barbara, please, stay a little longer."

"No, thank you. It was good of you to receive me."

"I promised your aunt, Lady Eglinton, I would send
word if I saw you." It was almost the truth. She hesitated
to bring up Adam's name.

Barbara shrugged. "Do as you will. Please convey my
best wishes to Lady Eglinton."

"I beg of you," Fabienne said, "remember that I am
your friend. I am here if you have need of me. I—"

"Good-bye." Barbara fairly bolted out of the room.

Fabienne stared after her, sick at heart. She had failed,
driving Barbara away with her bluntness. She sat at her
desk and penned a quick note to Lady Eglinton, saying
merely that she had seen Barbara, but did not know

where the family lodged. After it was sealed and handed over to her footman for delivery, she opened the secret compartment in her desk drawer.

There had been so many letters, one or two a day, some small notes, others crossed almost to illegibility. She gave the bundle of letters tied with ribbon a brief caress before picking up the sheet that lay atop, the latest missive from Sybil Ravenwood.

My dearest Fabienne,

I must speak. I can barely describe the effect your words have on me. As I read, I imagined a lover's touch on my own skin. I was aroused, intrigued, moved.

I marvel at the degree of intimacy we have reached, although there is still so much we do not know about each other. Fabienne, I cannot withdraw from you now, but I fear you will feel only the gravest anger and disappointment when we meet. I give you the opportunity to end this correspondence, although I yearn for your letters, and my heart leaps within my breast at the sight of your writing. I am too weak to end our exchange of letters, although I tried once, but I cannot resist you. I ask you to do it, thus saving yourself inevitable pain and embarrassment. I will bear the loss as best I may. If you refuse, and my heart both hopes and dreads you will, I beg of you, do not ever reproach yourself for what has passed between us. It is I who will be to blame, and you shall know why, and I do not expect forgiveness or mercy.

And yet I am in so deep now I cannot, do not wish to, escape. I have never had a friendship as profound, as innocent, and yet as passionate as this, and I fear for both of us.

It pains me to know that this admission is grounds enough for you to discontinue our correspondence immediately; that even were a man to address a woman he barely knows in this way, it would be grossly improper. As for the two of us, well, my frankness may well be the end of it. I cannot blame you, and neither can I blame myself.

*Love is not something we control, but its expression
is our choice, and I know I may make a terrible mistake in this. I suspect I have done so ever since we first
encountered each other.*

Forgive me, but I beg of you, write to me.

Sybil.

*It's a love letter. A love letter from a woman. I must be
mad, or she is, or we both are.* Fabienne's breath came
fast and a tide of heat rushed to her face. *It's strange,
but I feel no distaste, no shame. Only a deep longing.* She
touched a curl of hair that trailed over her collarbone as
desire burned in her belly. She wanted to stretch like a
cat in the sun, give herself over to the sweetness of a
lover's embrace.

The door opened. Ippolite gave her a curious glance
as she tucked the letter from Sybil Ravenwood into her
bodice. "Are you well? You look very flushed." He
tossed an envelope onto the table. "It seems we are
about to enter the world of the *ton*."

"We are?" She tried to collect her thoughts as she
examined the wax seal on the letter. "Lord and Lady
Eglinton have invited us to the ball for Tillotson's coming
of age. Well, well."

"Why are you surprised?"

"They're too grand for us, and I suspect they don't
know Luke courts Elaine. I told you how enraged Luke's
godfather was when he found out about them."

"Ah, yes, your Mr. Ashworth. I wonder if he'll be
there."

"He is not *my* Mr. Ashworth." Her sharpness surprised her.

Ippolite drew back, curiosity on his face. "I did not
mean to offend you."

"You didn't." She patted the papers on her desk into
a neat stack. The letter from Sybil Ravenwood scratched
with a delicate insistence against her skin. "I need to
walk." Fabienne rose to her feet. "I'll go with Susan to
collect Elaine."

"Should I accompany you?"

"No, there is no need. We shall be perfectly safe."

"I trust you are right. Has she mentioned again that she is afraid that someone follows her?"

"No, I think she fears to make me nervous. Walk with me if you will, Ippolite, though I don't feel much like talking."

"Very well." He waited while she arranged her bonnet and shawl. "I shan't be so indiscreet as to ask who your lover is. I saw you hide that letter."

"I don't have a lover." Crimson heat washed over her face as the paper caressed her skin.

* * *

Fabienne,
Forgive me for the brevity of this note, which I send in haste from my publisher's office. As you see, I am in London. I will be at Tillotson's ball.

S.R.

* * *

My dearest Sybil,
At last we shall meet. We must be together and I long to talk with you. As ever, I am your beloved friend,

Fabienne.

* * *

I cannot wait to meet her. And then what? Fabienne was wild with longing, hoping and dreading that Sybil would call on her. Would they find themselves unable to cope with emotions expressed so eloquently during the past few weeks? Would they kiss like old friends or shrink from each other in embarrassment? Would further intimacy be a clumsy disappointment or a revelation?

She was grateful that the last few days had been frantically busy. Elaine, after much thought, had agreed to attend the ball, and after more soul searching, scrubbed the paint from her fingers and allowed Fabienne to buy her a new gown.

As the young woman came down the stairs of the house, Susan followed behind her, clucking like a worried hen. Elaine's hair was curled and interwoven with rosebuds, and her light blue gown was of modest, simple cut by fashionable standards. It had caused her to blush when she first looked in the mirror, but Fabienne noticed with some amusement that Elaine sought out her reflection when she thought no one watched.

"I am afraid," Elaine said.

"Why?"

"That Luke will not really want me there. Maybe he has just invited us to be kind."

"If he doesn't make you an offer tonight, he is a fool," Ippolite said. He handed Fabienne and Elaine into the hackney carriage with a nod of approval. "You look quite ravishing."

"Thank you." Elaine blushed and examined the spokes of her fan as the carriage drew into the traffic.

Well, that would certainly enrage Adam Ashworth. Fabienne believed that Lord and Lady Eglinton were Luke's other godparents, and they were certain to disapprove even more strongly. But she didn't care. Tonight she would meet Sybil. Had either of them been less giddy, or had more time, she would have thought to ask Sybil what she looked like. She harbored a silly notion that they would immediately know each other.

Of course Adam would be there too, and perhaps that explained Sybil's sudden arrival in London, as well as her refusal to meet, despite Fabienne's continued pleas. Fabienne had purposely not mentioned her former liaison with him again, and she suspected Sybil, from natural delicacy, also did not mention her protector. Fabienne had never been entirely sure that Sybil and Adam had broken off their connection; there had been the first mention of someone dear to her heart who was now lost, and much sadness and loneliness in her letters. Now, with Sybil suddenly in London, it seemed that she was once

again Adam's mistress, if indeed she had ever ceased
to be.

The carriage jerked to a halt.

Ippolite opened the door and stepped down. "There's
a devil of a crush. We'd better walk from here. It's but
a few yards."

Fabienne hoisted her skirts and stepped onto the
street, avoiding piles of refuse and dung, with Elaine
following behind. Elaine grasped her hand. "Why, Fabienne, you shake almost as much as I do."

"You imagine things." Fabienne smiled with an effort.
"There is no need to be nervous. Luke will be there, and
many others you know, I expect. I will look after you,
and so will Ippolite." She doubted it. Ippolite would be
off flirting and gambling after the first few dances, and
they would probably not see him until the next day.

Inside the house wax candles blazed, reflected in the
gleaming marble of the entrance hall. As they joined the
crush of guests on the steps, common people loitered in
the street, children offering to hold horses' reins, a few
beggars, some staring passersby.

*Oh, please let her come to me. Please let everything
be well.*

The two women stopped in the ladies' cloakroom to
leave their outer wraps, Fabienne fighting impatience as
Elaine lingered in front of the mirror.

"It is vanity." Elaine was pale, and her hand cold when
Fabienne took it.

"Don't be ridiculous. You look very well, and I assure
you, you are the least vain person I know."

"I cannot be here. I want to go home."

"You are nervous—that is all. Come, take a deep
breath."

Elaine stood frozen. "This dress . . . it is unseemly."

"For heaven's sake, look around you. Look at me. You
are exceedingly modest by comparison. Now no more
nonsense." She grabbed Elaine's hand and hauled her
outside into the ballroom.

They approached Lady Eglinton, whom Fabienne rec-

ognized from chance sightings at the theater, flanked by
her two daughters. Fabienne smiled, and nudged Elaine
into a curtsy. "Lady Eglinton, we are most grateful for
your invitation."

"You are welcome, Mrs. Craigmont. So this is the
young lady artist. These are my daughters, Mary and
Sylvia."

Fabienne and Elaine curtsied again, murmuring polite greetings.

"I should like to talk to you about a portrait, Miss
Twyford," Lady Eglinton continued. "Mrs. Craigmont, I
thank you for the service you have done my family. You
know to what I refer. You are welcome at our house."

"Thank you, my lady." Fabienne breathed a sigh of
relief. Lady Eglinton might look and behave like any
other conventional *ton* matron, but her eyes, a familiar
blue-gray, were shrewd and knowing. It was she who had
summoned Luke's irate godfather to town, and doubtless
she knew all the family secrets.

Ippolite escorted them to a couple of empty chairs at
one side of the ballroom, a brilliant scene of color and
movement, marble and gilt hung with greenery and flowers.
Fabienne spotted Luke among the dancers, and saw a few
other familiar faces. Ippolite offered to fetch refresh-
ments, engaged Elaine for the next dance, and then left
to find other partners.

As Fabienne watched the dance, she tried to identify
Sybil Ravenwood. What did she really know of the
writer? Fabienne had no clues as to her appearance, or
her age, although she suspected from Sybil's statement
that her heart had been untouched for some years and,
from a mention of a marriage of ten years' duration, that
she must be at least thirty. Yes, she might well be like
Fabienne, sitting alone and watching younger and more
beautiful women dance and flirt.

When the dance ended, Luke came to greet them. He
stared at Elaine openmouthed before engaging her for
three dances. He looked slightly affronted that she was
already engaged to Ippolite for the next dance, and Fa-

bienne thought that a little competition would do him no harm at all.

"And how are you, Mrs. Craigmont? You look most handsome."

"Thank you, Luke—or should I now address you as 'my lord?'"

"Good heavens, no. We are better friends than that, I hope." He raised her hand to his lips.

"And who taught you to flirt so? But tell me, have you met Mrs. Ravenwood yet tonight?"

He frowned, confused. "Mrs. Ravenwood? Here? Are you certain?"

"Absolutely. I was assured she would be here."

"That is—no, you must be mistaken." He looked uncomfortable, as though caught out in a half-truth.

"No matter," she said. "Go and talk to your guests."

She watched him leave and turned her attention again to the dancers, almost sick with disappointment.

Then she felt it—a thrill of anticipation, desire, and dread that licked up her spine, ice turning to a burn.

You're here. At last.

Chapter Seven

A shaft of moonlight illuminated an asymmetry in the elaborate carving of the wall, and Serena watched with a thrill of horror as, with a ghastly creak, a section of paneling swung open. She gave a gasp of terror. It was not the beloved form of Roderigo that appeared, but a knight clad in armor as black as night.

Was it a phantom?

But no. He spoke. "Beware, lady. Abandon your quest. You are betrayed and only sorrow can follow."

—*The Spectre of the Abbey* by Mrs. Ravenwood.

"*M*rs. Craigmont."

Adam stood beside her. The last time she had seen him, he had been unshaven and distraught, dressed in a soiled and crumpled shirt and breeches, his hair disordered. Now he wore a finely tailored dark blue coat and breeches, and a sapphire glittered in the folds of his neckcloth.

"Mr. Ashworth." She shivered as he took her hand and she felt the heat of his lips through her glove. Bitter disappointment welled within her, followed by rage at his untimely appearance.

"You look very well, Mrs. Craigmont."

"Thank you. As do you."

"Ah, well, sometimes I brush off the country mud and leave my pigs." He hesitated. "Will you stand up with me, Mrs. Craigmont?"

"No, sir. I am merely here to observe, and act as Miss Twyford's chaperone."

"Of course. Your charge looks remarkably well tonight." He stared at Elaine, a thoughtful expression on his face. "It is a most strange thing. For a moment there, she almost had a look of Babs about her."

"They are both unusually tall women."

"Not so much that, but in the way she moves, her gestures." His gaze was steely blue when it turned back to Fabienne. "How old is Miss Twyford?"

"Nineteen," she said, before realizing her folly.

For a moment she saw a curious mix of emotions on his face, shock, relief, sadness. He cleared his throat. "Well, we may as well continue to talk while we dance." He bowed and held out his hand. "We can join the set here."

"Very well," she said. "I daresay it will not cause too much talk, that a chaperone stand up."

"As if you cared for that. I hope you still like to dance," he commented as the music began.

"I do. If I could, I would dance every dance." They circled, crossed, and were separated for a brief time.

"If it would not cause scandal, or ruin my chances of matrimony, Mrs. Craigmont, I would request you as my partner for the whole evening."

She laughed. "Matrimony—that is why you are in London?"

"So my sister likes to think. You know why else I am here, of course. We'll talk of that later, and not have our dancing interrupted by serious business."

"I didn't know you liked dancing so much."

"Like so many things, it depends on who one's partner is."

She raised her eyebrows. "Indeed. I would say it depends on a great many other things—the size of the room, the company, the expertise of the musicians."

He smiled and took her hand as the dance demanded. "You may be right, though I admit I find it pleasing for another reason. It reminds me of mathematics."

"How? I do not see how there can be a connection."

"Observe the patterns we make, the variations. This is what the study of mathematics used to be like for me. It was like strolling in a pleasant garden, where all was harmony and symmetry."

"Barbara showed me the knot garden at your house," Fabienne said.

"That is exactly what I mean—contrived yet full of grace. Of course, I was cast out of the garden of mathematics some time ago."

"How can that be?"

The lines of dancers crossed, interwove, and broke into sets again. "I lost the gift," he said when they next met. "It happens to many who flourish early in mathematics. By the time I was twenty, I had been at Cambridge some four years and found it harder each time to wander the paths of the garden, and knew that soon its gates would be closed to me."

"What did you do then?"

He took her hands to lead her down the line of couples. "My father suggested I take the Grand Tour, and when I returned to London, I met you."

"You never told me any of this before."

"Well, we did not talk much then, did we? As for the mathematics, I can still do work far beyond the ability of others, and I dabble in a gentlemanly sort of way— when I am not tending to my pigs, of course."

"Ah, yes. Your treatise."

"So," he said, when the dance brought them together again, "you have seen into my soul, Mrs. Craigmont. And of course you know the worst of my family, too."

"I am not sure whether that is a privilege or a responsibility, Mr. Ashworth." She wondered at his sudden openness.

"Forgive me if I mention it, but you look around as though there were someone you seek."

"I do. You must think me abominably rude."

"Not at all. May I ask who it is?"

The dance separated them before she could make, or evade, a reply. When they were together again, hand in hand, face-to-face, it was to the last measures of the music.

He bowed over her hand. "Will you walk awhile with me, Mrs. Craigmont? Possibly you will spy this person whom you seek, and besides, you and I must talk."

"But Elaine—"

"She is with Luke, and I assure you she could not be safer. I believe they are to dance at least the next three dances together. Tongues will certainly wag then, and if you are worried about your reputation, anything we two could do will be of little consequence."

"Very well."

He should tell her. Of course he should tell her, and that would be the end of it. And after he had suffered her anger and scorn, seen her mortification, she would leave and they might never speak again.

He escorted her to where Elaine and Luke stood, and watched as the two women had a brief conversation. Meanwhile he went in search of some wine, and returned to find the next dance under way. Fabienne, seated at the side of the room, looked composed, but one hand clenched the handle of her fan so hard he wondered if she would break it. Her gaze shifted around the ballroom, and he knew her distress was his doing.

He could not help stopping a little distance away to admire her. She was simply ravishing, dressed in a soft gold that glinted bronze and copper in the light—silk from her Indian nabob, of course—the sumptuous fabric cut in a simple style. A length of the same silk was twisted into her hair with a rope of large, opulent pearls. The effect was one of stunning simplicity and sensuality, as though an Eastern queen had plucked items from her treasure chest, twisted a few riches into her hair, and gone forth to amaze her subjects.

She started as though someone touched her shoulder and turned her head. Again he saw a flash of pain and disappointment in her eyes.

He offered her his arm and led her out of the ballroom and onto the terrace into the London night air, her gloved fingers warm and light on his sleeve. Had he made a mistake, bringing her out here? It was too much like that evening at his house, not to mention other times twenty years ago when he lured her away from polite pursuits to get his hands up her skirts.

She turned to him with a faint smile and took the glass of wine he offered.

He breathed a sigh of relief. It was all right, then. "I must ask your forgiveness," he began and lost his nerve entirely. Well, God knew he had other things to apologize for. "I behaved in a monstrous fashion to you at my house. I abused my position as your host. I insulted you—"

"Pfft." She waved her free hand in the air and let out her breath in a sort of puff that sounded entirely French. "So you did. Let us forget about it."

"You behaved with great fortitude. You approached a madman with an ax, and you spoke some words I did not wish to hear, but which were entirely true."

She shrugged. "Ah, as to that, I had no right to say such things to you. I tend to be blunt and too open. It is a failing."

"On the contrary, it is a virtue in you." Had he dared, he would have kissed her hand. The old, or rather the young, Adam Ashworth would have done so. He stood frozen to the spot, a yard from her.

"Possibly. Have you seen Barbara?"

"No. They left their lodgings. I have some contacts, old friends, who will help me find her. Thank you again for letting my sister know."

She bowed her head in acknowledgment. "And do you plan to stay in London?"

"I have thought I should, to make sure Sanders keeps up to scratch. I'm staying with my sister while I look for a house."

"I am sure the pigs will be inconsolable," she murmured. She placed her glass on the wall of the terrace and turned to face him. "Call on me, Mr. Ashworth. I told you I will ask a favor of you."

"Certainly." He added, in a teasing tone, "I should

not wish to compromise you, however." Did she really know quite well who Mrs. Ravenwood was, and did she intend to act upon her feelings? He wished he could divine her thoughts, and regretted that he lacked the courage to reveal himself to her.

She fluttered her fan at him. "Why, sir, whatever could you have in mind?"

He grinned. "At my age, not much, so don't flirt with me, Mrs. Craigmont."

"Indeed, sir, you must save your waning strength for the demands of society, if you are to stay in London."

"Ha. If my sister had her way, I would have been engaged ten times over this evening, and most likely to a silly chit younger than my daughter."

"You're not so bad a catch," Fabienne said. "Despite your long hours in the library and pigsty, I am sure the mothers with eligible daughters in London will be all over you like flies on a dead dog."

"What a charming turn of phrase, Mrs. Craigmont." Something in him, the devil that had made him reply to her letters and pour his soul out to her, caused him to blurt out, "I am damnably lonely."

She raised her eyebrows.

He had to say something, even if he could not tell her the truth about himself. "I remembered tonight how you looked the first time I saw you. How ravishing you were then, and still are now."

"I am not the same person, certainly not the same silly girl." Her voice was cool.

He put his wineglass down next to hers and took one step closer to her. Her eyes widened. God only knew what sort of expression he had on his face, as desperation and ravening hunger for her raged through him. He took her hand, raised it to his lips, and pressed his mouth to her palm through the kidskin glove.

She drew her breath in, sharp and quick. "My affections are engaged elsewhere." Her voice wobbled but she did not draw her hand away. "And yours too, I believe."

"No," he said. "You are mistaken."

She snatched her hand away, and ran from the terrace, back into the house, leaving him alone, elated and ashamed.

Cartwheels on cobbles, chiming bells, the cries of street vendors—the sounds of London waking up, or in the case of the *ton*, London retiring for the night. Adam stifled a yawn and approached the man who stood on the steps of the Eglintons' house. "Good morning, sir."

God, he is changed. Greenmore looked ill and ravaged, a yellowish cast to his skin, his eyes weary in discolored hollows. He looked at Adam without recognition. "Good morning, sir." He turned his attention to the traffic again.

"Will you take some breakfast with the family, sir?"

Greenmore snorted. "I think not. My physician expressly forbids breakfast, among other things. Wait, sir. I know you. Why, Adam Ashworth, of all men."

Adam took his offered hand and raised it so their branded wrists touched. "Brother," he said softly.

"Aye, brother. So where have you been these twenty years? In country exile?"

"Yes. I'm sorry I did not get a chance to speak to you at the ball. I only saw you from afar. How are you?"

"Dying, or living, if you prefer. So are we all, from the moment we're dropped from the womb. What brings you back to town—and back to the fold?"

"So the brotherhood still exists?"

Greenmore laughed. "Somewhat changed, yes. We're a more polite band these days. You should join us one evening. I'll send you an invitation."

"Thank you." Adam stood back as Greenmore's carriage drew up. "I should warn you, sir, that I intend to call in some old debts. I need help in finding one dear to me."

Greenmore lingered. "A woman, I suppose."

Adam fought to keep his voice as casual as Greenmore's. "The woman I seek in this case is my daughter. She is married to a Captain George Sanders."

"Your daughter? Adam Ashworth, a pillar of respectability—but who knows what lies beneath? Welcome back, brother. Captain Sanders, you say. That sounds familiar. You will hear from us. I wish you good night—or good day."

Adam watched the carriage bump along the street until it was out of sight, and turned to go back into his sister's house.

The wheels were in motion.

The candle flame flickered weak and pallid in the early-morning light. Fabienne glanced at her reflection in the mirror, her skin dull, shadows beneath her eyes. The gold scarf and rope of pearls from her hair and her fan and gloves lay on her writing table, surrounded by crumpled sheets of paper from earlier, discarded attempts.

> *Madam,*
>   *You said it was to be my decision to end this—I do not even know what to call it—our association. We have left many things unsaid, but I thought that in one instance, our deep regard for each other, we were as frank and open as any could be. Yet you did not seek me out last night, I return home to find that you have not sent me word, and all I have to find you in London is your publisher's address.*
>   *It goes against my heart and my inclinations, but I beg you not to write again, nor seek me out, although now I doubt that was ever your intention. I wrote from my heart, and you, I now think, did not. It is best that we put an end to this folly.*
>   *I should be obliged if you return my letters.*
>
>   *Yours etc.,*
>   *FC*

A tear dripped onto her letter, blurring the ink, and she swiped at her face with one hand. How could she have been so foolish, to pour her heart out to a stranger, to give her trust to someone so reluctant to reveal herself?

But there was true regard there. I am sure of it. She

folded and addressed the letter, added some drops of sealing wax, and it was done, over, finished.

She rang the bell for Susan and snuffed out the candle flame with thumb and finger, holding the smoldering wick for its small, lingering pain.

Chapter Eight

"I will put you to the test, madam."
Alicia struggled in vain against the cruel chains that marred her ivory flesh, as her captor's shadow loomed dark and sinister on the noisome dungeon wall by the lurid light of flickering torches.
—*The Curse of the Molfitains* by Mrs. Ravenwood.

"**Y**ou are not listening," Elaine said with some exasperation, as the carriage lurched along the London streets.

"I beg your pardon," Fabienne said. "I was far away."

"I was telling you, today Lord Greenmore called on Lady Eglinton while I sketched her daughters. He much admired my work and wishes me to paint his portrait, but I don't want to."

"Why is that?"

Elaine gathered her shawl more closely around herself. "I don't like him. I don't believe I could paint him and not have my dislike show through."

"If he becomes insistent I shall tell him you're far too busy to take on another commission," Fabienne said. "And I agree with you, he is unpleasant."

"I like Lady Eglinton," Elaine said. "She prattles on about nothing, but notices everything. And Mr. Ashworth is most kind. He tried to explain a mathematical puzzle to me, but I could make neither head nor tail of it. He is very clever, isn't he?"

"So they say." Fabienne stared out of the window.

"I should like to paint Mr. Ashworth," Elaine continued. "He has an interesting face. When did you know him before?"

"A long time ago. I doubt whether he could afford a portrait. He's only a country gentleman whose sister married an earl."

"Oh, no. He is quite wealthy. He has leased a house on Harley Street. Lady Eglinton told him he had all the signs of a man come to London to marry."

"And what did he say?"

Elaine giggled and gave a passable imitation of Adam's Sussex accent. " 'Prissy, I swear nothing but gowns, bonnets, and matrimony bounce around in your head.' "

So Adam looked for a wife. Why did that cause her so much pain, make her want to dig her nails into her palms and scream? Was it because she could not bear to think of anyone else finding happiness? She was on her way to becoming a bitter, aging woman. She needed— something. A new gown, a new bonnet? Or a new lover?

"It looks like hell." Adam ripped off the neckcloth and glared at his manservant.

"It's the latest fashion, sir," Dimmock said.

"What would you know of fashions? You're a country gentleman's manservant, not one of these fop's fops."

"I'm trying to better myself, sir, as you suggested. Another gentleman's manservant, one I met playing skittles, showed me this. It's quite the thing, he told me."

"When I suggested you better yourself, I meant you might try attending an exhibit, or the theater. You could play skittles at home."

Dimmock shrugged, and took a fresh neckcloth from the drawer. "If I like skittles in the country, sir, it stands to reason I should like them here. I did go on a rat hunt with Lord Eglinton's valet, but I like skittles better."

Adam turned his attention back to his neckcloth. "Tie it the usual way, and not too tightly. I intend to breathe."

He looked at himself in the mirror, noted with approval his flat stomach, and wondered if his gray hairs made him look distinguished, or merely old.

"You could dye it, sir," Dimmock, the mind reader, said.

"Mind your place," Adam snapped.

"I beg your pardon, Mr. Ashworth. The Earl of Greenmore's valet told me his master does. He recommended—"

"Enough," Adam said. "I won't have the village speculate on the color of my hair when we return."

"Ah, sir, is there, ah . . ."

Adam knew his servants carried on a lively series of bets, as to how soon, and to whom, their master would propose marriage.

"Not yet."

Dimmock nodded with enthusiasm. "Very good, sir. May I wish you the best of luck, sir, this afternoon."

"Thank you."

If only Dimmock knew the truth of it, exactly what sort of mess Adam had blundered into.

Fabienne's salon was held in a large space in her house, created by opening doors between two adjoining rooms. She had a liking for statuary; a strange mix of both classical subjects and pagan pieces from India were in shallow alcoves, and in one corner of the room an orange tree stood in a brightly painted pot. Ornately patterned rugs hung on the walls beneath gilded plasterwork. The combination of styles, exotic and classical, should have clashed, but the juxtaposition of such items seemed playful, a wink in the face of fashion. Her guests were as mixed a collection as her sculptures—members of the *ton*, a few soberly dressed men who might be tradesmen, others who affected a fashionably artistic disarray of dress and hair, and several women who appeared to be unescorted.

Adam yawned, stuck his hands in his pockets, and tried to get comfortable in his elegant gilt chair as a tremulous young woman read poetry to the assembled company.

After the poetry reading, apparently the last event of the gathering, Fabienne stood and spoke a few graceful words of thanks, and he watched as she moved around the room, smiling and chatting. She wore a fringed and beaded scarf around her head, a compromise to the turbans most women of her age and station would wear. It was peacock blue, with a fringe of gold beads that trailed onto the bare skin of her neck.

"It is a pity you came so late, Mr. Ashworth," she said. "You missed entirely our discussion of parliamentary reform."

He kissed her hand. "I regret I would not have much to say. I'm only a simple country gentleman, Mrs. Craigmont."

"Your false modesty does not fool me. Did you enjoy the poetry?"

"Very much."

She cocked an eyebrow at him. "Indeed?"

"Yes, it was most conducive to peaceful reflection."

"So that is why your eyes were closed."

"It was very pleasant." He leaned toward her. "I am at your service, Mrs. Craigmont, if you wish to call in your debt."

"I do." She hesitated, and before moving away, whispered, "Stay after the others have gone."

"Sister, I'm invited to dine out," Adam heard Argonac say. "You expect Miss Twyford back soon, I suppose."

"No, she dines tonight at the Eglintons'. As for me, the servants have the night off and I shall have a quiet evening alone."

Fabienne directed the footmen as they moved furniture and took out dirty china and wineglasses.

Another servant showed Adam into a small, upstairs room with a doorway that he was fairly sure led to Fabienne's bedchamber. The walls were covered with an intricate paper, and a dark, richly patterned carpet lay on the floor. In the light of the lamp and fireplace the room had a deep, feminine glow that reminded him of its owner. Papers and books lay scattered on a small desk, more books on a small bookshelf, and one lying face-down on the sofa by the fireplace; he turned it over.

Naturally the writer was Mrs. Ravenwood.

Fabienne entered the room, accompanied by a servant, who carried a tray of wine, fruit, and biscuits. When they were alone, she held her hands to the fire, and said, "I have need of you, sir."

He could only gape at her. What should he do? Fling himself at her feet, bear her onto the sofa in a passionate embrace? Her directness both appalled and excited him. He must be mistaken. He cleared his throat. "In what capacity, Mrs. Craigmont?"

"Please sit down."

He sat on the sofa and she sat at the other end, hands folded on her lap. She did not look particularly approachable, her face stern, back ramrod straight. "Will you have some wine?"

He accepted, and rose to pour them each a glass of madeira.

She took a sip that was almost a gulp, and said, "This is very difficult for me. I beg of you, be patient."

The fire crackled and a clock ticked in the otherwise quiet room. She gazed at her folded hands, and he looked at her, at the gold beads that brushed her neck like a caress, moving slightly with each breath she took. Her peacock blue gown had a gauze inset at the breast, hinting at what was beneath. He imagined pressing his lips to the white fabric, absorbing the warmth of her breasts.

"I need to know who the surviving Sons of Prometheus are." She laid her hand briefly on his sleeve. "No, do not deny it. I know you carry the mark here."

"I took vows," he said, taken entirely by surprise at her request, and startled by her touch. "And why? What are you about, Mrs. Craigmont?"

"So you will break some vows, but not others?"

"What do you mean? I keep my word, madam."

She curled her lip and looked away.

"Fabienne, why do you wish to know about the Sons?"

She turned her face to him, troubled. "I cannot tell you. Please believe me that it is of vital importance to my well-being."

"And I cannot break my word."

"But you do. You said you would repay the favor I did your family."

"I would never have made such an offer—and it was only an offer, nothing more than that, and certainly not a vow—had I realized what you would demand of me." He placed his glass on a small table and stood. "I regret I cannot help you, madam."

She stood, face-to-face with him, her lips pressed tight together. "I see. I shall give you some time to reconsider that, sir, for I know about you and Mrs. Ravenwood, and I shall not hesitate to use that to my advantage. Now, if you will excuse me, I shall see to some household matters for a few minutes. Please help yourself to more wine."

She swept out of the room in a rustle of drapery, and with a faint waft of perfume, leaving him flabbergasted.

She knew. She'd known all along, and she was going to expose him in the most humiliating way possible. How subtly she'd fired his imagination with her hints and innuendos and reduced him to a state of priapic idiocy.

She hadn't meant a word, not one sweet, loving word. She'd played him for a fool, and now planned to make him an even greater one. Adam Ashworth, respectable country gentleman, was to be revealed to society as the creator of silly novels for silly women. He, who prided himself on his learning—yes, he could have stayed at Cambridge, and pursued a respectable, if not spectacular, career as a don—had debased and prostituted his gifts. He would become a laughingstock, regarded as unmanly and effeminate. What would Barbara think? Or Luke? Or his sister? Particularly his sister. He shuddered.

Damn Fabienne. What on earth was he to do?

And the letters. She still had his letters, those incriminating, embarrassing, ridiculous letters.

Fabienne leaned against the closed door and took a deep breath. Her heart pounded.

She had flung down the gauntlet.

She could imagine the drawing room gossip; a few words, dropped in the right ears, would start the vicious cycle of innuendo and malice. . . . *Adam Ashworth keeps a mistress. Or rather, she keeps him. Oh yes, he's so respectable now, but he was very wild as a young man. And you'll never guess who his mistress is. Perhaps it will make you think twice about buying her next book. Yes, Mrs. Ravenwood. No wonder she does not move in society. And to think he is in London to find a wife. You know he has rather more money to throw around in town than a country gentleman of modest income should, and it has to be hers; why, he's little better than a pimp.* . . . The mamas would swoon in shock and whisk their darling daughters out of his way.

He and his mistress would regret their game.

Pausing on the staircase to admire her reflection in a mirror, she tore away the piece of gauze tucked into the neck of her gown to reveal the swell and shadow of her breasts. She loosened a few locks of hair to fall artfully from the scarf she wore around her head, twisting them in her fingers to give them some curl. She saw the smile and parted lips of a woman who anticipated satisfaction. For the first time in days, she felt alive, powerful, capable.

When she returned to her room she was at first outraged and then amused to find Adam rifling through her desk, his coat flung onto a chair. He looked up as she entered, fury on his face.

"Damn you. Where are the letters?"

She sauntered over to the sofa and sat, one arm along the back, her gown pulling taut over her thigh. "Not there. Have a care, Adam. Those bills are in order."

He tossed them onto the floor. "Not anymore, madam." He paused and examined her, his gaze sweeping her from head to toe, lingering at her bosom. "Is this for my benefit?"

"I beg your pardon?"

"This blatant display of your feminine charms," he growled.

"I apologize if it offends you." She leaned forward to give him a better look.

He muttered something under his breath, flushed, and shifted from one foot to another. She could see why; his close-fitting trousers betrayed him.

"Who is your tailor?" she asked, staring at the area in question. "He's very good, but the cut of your trousers leaves something to be desired."

He glared at her, and then reached down, taking his time, and adjusted himself, matching her crudeness with great deliberation. She was aware of a tight thread of sensuality between them, a hum in the air, the awareness of each other as man and woman.

He looked back at her desk and the moment was broken. He plucked his spectacles from his waistcoat pocket and began to read. A grin spread over his face. "Dreadful stuff," he commented. "I particularly like the line where he compares you to a robin. They are extraordinarily aggressive and unpleasant birds."

"He is only nineteen." Fabienne stretched. Her gown slipped up, revealing one ankle. "He has . . . other talents."

Adam dropped the sheet as though it were on fire. "And the letters—where are they? In your bedchamber? Crushed beneath the drained bodies of bad poets scarce out of the schoolroom?"

"Good heavens, what a turn of mind you have. No, they're not in this house. They're quite safe from you."

"Damn you, Fabienne." He pushed the disordered contents of her desk into a pile, stalked back to the sofa, and took his original place, glowering. "Now what?"

She shrugged, ran a finger along her collarbone, then toyed with a lock of hair. He'd touched her that way in his library; did he remember? His sudden, sharp breath gave her the answer.

"Listen, Adam. I am not unjust. I will tell you what I know of the Sons of Prometheus, and you may decide whether you must indeed break a vow."

He gave an impatient snort. "If you ask me to name names, of course I do."

"Hush." She leaned to place one fingertip on his mouth.

He became absolutely still at her touch, then smiled and lifted her hand away. "So speak, Mrs. Craigmont."

"Very well. The Sons of Prometheus bear a brand, here, as you do." She laid her hand on his forearm, warm and solid, his linen shirt smooth to her touch. "You expected the revolution to come at any time, and a new age of freedom and equality to be born. So we believed in France, as my father still did, even at the end when he mounted the scaffold."

"I wept when the Bastille fell," Adam said. "I walked the streets of Cambridge all night when I read the news, and wept and laughed like a madman. I was nineteen and I thought the world would change. It seems a long time ago now."

"I believe the members of the Sons were mostly men of the aristocracy, and a few others, gentlemen, clever learned men. There is an initiation of some sort."

Adam nodded. He seemed lost in thought.

"And there was wild talk of revolution and secrecy, as well as much libertinism and depravity. You are the only one I know who can help me, because I know you to be a member. I seek a man of about your age, and one a few years younger."

"Naturally I should deny any names you may suggest." He turned to her then, giving her his attention. "What is the purpose of this? You know that if you wish to harm one of my brothers, I shall remain silent to the grave."

"Not even if I sought to right a wrong?"

"Not even then." He sighed and leaned back, one arm against the carved wooden back of the sofa, his fingers a few inches from hers. "Well, Mrs. Craigmont, to be quite honest, I should very much like to see this matter of the letters cleared up before I proceed any further." He yawned. "That is a most attractive scarf in your hair. It is from India, I suppose."

"Yes, it—what . . . ?" She struggled against him as he whipped the scarf from her hair, grabbed her wrists, tied them together, and looped and knotted the ends through the carving of the back of the sofa. It happened within a heartbeat. One moment she was lulled by the smooth, deep cadence of his voice; the next she was his prisoner.

"My son's a sailor," he said, as though in explanation.

"He teaches you to tie up women?"

"No, no, he's only a sweet, innocent lad. He taught me the knots. Don't struggle, Mrs. Craigmont. You'll tighten them."

"You whoreson! I'll scream for help!"

"Do, if it makes you feel better. Everyone is out tonight, I believe."

"Bastard!" She twisted to sit sideways and aimed a kick at him. For good measure, she opened her mouth and let out a piercing shriek.

He winced. "My dear Mrs. Craigmont." His voice was a soothing rumble. He turned toward her, hooking his leg around hers and trapping it against the edge of the sofa. Her other leg was still bent at the knee from her ineffectual kick, her foot resting near his thigh.

He stroked her ankle and removed her slipper. "The letters, if you please, Mrs. Craigmont. All you need do is tell me where they are, and you'll be released. It's quite simple."

"You think to frighten them out of me? How very ungentlemanly."

"No. I plan to pleasure them out of you." He cradled her stockinged foot in his hands.

"I beg your pardon?" She drew herself up with as much dignity as she could, and stopped as she realized the action parted her legs. "You mean to force me?"

"Of course not." He laughed. "You forget our history, Fabienne. I made you do a lot of things you'd never dreamed of doing, once. And you weren't unwilling. You were very willing, in fact. And you can protest all you like, but I know what you look like when you're roused, and I can see it in you now."

"Oh, you are mistaken. You are very much mistaken. How dare you—"

"Do you remember the time I—"

"Stop!" She managed to thud her heel into his thigh and was rewarded with his grunt of pain.

"Oh, Fabienne, don't fight me." His hand moved on her ankle, pushing up her gown and petticoat, his fingers tickling around the back of her knee and above. She became still, scarcely breathing, and watched his fingers peel off her stocking—he took the time to examine her garter, nod approvingly, and drop it into his pocket. As his hand slid down her leg and his fingertips traced the arch of her foot, she sank back against the sofa, appalled at her reaction. Yes, he was right. Damn him, he was right. She was angry but she was also aroused.

His hand moved on her foot, a torment, fingertips teasing.

"Adam?" She could barely speak.

He gazed into her eyes, his voice low and seductive. "And the letters?"

"Pig." She gasped for breath.

"You're enjoying it, aren't you? How about this?" He raised her foot to his mouth, and she felt his breath and then his mouth. It was shockingly intimate, wicked, his tongue curling on her skin, the wet, hot suck of his mouth. He stopped just long enough to murmur, "Tell me, sweetheart."

When he nipped her toes with his teeth she shuddered, no longer caring that he saw her reaction. He raised his head and danced his fingertips over the sole of her foot. "I wonder if you'll climax first. You look as though you could."

"You filthy pervert!" she gasped. Heat pooled in her belly, simmered at her nipples. She arched her back despite herself and panted, trying to draw her foot away. "I won't tell you."

"No? Come, Fabienne. Tell me. Release your secrets for me."

The doorbell rang.

Neither of them moved for a second, frozen.

"Oh, good heavens, it's Elaine—it must be—back early. There's no one to answer the door. For God's sake, let me go." Fabienne struggled against him as he leaned between her outstretched legs and pulled the scarf loose.

He was laughing, damn him.

"My stocking, where is it?" She bundled her hair up and tied the scarf around it.

Adam plucked her stocking from the floor and tossed it onto her lap.

"And the garter," she snapped.

"No, I'll keep that."

"You will not. Give it to me, if you please. How can I put the stocking on if I do not have the garter?"

The doorbell jangled again.

"It joins my arsenal," he said. "I'd be happier still if you gave me its fellow, and in heaven if you gave up the letters. Have pity on a poor, lonely widower. Think of it as fairly won in the jousts of love."

"You intend to tie it around your lance?" She was mortified by his burst of ribald laughter. Furious, she stuffed the stocking into her pocket, found her slipper on the floor and jammed her foot into it. She took a quick look in the mirror—God, she looked half-ravished, her cheeks flushed and her hair in wild disorder—then ran downstairs to let in Elaine and Susan.

Susan looked at her and giggled.

"You're home early," Fabienne said to Elaine, ignoring her maid. "I thought you were to stay for dinner?"

"I had a headache. I wanted to come home."

"Oh, sweetheart." Fabienne laid the back of her hand on her daughter's forehead. "I don't think you have a fever. Come upstairs and Susan will fetch you some tea and something to eat." As Susan left for the kitchen, Fabienne said, "What's wrong? Is it Luke?"

"Yes." Elaine trudged up the stairs. "He goes to the country soon, to visit his estate, and I know he has much to do there, but he did not tell me he was to go. I heard it at Lady Eglinton's, and then all the talk was of this and that heiress, and how many times he danced with them at some party. And then I once again thought someone followed as we walked home."

"You should have taken a hackney carriage. Why do you risk yourself so?"

"I thought the walk would do my head good."

Fabienne longed to take her daughter into her arms. "Come, you're tired. You'll feel better soon. Mr. Ashworth is here, but he won't stay for long."

"Why are you wearing only one stocking?"

Fabienne cursed silently to herself. "I was darning it."

"While Mr. Ashworth was here?"

"No, of course not." Fabienne pushed Elaine into her room, where Adam, coat on and perfectly composed, bowed to them both.

"Miss Twyford is not well," Fabienne said. "I'll bid you good night, Mr. Ashworth."

"Good night, Mrs. Craigmont. Thank you for a most interesting evening. I hope you feel well soon, Miss Twyford." He paused to kiss Fabienne's hand and murmured, "The letters, madam. That was but the smallest weapon at my disposal."

"You shall not have them. You may tell Mrs. Ravenwood, since you act as her spokesman, that I will consider it only if she returns mine, first, and in person."

His eyes were cold. "Believe me, Mrs. Ravenwood will never agree. Good night, Mrs. Craigmont."

Chapter Nine

His senses reeled at the unimaginable delights that lay beyond. As he was about to enter the chamber of forbidden pleasures, an image of a pale, pure maiden rose in his mind, her tear-filled eyes begging him to remain unsullied.

"Away!" Roderigo cried. "I shall plunge myself into delightful sensuality!"

—The Spectre of the Abbey by Mrs. Ravenwood.

*I*n the morning room of Adam's house next day, the air was full of heavy sighs and the clink of silver on china. Luke, whom Adam had invited to breakfast on his way out of town, produced most of the gusty exhalations as he worked his way methodically through a large plate of food.

Adam, meanwhile, drank coffee and regarded his godson's woebegone expression and undaunted appetite with some amusement. "What's wrong, Luke?"

"I fear I shall lose Miss Twyford if I go to the country."

"Is she yours to lose?"

Luke shook his head and accepted another helping of eggs.

Adam hesitated. He remembered Fabienne's scorn at what she perceived as his hypocrisy. *How well you play the moralist, Adam. . . .*

"Luke, I must tell you something in the strictest of confidence regarding Miss Twyford. I have reason to believe she is my daughter, and Mrs. Craigmont, as you have probably guessed, is her mother. I beg of you, not a word to a soul of this. Later, I'll tell you more."

Luke's mouth dropped open. "But . . . but . . . *you,* sir?"

"It's just as well you're no blood relative of mine," Adam said. "But you must consider what you are about with Elaine. She is an excellent young woman, and I would not like to see her heart broken."

Luke sighed, bewilderment on his face. "She seems to like her painting more than me. I fear she will turn me down again."

"Good God," Adam said. "Cheer up and stop playing the mooncalf. Either propose to her or look for a wife elsewhere."

"Yes, sir." He hesitated. "I have met no other woman I like as well."

"My sister has introduced me to several very pleasant young women," Adam said. "Surely you have met some too?"

"Sir, you have not yet made anyone an offer either."

"Nor am I likely to. I'm here to find Babs. Although my sister may tell you otherwise, matrimony is the last subject on my mind."

"What about Mrs. Craigmont?"

Adam's cup clattered on its saucer. "What?"

"Well, sir, she is a very beautiful woman, and very kind. When I first came to town, I told her of my aunt Margaret, how much we loved her, and—"

"Never talk to her of my wife again!" Adam shouted. He made an effort to steady his voice. "Do you understand?"

"Sir, I did not mean to offend you or break a confidence. She—there is something about her that compels confidence—she only asked me how long I had lived with your family, and so on."

"I'm sorry, Luke." Adam came round to his side of the table and patted his shoulder. "I was wrong to shout at you."

"I beg your pardon." Luke stood. "I should go, sir, so I may arrive home in daylight."

"Keep out of trouble." Adam folded his godson in an affectionate hug, wishing he could give himself the same advice.

After Luke had gone, he read again the invitation that had been delivered a few hours earlier. Tonight he was to meet some old friends.

"Brother," Adam said quietly, and raised their joined hands so his branded wrist touched Greenmore's.

"Welcome back. It's a good evening to join us. Tonight we initiate a new member."

A footman pushed open a door. Adam looked around at an all-male gathering, as determinedly masculine and staid as any gentleman's club, with no masks or bared flesh in sight. "Why are there no women present?"

There were some smiles and sideways glances from men standing nearby. "You are so refreshingly old-fashioned," Greenmore said. "We decided there were to be no more females—oh, a decade ago. Not for purposes of serious discussion, at any rate. Their minds, you know, are not suited to such activities."

There was a murmur of assent. Adam opened his mouth to disagree before he remembered to his shame how he thought of his own daughter, and many other women, the same way. *Ha ha, Ashworth, so you're Mrs. Ravenwood—how well you simulate the female mind in all its vapidity and absurdity.*

"I remember some remarkable women I met here," he said. "Women who had wit as well as beauty, who could hold their own in conversation as well as sensual activities. Besides, at the initiation . . . ?"

"The ceremony has changed somewhat."

A servant murmured discreet words in Greenmore's ear, and the company was summoned to dinner.

Adam listened, astonished, to the conversations around him. He was seated next to Lord Charles Landon, who twenty years ago had more hair and less paunch. On his other side, an overweight man, his face flushed, complained of his tenants' drain on his property.

"Enclose the land," someone suggested. "You'll be rid

of them, and they'll be forced to shift for themselves. They'll wish they had been more grateful to you for your stewardship."

"An excellent idea," Adam said. "I daresay they'll thank you with their dying breath as they expire in a ditch, or with the noose around their neck for stealing to eat. Why not hang them all to begin with?"

"Now, Ashworth . . ." Landon remonstrated with a smile.

"Or, as Dean Swift suggested for the Irish, they could eat their children." Adam began to enjoy himself.

"How could anyone jest about such an unnatural act?" asked a fair-skinned boy opposite, whom Adam guessed was the new initiate.

"Perhaps you had best change your ideas of what is natural or unnatural, given the step you take tonight," Adam replied.

"Come, Ashworth, do not frighten the lad," Greenmore called down the table. "No, Barton, we do not eat children here. You must forgive Ashworth. He's rotted too long in the country. What have you been doing there all this time, Ashworth? Spawning bastards in the dunghills?"

"Hardly. I write a mathematical treatise, I breed pigs, and I look after my family and land. I'm just an ordinary country gentleman." He smiled at the young man opposite. "And you, sir, why do you join the brotherhood?"

"My father told me it would help me advance. I am a younger son, and I seek a career in the Church."

"A career in the Church?" Adam was further astonished. "Did you not know most of us are—were—atheists? Do you not understand the origins of this organization? Or the activities?"

Landon laughed. "I assure you, sir, things are very different now. Your godson Tillotson should join us."

"I doubt it would suit him," Adam replied, wondering if Luke might be safer in the Brotherhood than outside it.

The conversation now turned to a discussion of their sons.

"They are insolent young pups," a man complained. "All they care about is the tie of their neckcloths, and the fit of their coats. Do you not find it so, Ashworth?"

"My son's too young for that. He's a midshipman, at sea." He felt a pang of loneliness and worry for Jon.

"You only have one son? And he's in the Navy?"

"It was what he wished to do, ever since he was a child, and I would not stand in his way. I'm not sure where he gets his sealegs from, but I'm heartily proud of him."

There was a silence. He guessed that he might be in a minority, having a son of whose exploits he could boast. He added, "Do you not think it hard on young men today? Look at the advantages we had—we could travel, we could broaden our minds, and new ideas and thoughts were in the air. Barton, all your life, I'd think, you've lived in a country at war, with no chance to take the Grand Tour as we did. Do you plan, when we are at peace again, to travel, and see the places you read about at school?"

"Not really, sir. I enjoy London." Barton looked affronted.

"But there are other cities—Venice, Rome, Paris. We thought travel a necessary part of a gentleman's education."

"And times have changed," Landon said with a frown. "Why, you'll make the boy dissatisfied, and then what will he do?"

"If we were not dissatisfied, we would never change, or seek new experiences," Adam replied. "What do you think, Barton?"

"I am quite content as I am, sir. I believe travel to be overrated. I can read all I want to in books."

"Speaking of books," another man said, "I happened to pick up my wife's copy of *The Ruined Tower*, and found it is surprisingly well written, for a woman."

Adam took a large gulp of wine.

"I thought it immoral," Barton commented. "I was much shocked that my mother and sisters are mad for the book. There is, I believe, some hint of illicit unions, and the heroine spends much of her time in a state of undress."

"It is drivel, mere entertainment for women," Landon said. "Although I must admit the author has a ready turn of phrase and seems to have some education."

To Adam's relief the conversation was halted by an announcement that they should retire to an adjoining room.

The beginning of the ritual was as Adam remembered it. In the dim, flickering light, it was almost as though it was twenty years ago, when the world seemed full of hope and possibility.

"You no longer strip the initiates?" Adam asked. "How else can it signify a rebirth?"

"Good Lord, no. Couldn't have a future bishop naked in our midst," Landon replied with a grin.

Barton's voice was eager and nervous as he swore to brotherhood, secrecy unto death, and the pursuit of liberty and pleasure. Other men helped him off with his coat, and rolled up the young man's shirtsleeve. Barton licked his lips and stared at the glowing brand in Greenmore's grasp.

The brand descended toward the pale skin of Barton's arm and Adam braced himself for the hiss and reek of burned flesh. Neither occurred; the branding was reduced to a piece of playacting, with no pain involved. There was a burst of applause as Greenmore clasped the young man's hand, and spoke the ritual words of welcome.

Adam joined the men who clustered around Barton to offer congratulations. He offered a few, formal words, and stepped back.

He thought back to his own initiation, standing there, stark naked, triumphant. The brand on his arm had hurt like hell, and he knew that any woman in the room would give herself willingly to him that night.

"We are not totally devoid of female company," Landon murmured from next to him. "In the next room, in fact, if you would care to accompany me."

The group had begun to disperse, some leaving for the card and billiards rooms, while others stayed behind for serious drinking. Adam followed Landon out, and a footman, face impassive, opened a door into a dimly lit room.

At the far end, three nearly naked women in gauzy drapery posed. As he watched, they shifted position, arms around one anothers' shoulders, drapery sliding to reveal breasts and buttocks.

"Classical poses," Landon said. "The Three Graces."

Adam was aware now of other men seated in the shadowy recesses of the room, and some stealthy movement there, the gleam of bare female flesh.

"This, of course, is what many find most arousing." Landon indicated a spot to the side.

Adam stared at the two young women twined naked on the floor. At the moment he could not recall which classical scene they could possibly represent. One raised her head to give the two newcomers a bright, welcoming smile.

"Get on with it," gasped an urgent voice from the shadows.

"Beg your pardon, sirs." The girl bent to her task again.

Adam, torn between laughter, lust and embarrassment, hoped his face did not have the same look of slack-jawed idiocy as Landon's.

He edged toward the door. "It has been a most pleasant evening, Landon. I'll bid you good night." Reluctantly tearing his gaze away from the naked women, he left the room and went to bid his host good-bye.

"Leaving so soon, Ashworth?" Greenmore looked up from the card table.

"Yes. I keep country hours. I thank you for an interesting evening."

"Do you find us much changed?"

"I do. Whether it's for the best or not, I can't say. We were once so full of hope."

"You've become maudlin. I have found your missing Captain Sanders, by the way. I hear you've been frequenting gaming hells in search of him, and doubtless you would have found him eventually. I have saved you your estate." He chuckled. "He will be found at the cockfight at Mrs. Craven's house in Moon Street in Covent Garden tomorrow night. Why do you wish to find him?"

"He beats my daughter, his wife." He couldn't explain why he felt compelled to answer Greenmore directly—maybe because of the bond they had in the brotherhood. He had blurted it out to Fabienne too for even less reason.

Greenmore frowned. "I am most sorry to hear it. I thought Sanders had much promise in his youth. Well, I'll bid you good night."

Adam climbed into the hackney carriage, restless and dissatisfied. Part of it, he knew, was unsatisfied lust, pure and simple. The classical poses, despite his amusement and embarrassment, had stirred him. Altogether, the evening had brought back too many memories of the Brotherhood, nights when he could drink and make love and talk and emerge bright-eyed into the dawn, ready to catch a few hours' sleep and start all over again. He had changed, and so had the Brotherhood.

Now he was to return to the unwelcoming atmosphere of his leased house, an empty bed, and his gnawing anxiety about how soon Fabienne would publicly unmask him.

He rapped on the roof and told the driver to take the long way home, at least half an hour's drive. With a rueful smile, he knew the man would probably drive through the Strand and Covent Garden, thinking Adam wished to find himself a whore. Twenty years ago, Adam would have considered it.

The coach slowed as they drove through Covent Garden, and Adam could not resist looking out of the window. Oh yes, he remembered it only too well—the slow drive, assessing the gaudily dressed and painted women.

The women strolled in pairs or groups of three or four, looking about them boldly, breasts exposed, their gowns almost transparent, eyes painted and watchful.

One tossed her hair and smiled at him. Under the paint she seemed quite young and her smile was warm and bold, even though it revealed the gap of a lost incisor. She laughed, and began a seductive sway toward him, picking her way daintily through the refuse. A second later, she swore violently and fell flat on her backside in the street as another figure, cloaked and hooded, pushed her out of the way, and fell into the carriage, sobbing incoherently.

"Oh, Mr. Ashworth, thank God you are here!"

Chapter Ten

"Soon, dear child, you will taste delights beyond your wildest dreams, and passion beyond imagining. Cast off those maidenly reservations, I beg you."

The fumes from the goblet the count handed Alicia swirled thick and intoxicating to her senses, as she struggled within his grasp. "No, sir, it is unseemly. I cannot!"

—The Curse of the Molfitains by Mrs. Ravenwood.

"*G*ood God, Miss Twyford, what are you doing here?" Adam disentangled himself from the folds of her cloak, and pushed his handkerchief into her hand as she burst into hysterical tears.

"Oh thank God. Thank God, you rescued me." She choked and hiccuped, clutching his coat. "It has been so dreadful. Those women threatened me; they said it was their street. I was so afraid."

Adam patted her arm, relieved that the shock of her sudden arrival had shrunk away his lust as effectively as a block of ice. "Now, now," he said in as comforting a tone as he could muster, "I'll take you home. Don't cry. You're safe."

He instructed the driver to go to Fabienne's house, and waited for Elaine to calm herself.

She gazed at him with luminous, grateful eyes. "You have saved my life, Mr. Ashworth."

"What has happened to you? Why are you alone here?"

"I was at Lady Eglinton's house, and since I did not need a chaperone while I was there, and they had invited me to dine, Fabienne said she would send Susan for me later. So, when the Eglintons' footman announced a carriage had arrived, I got into it, and—" She gulped, and began to cry again.

"It's all right. You can tell me."

"There was a stranger already in it, and he tried to tie my hands and put a gag in my mouth." She clutched Adam's sleeve and wept against his shoulder.

He put his arm around her, patted her, and made soothing noises. Poor child, no wonder she was distraught.

"He would have overpowered me, but I remembered I had put a paintbrush in my pocket. I jabbed it into—into—his private parts." She whispered the last few words.

"Brave girl." Adam winced.

"And then I opened the door, and jumped out and ran as fast as I could. I did not know where I was. I met those horrible women, and some men shouted obscene things at me. I thought I would be killed or worse. Someone stole my purse while I was in the street. I was desperate. I prayed to God to save me, and then you came along. You are like an angel, sir."

Somehow he doubted angels drove around Covent Garden sizing up whores. "You're safe now. You'll be home soon."

She sighed and snuffled against his shoulder, his handkerchief clutched in her hand. "Sometimes I wish I was back in the country with my mother. I was happy there."

"I miss the country too," he said. "Where did you live?"

"Near Lichfield. Fabienne had some connections with people there. When she returned from India, she was greatly impressed with the painting I did for the pottery. My mother said I should accept her offer to go to London for painting lessons. But I miss my home."

She was quiet then, and Adam thought she might have fallen asleep on his shoulder like a tired child. The carriage drew up at Fabienne's house, and Elaine straight-

ened up, wiping her nose, as the footman opened the
carriage door.

Fabienne, wearing a nightgown and shawl, her hair
loose, burst from the house. "Where have you been?
Susan came home hysterical because you disappeared.
Ippolite is out looking for you." She gathered Elaine to
her in a close embrace.

"It is not my fault." Elaine started to cry again. "I
have been so frightened. I thought I should die."

"Mr. Ashworth, what are you doing here with her?"
Fabienne stared over Elaine's shoulder at Adam. She
looked rumpled and fierce, and close to tears herself.

He stepped forward, arms outspread, responding to an
urge to embrace both women, to offer protection and
comfort.

"What has happened?" Fabienne looked at him with
horror.

"Have your maid put her to bed," Adam said. "She's
quite well, apart from being frightened half to death."

"Mr. Ashworth," Elaine broke free from Fabienne's
arms. "Thank you. I shall pray for you." She darted up
to him, kissed his cheek, and ran into the house.

He could not prevent a foolish grin breaking out on
his face.

"You're drunk." Fabienne gathered the shawl around
herself.

"Slightly, yes, madam. Not so drunk that I could not
look after this young woman, which you seem unable
to do."

She ignored his rudeness. "Please come in. I shall see
Elaine to bed."

He was shown once again into her private room and
sat on the sofa, where only a few days ago he had made
Fabienne writhe with pleasure. A servant offered him
coffee served with small, rosewater-flavored biscuits.
After a while, Fabienne, with her hair now pinned back
and the shawl knotted at her breast over the nightgown,
joined him.

"I beg your pardon," she said. "I owe you an apology.
Thank you for what you did tonight."

She sat down and nibbled absently on one of the biscuits. He watched her tongue as it captured crumbs from her lips.

"I don't understand it," she continued. "If she were an heiress, there would be a reason to steal her away. Yet it all seems as though this were not by chance—someone must have known her movements, and planned this. Thank God she is safe. Where did you find her?"

"In Covent Garden. I was on my way home."

"She wept for her mother when I put her to bed. Maybe it was a mistake to bring her here. London is not a safe place for a young woman, whatever else its advantages for her may be. She has thought for some time that she was being followed, and to tell the truth I did not take it seriously." She wrapped the fringe of her shawl around her fingers and stared into the fire.

"Who would follow her? You don't suspect Tillotson, I hope. He's completely harmless."

"Not that harmless. He's a man. But no, I think Luke would do anything to protect her." She fell silent and lifted the coffeepot, offering him another cup.

He shook his head. "May I suggest you hire another servant to protect Elaine—someone larger and more threatening than your maid? I should be willing to—"

"No, I shall find someone. Thank you."

"It's late. I should not keep you from your bed. You look tired."

"I have been half sick with worry—that is all." She licked a few stray crumbs from her fingers. "I trust it did not interfere with your evening's entertainment."

"What the devil do you mean?"

She shrugged. "There is only one reason why a man should drive through those streets and open his carriage door for a woman he could not possibly recognize. Elaine told me she had her cloak hooded over her face."

"That is my business," he said. "Unless you're jealous, Mrs. Craigmont."

"Jealous? Why should I be jealous? You have an extremely high opinion of yourself, Mr. Ashworth." She sighed. "Oh God, why do I rail at you, when you have preserved my—the one I hold dearest in the world? Forgive me."

She was asking him for forgiveness? He stared at her in confusion, then grinned. "Ah, so you will give me the letters?"

"Absolutely not. And I trust you will behave like a gentleman tonight." She gave him a clear, candid gaze. "I should hate you. I was angry with you for so many years, and I thought I had rid myself of that burden. But since you have come back into my life . . ."

He waited, breathless, for what she would say.

"May we declare a truce?" she asked.

"A truce? You mean you will not expose me to the world, or blackmail me?"

"Not for the moment."

He leaned back against the sofa and laughed aloud. "And who decides the end of the truce, Mrs. Craigmont?"

"Why, I do."

"That is absurd. What benefit do you think this truce will have for either of us?"

"I cannot find peace in my life if I hate you, or anyone. So, please, humor me. Can we not be kinder to each other? It seems we are brought together more often than we wish, and until Luke and Elaine resolve things, so it will be. Grant me this."

"A truce." He was still unsure what she meant, but if it would delay her exposure of him as Mrs. Ravenwood, he should agree to it. "You are the one who opened hostilities, madam."

"True. I humble myself before you."

"Balderdash, Fabienne. You humble yourself before no one."

She smiled. "A truce. Please?" She held out her hand.

"It seems I have little choice." He took her hand, her fingers warm and small in his clasp, and raised it to his mouth. She started but did not pull away as he kissed each knuckle.

"Adam," she whispered as he turned her hand over, carefully unfolding her fingers, and pressed his lips to her palm. Her fingertips curled around his jaw in a light caress.

"I beg your pardon. I'd best go." He dropped her hand and stood.

"Yes, it's late." She rose, her hands clasped at the knot of her shawl.

They faced each other, Adam more aroused than he had been all night, praying that her gaze would not drop to his groin, while half hoping that she would see his desire for her. He wasn't sure who made that first step forward, but they met, body to body, mouth to mouth, and she was in his arms, pressed against him. Her mouth was hot, imperious, demanding, her hands at his neck and shoulders insistent, pulling him against her with a greed that rivaled his own.

He broke away. "This is more than a truce, Mrs. Craigmont."

She sucked in a deep breath, her mouth wet from his. "Yes. I think I am mad."

"What now?" Every fiber in his body urged him to continue, while his mind tolled a solemn warning that what he was about to do was unwise, unseemly, and senseless.

She whispered his name, raising her hand to the shawl knotted at her throat. The folds of delicate wool fell away, revealing her lawn nightrail.

"You asked me, but moments ago, to behave like a gentleman." He stepped back, away from her, trying not to stare at the dark shadow of her nipples revealed by the thin fabric.

"So I did." She took his hand, tugging, her glance moving toward the door that led to her bedchamber. "What's wrong?"

"This is impossible. I cannot . . . I should leave."

She shrugged. "If that is what you wish." She bent to pick up her discarded shawl and wrapped it around herself.

"No, it's not what I wish. I—" He stopped, appalled,

before he could blurt out what he wanted in the crudest of terms.

She breathed his name and pushed him back onto the sofa.

He pulled her to him, kissing her with a ferocity that astonished him almost as much as her equally avid response. He groaned into her mouth—*Oh God forgive me. I may never do this again. I want her so much I think I will die*—before he tore at the buttons on the placket of her nightrail.

She helped him slide the fabric from her shoulder as he latched onto one breast, her hands at the back of his head and then scrabbling at his neckcloth and coat.

I can't do this. What if . . . ? "Stop!"

She drew back, lips parted, her hair collapsing onto her shoulders, one breast still cupped in his hand.

"Yes, we should—" She pulled at her nightrail.

"No." He attempted to hoist her off his knees.

"Adam?" She looked at him, astonished. "What is wrong?"

"This is wrong. All of it."

She stared at him, then at his hand on her breast.

He let its sweet weight slide from his hold and tried to think of a way to turn her down without offending her. "I'm sorry. I beg your pardon. I cannot."

"You cannot?" She leaned back, reached down and ran her fingers over his erection. "Oh, I think you can."

"No!" He grabbed her hand and tipped her off him so that she landed in a heap of flailing limbs and fabric on the floor. He glanced away from her parted legs. "I'm sorry. I didn't mean to hurt you. I—"

She scrambled to her feet, eyes cold. "Get out!"

He stood, attempting to straighten his neckcloth and coat, sick at heart. "Forgive me."

"Go!" She raised her voice.

Footfalls thundered on the stairs.

"Mrs. Craigmont, ma'am, what's wrong?"

Damn, it was her maid, who took one horrified look at Adam and then at Fabienne's disheveled appearance and grabbed the poker from the fireplace.

"Don't be a fool, Susan." Fabienne pulled her nightrail back onto her shoulders. "Good night, Mr. Ashworth."

"Good night, Mrs. Craigmont." He bowed and left. There was little else he could do.

Chapter Eleven

"Honor, sister, demands that I meet him, and restore the spotless reputation of your unsullied maidenhood."

Her head was bowed, the lily white of her cheek suffused with crimson. "I cannot tell you—but I must—it is too late."

Roderigo fell back, his manly complexion as pale as death. "Too late! Oh, would that it were not so!"

—The Spectre of the Abbey by Mrs. Ravenwood.

Susan picked up the shawl from the floor and wrapped it around Fabienne. "Why, ma'am, you're all a-tremble."

"I'm well enough." Her legs were weak and shaking. She sat on the sofa and held her hands out to the fire.

"Did he hurt you, ma'am? Shall I send for the doctor?"

Only my pride. "No, don't be ridiculous."

"Monseer said it was Mr. Ashworth who brought her home. Shame on him for taking advantage of you so."

"Yes, he rescued her. I am most grateful to him for that."

"Would you like me to brush your hair? And Polly's brought up a warming pan for the bed."

"Thank you." Fabienne let her maid fuss over her and help her into the warm bed. She sank into a pleasant darkness somewhere between sleep and wakefulness. Maybe she wouldn't dream. Maybe . . .

*   *   *

She was seventeen again, wildly in love, and terrified of the future.

She walked toward a doorway from which candlelight and music and voices spilled out. Inside, the air was thick with sweat and perfume. She saw no one she knew nearby, and stood alone, watching the dancers, looking for Adam, too shy to push her way through the crowded room. Most of the people there were masked, as she was, but she knew she would recognize him by his height, the gleam of his blue-gray eyes, and his hands. She shivered at the thought of his hands, and a thrill of anticipation, desire and dread ran through her, ice turning to a burn, as he approached her. "I wish you did not do that, Mr. Ashworth."

"I do nothing, yet. What do you mean?"

"When you are nearby, I feel it in my skin, my heart."

"I know. I feel it too." His lips seared her wrist. "Do not deny me much longer. I shall go mad."

"My mother thinks you will propose marriage to me," she lied.

"I imagine the comtesse has her sights set higher than that." His eyes, behind his mask, were cool. "Do you wish to dance? No? Then you had best have some wine. Wait here."

He left her side and returned with two glasses. He tossed his back with an ease that suggested he had been imbibing for some time. In the crush of the room, Adam moved closer to her, his hip bumping hers, his arm around her waist.

"Come with me, away from these people." He took her glass, drained it, and tossed it under a chair.

Outside in the coolness of the corridor, a servant sprang forward to open a door.

"Oh," Fabienne said as her eyes adjusted to the half-light inside the room. Naked couples, their pale flesh gleaming, lay against pillows on the floor. In the far shadows a woman cried out, a panting sob that Fabienne recognized.

Adam laughed, and drew her forward. "Come, sweetheart." He bent his head to hers. His lips took hers, probing her mouth open. He tasted of wine and himself, an essence of maleness and his own scent that made her tremble with desire and fear.

"No." She pushed him away. "Not here. Not with them. No."

"Very well." He opened the door and bowed. "You have made me wait long enough, and I believe I'll last a little longer. Please take a look at as many rooms as you wish, Miss Argonac."

"Thank you, Mr. Ashworth. I shall."

He laughed and pushed her against the wall, his lips searching hers again. She opened her mouth to the tease of his tongue, melting with desire, and laced her fingers in his hair.

"Enough." He pulled away from her, his breathing uneven. "I've changed my mind. I'll take you here in front of the servants and anyone else who cares to walk by, if we do not find a place soon."

He took her hand and led her down the corridor, to where lights grew more infrequent. There were no servants stationed here, and the sounds of music and voices had all but faded away.

"Here." Adam kicked a door open. The room had no fire, and a pair of candles provided the only light. He grasped her by the waist and lifted her onto the table. "I had hoped for a bed, but this will do."

He tossed off his mask, coat and waistcoat and threw them onto a chair.

Fabienne removed her mask. So this was it. She was about to take that final step with a man who made no promises, no commitment of honor or love.

"You do not become coy, I trust, Miss Argonac." Adam frowned.

"No. I—"

"Ah, Fabienne, I burn for you." He took her in his arms then, pressing her back onto the table, his lips at her throat.

She abandoned herself to her ravenous hunger for him, hands pulling at his shirt. She stroked the smooth muscle of his back and pushed the linen of his shirt up to touch her mouth to his chest, hearing his sharp intake of breath. *He wants me. He truly wants me. I have power over him. I can make him do what I want.*

He unlaced her gown and stays enough to bare her breasts and suckle them, something he had done before, but never with this single-minded urgency. Fabienne buried her fingers in his harsh, springy hair, tugging as it sprang free of its ribbon.

"Tell me you want me," he said, before his mouth returned to hers, stopping any answer she might make. "Tell me."

"Yes. I love you. Please."

He laughed, and let go of her to undo his breeches.

"I want to touch you," she said, finally bold enough to voice her desire.

"Very well."

She reached into his breeches and freed that part of him she'd felt pressed up against her, nudging against her hip, or rubbing her legs apart through their clothing. *How strange it must be to be a man,* she thought, *to live with such a thing growing and coming to life all on its own.* He swelled dark and hard, warm against her hand. She brushed her fingertips over its head, smooth and silken, stroked her thumb against a blue vein that pulsed down the length.

"What do you think of that, Miss Argonac?"

"It is very strange."

He took her hand in his and wrapped her fingers around him. "Like this. Touch me like this."

She moved her hand as he showed her and heard his breathing quicken. "Does this please you?"

"It certainly does. You have considerable natural ability, Miss Argonac. But you'd best stop now." He pushed up her skirts.

His thumbs found her and parted her, fingers probing. He had touched her so before, but never looking into her eyes, his own nakedness exposed.

"Adam," she said, uncertain and yearning, "tell me you love me."

"I want you more than life itself."

The table was cold and hard under her exposed skin, and she slid as he pushed into her. Cursing under his breath, he grasped her and shoved. There was no pain, to her surprise, just tightness and pressure, and Adam filling and stretching her. She gripped his arms.

"Do I hurt you?" He slowed, and lifted a hand to her face.

"No. I . . ." She wanted him to say he loved her, but she knew he would not. "Will you kiss me?"

"Fabienne, sweetheart." He bent his head to hers and kissed her, one hand at her breast, then pulled away, his head thrown back. She knew she had lost him; he'd leaped ahead of her into the dazzle of a pleasure he'd long denied himself, as he groaned and shivered against her.

And that is all? she wondered, bewildered and disappointed. *All these weeks of kisses and caresses, and what he wanted, and I too, and it ends so fast, like this?*

"Oh, God." He sagged against her, panting, his heart pounding wildly. "Too fast." Then he grinned. "It will be better the next time."

The next time? Maybe she had been wrong, and he intended more than a pursuit and conquest. If only he would tell her he loved her.

"Did I bleed?"

"No. You're hardly a virgin after all we've done. My fingers took care of that, sweetheart, while you held me off all this time." Then he smiled and pushed into her again, his penis firming inside her, and she knew his definition of the next time was right now, and love had little to do with it.

The man looming over her changed. He wore a mask and thrust into her with a savagery that would have made her scream if the other one's hand had not been over her mouth. She bled now—certainly not a virgin anymore, not a silly, trustful girl.

Let me go. I promise I will tell no one. Please, let me go, I beg of you.

"Fabienne!"

Now she could speak. *"Aidez-moi!"* Help me.

"Fabienne!"

She gulped and opened her eyes. Her brother sat at her bedside, holding her hand, while Susan stood behind him, her eyes wide and terrified.

"Ma'am!" Susan said. "Oh, ma'am, you cried out so loud, I thought you were murdered. And in French too."

"Go back to bed," Fabienne said, her tongue thick in her mouth. Light seeped in through the curtains; Ippolite was dressed and smelling of cigars and wine.

"I'll brew you some chamomile," Susan said.

"Did I wake Elaine?"

"No, she sleeps like a baby, ma'am. My Lord, you may go to bed now, and I'll look after the mistress."

"I don't want chamomile." Fabienne knew she sounded fractious, but she wanted at all costs not to sleep again. "Go back to bed, Susan. There's no need for you to be up so early."

"Maybe we should call the doctor," Ippolite said after Susan left.

"You want to see me in Bedlam?" Fabienne saw the fear and grief in his eyes and regretted her flippant remark. "Please, trust me. I believe I am to solve the mystery of these dreams soon. I regret I disturbed your rest once again."

"On the contrary, I have been home some two hours and, as I usually do, stay up until Susan is awake, so that if you dream I can be here."

"Thank you. I had no idea." She blinked back tears and patted her brother's hand. "Please, go to bed. I am quite well now."

And so she would be, as long as she was awake.

"Mr. Ashworth?" Dimmock asked. "The blue or silver waistcoat?"

"Blue. No, silver. Whichever you think would be best."

Dimmock made a great show of hovering between the two waistcoats, lips pursed, as though it were the most important thing in the world, and his master derelict in his duty.

"I'm going to a cockfight," Adam said. "I doubt

whether there will be any connoisseurs of fashion present."

"Very good, sir." Dimmock's voice was rife with disapproval. Adam wasn't sure whether it was his destination or apathy on sartorial matters that offended his valet.

While Dimmock fussed around, brushing clothes, Adam's mind returned again to the previous evening. He was a fool, pure and simple, and worse, a cowardly one.

He was too afraid to tell Fabienne the truth, fearing her contempt or pity, and now whatever sort of understanding they had was gone, destroyed. Damn his scruples, damn her, damn her string of lovers—or at least the string of lovers he imagined. And she held the means to ruin him, to make him an object of ridicule to the world. He was a fool twice, thrice over. Had he left her purring with satisfaction the truce would have continued.

God, that was even worse. He was willing to prostitute his body just as he'd prostituted his intellect to write his novels.

The writing had begun as an innocent diversion— stories told to Mags as they lay abed—romantic, silly, erotic tales. Later, as she lay in bed alone, fading away from him, he had spun out long and complex plots. It was the only hope he had, when science and medicine failed, to make her stay with him a little longer.

Write them down, Adam, my love. . . .

So he had, and the works of Mrs. Ravenwood had become more than a pastime. Now they owned him, and he'd lost Mags.

He might have lost Fabienne too.

He stopped himself from groaning aloud with lust and regret as he became aware that Dimmock needed his attention again.

"Your boots, sir."

Adam submitted to his valet's demands with a heavy sigh.

In the courtyard behind Mrs. Craven's house, a motley crowd milled around, shouting and placing bets—

members of the *ton*, ragged barefoot urchins, and a few women whose garish dress and forthright manners betrayed their profession. Adam nodded to the few men he knew and threaded his way through the crowd, keeping an eye out for pickpockets.

"Mr. Ashworth?"

The man who addressed him was not tall, but lithe and athletic in appearance, olive skinned and with familiar almond-shaped eyes—Fabienne's brother, the Conte d'Argonac.

"How do you do, my lord?" Adam said.

"Call me Argonac. I have a fencing academy nearby. I should be honored if you care to drop by for a bout. Tillotson says you taught him, and that you studied in Rome and Paris."

"Thank you. I should enjoy that, although I fear I'm slower than I used to be." Adam wondered what else Argonac knew about him—that he dishonored the Frenchman's sister at twenty-year intervals, for instance?

After bets were placed—for surprisingly high stakes—the two fighting cocks were released into a central, shallow pit, where they strutted for a few brief seconds. After a short flurry of wings and spurred feet, one lay limp and bloody, while the other stretched its neck and crowed in triumph.

"Not a female in sight, yet they fight all the same," a familiar voice commented. "Good evening, Ashworth. I believe you know Captain Sanders."

"Good evening, Greenmore." Adam bowed and turned to Sanders. "I trust my daughter is well."

"Well enough, the last time I saw her." Sanders gave an insolent smile as he turned to leave. "Good evening, Father-in-law."

"Not so fast." Adam stepped in front of him. "Where is she?"

"At our lodgings. Your daughter's a whining wretch, Ashworth, the children too. I should have left them in your tender care." Again Sanders turned as if to leave, but stopped. "You know, I've always wondered about the youngest, the girl. She bears such a remarkable resemblance to you I wonder whether there's a closer relationship between my wife and her father than is natural—"

"Ashworth—" Greenmore stepped forward, a restraining hand on Adam's arm. Adam shook him off, aware only of a burn of cold anger. His fist clenched. He stepped forward, swung his arm, and his fist made a satisfying contact with Sanders' nose. Sanders staggered and fell to the ground.

"A mill! The gentry coves have started a mill!" a man shouted, and one of the whores gave an affected high-pitched scream.

Sanders got to his feet, one hand at his bloody nose. "I demand satisfaction, sir!"

Greenmore stepped to Sanders' side with a faint ironic smile. "Forgive me, Ashworth. Sanders is my guest tonight and I am obliged to act as his second."

"If I may, Ashworth?" Argonac touched Adam's arm. He said to Greenmore, "I'll call on you directly, my lord."

Argonac and Greenmore had arranged for the duel to take place in Hyde Park the next morning at dawn. Trees loomed through the early-morning mist, and the grass was silver with dew. This could almost be Adam's estate in the country, and there was some comfort in the thought that he would see trees and clouds at the end. He could not afford to think of his regrets, that he might not see his children or grandchildren again, and that he had never told Fabienne the truth.

The carriage horses snorted and stamped, their breath rising like smoke in the air. The physician, instrument case in hand, stood nearby, and two of Greenmore's servants—one a huge, hulking brute with a dirty wig perched precariously on his bald pate, his companion a skinny, gangling fellow—passed a bottle between them.

Argonac returned. "Fifteen paces. Good luck, Mr. Ashworth."

"Thank you." He gripped Argonac's hand. "Tell Fabienne—"

"Fabienne?"

"No matter." He'd written her a letter. He took the pistol Argonac offered, and sighted it, resting it on his wrist. A finely tuned instrument suitable for taking one of them to dance with the music of the spheres. He'd always liked the idea of becoming a constellation after death; it made about as much sense as anything else.

He and Sanders stood back to back, and Greenmore called out the paces.

. . . Fifteen.

Turn, sight, fire.

Chapter Twelve

Madeleine clutched the letter in her damask hands, a thrill of horror creeping o'er her senses. This was impossible. It could not be. She swooned into the arms of the knight who stood silent and forbidding before her.
—The Castle Perilous by Mrs. Ravenwood.

*F*abienne had moved beyond disappointment and embarrassment to anger. Adam had rejected her. He had caressed her and aroused her, and then turned her down. She knew she was desirable. She knew she could snap her fingers and have virtually any man begging for her favors. But she did not want any man; she wanted Adam—and he didn't want her.

She knew that any woman's advice—the advice she would give to another woman similarly spurned—was to show coldness and indifference. *Make him think you don't want him, chérie. He'll come running with his tongue hanging out.* She heard the faint echo of her mother's voice, and then the reply of her seventeen-year-old self—*But I love him. I love him so much. Why should I do that?*

She clenched her fists as she approached Adam's house, furious that she had changed so little.

She grasped the knocker and brought it down hard. There was a pause. She imagined the servants peeping through the shutters, debating whether they should admit

a lone woman at this scandalously early hour. She
knocked again.

Eventually the door opened.

"I wish to see Mr. Ashworth." She swept into the
house, past the footman. He clutched an apron and
duster in one hand, an expression of alarm on his face.

"I beg your pardon, ma'am. He's not at home."

"Then I shall wait."

He was out and in someone else's bed—Sybil Ravenwood's, most likely.

"Yes, ma'am. This way, if you please." He showed
her into a drawing room. "Would you care for some
refreshment, ma'am?"

"No, thank you."

Alone in the room, she prowled around, too restless
to sit, and examined it for evidence of Adam's occupation. It was disappointingly impersonal, with all the appearance of a room not often used.

The footman came into the room again, holding a silver tray. "Begging your pardon, ma'am, you did say you
are Mrs. Craigmont, did you not?"

"Yes, I am Mrs. Craigmont."

"Well, then." The man looked thoughtful. "I've been
cleaning the study, and noticed this letter for you,
ma'am."

"Thank you."

Something must be wrong. She broke the seal and unfolded the sheet of paper. It was crossed so tightly, every
inch of space covered, that at first it was almost illegible.
The familiar hand was scrawled as though the writer
were in a desperate hurry, with sprays and sputters of
ink where the nib had dug into the paper.

It was Sybil Ravenwood's hand.

No, it was Adam's hand.

Fabienne,
   *If you read this, it means I am dead, with many
regrets. Above all, that only now from beyond the
grave can I tell you in my own voice how passionately
I love you. Forgive me. . . .*

He knew about Elaine. He knew the deepest secrets of Fabienne's heart. He had received intimate confessions made to a person who existed only in her imagination.

And she had never guessed.

Her vision blurred and her hands shook.

The drawing room door creaked open, revealing Adam, dressed in black, silent and still. An icy shiver trickled down her spine. *But he's dead. He says he is dead.*

The letter slipped from her numb fingers in a long, dizzying spiral to the floor.

She woke to the sting of brandy in her mouth.

"It's all right," he said. "Don't cry."

"I'm not crying." Tears leaked down her face.

"I've ordered some tea," he said. "You fainted. I'm sorry I gave you such a shock."

"You said you were dead." She opened her eyes to find herself lying on the sofa, Adam beside her with a glass of brandy in his hand.

"I beg your pardon?"

"The letter. You said—"

"The letter? Damnation." He left her side, pounced on the paper, and flung it into the fire.

"Wait—I hadn't finished reading it."

"Thank God for that."

"Why did you say you were dead?"

"Because there was a good chance I would be." He sat in a chair opposite her and held out the brandy to her. "May I ask how much of the letter you did read?"

"Barely the first sentence, Mr. Ashworth. Or should I address you as Mrs. Ravenwood?" She struggled to sit, fighting dizziness and nausea. "How could you deceive and betray me so vilely? How could you do this to me?"

He shook his head and looked at her, surprise on his face. "You mean you didn't know? But—"

"I did not!" She tried to keep her voice from shaking. "You deceived me shamefully. I thought she was your mistress."

The footman, carrying a tea tray, entered the room, and they were both silent as he poured tea.

"Robert," Adam said to him, "if you wish to stay in my household you will not indiscriminately hand out letters I have written."

"I'm sorry, sir. I—"

"It wasn't his fault," Fabienne said. "How was he to know? You lie to me and deceive me, and then blame someone else for your misdeeds? That is unjust, indeed."

The footman glanced from her to his master, alarm in his eyes.

Adam glared at her and nodded to the footman to leave. "If you had not arrived uninvited at my house, none of this would have happened."

"I brought your spectacles back," Fabienne said.

"In person? I don't believe that was necessary." He poured more brandy. "What did you really want?"

"Why did you think you were going to die?" Shaking with rage, she put her teacup down on a small table nearby, grabbed the refilled brandy glass, and swallowed its contents. "How dare you do this to me? How dare you say you are dead and then walk into the room? You have the gall to tell me you love me—" She burst into tears again and fumbled in her reticule. "I should have Ippolite call you out. And here are your damned spectacles." She flung them at him, and heard the clatter and tinkle of breaking glass.

"Damnation," Adam said in a mild tone. "Fortunately I have a spare pair. Have my handkerchief, Mrs. Craigmont. It is far more practical than yours."

"How can you take this so lightly?"

"I do not." He stood and bowed. "If you will excuse me, I shall return in a moment."

In the few minutes that he was gone, she scrubbed at her eyes as fresh tears of rage and humiliation leaked out. She took another sip of brandy, hoping that the weakness and shaking in her limbs would pass soon and she could go, away from this man who had hurt her. She wanted to curl up under her bedcovers and cry undisturbed, abandon herself to grief.

"Mrs. Craigmont?" Adam stood in front of her, holding a bundle of letters—her letters to Sybil Ravenwood, the imaginary figure of her desires—tied with the garter he had taken from her. "They are all there, save one. I am afraid it met with an accident. May I sit down? I'm devilish tired." He dropped into his chair and refilled the brandy glass, his hands shaking.

A tear plopped onto the bundle of letters on her lap. "Oh, Fabienne, dearest, please—"

"Never use my Christian name again!"

"I beg your pardon." He tapped the wooden arm of his chair with his fingers, a nervous tattoo that made her want to leap up and slap him.

"What were you thinking of?" Fabienne demanded, her voice thick with tears. She really didn't care. He knew all about her, after all. "Did you mean to make me a laughingstock?"

"No. I think it more to the point that you intended me—or still do—to become a laughingstock. I tried to break off the correspondence several times as you may remember. We were equally guilty in refusing to do what was sensible. I can only admit that when you ended our exchange of letters I felt relief and great sadness. I fully intended to reveal myself at Tillotson's ball, but lacked the courage. There. You know the worst of it, now."

"I would have ended the correspondence sooner had I known Mrs. Ravenwood's true identity. There is no comparison."

"Truly?"

She hesitated and reached for the brandy glass. "I don't know."

He drained his teacup. "I have a grievance to address also."

"How can you possibly—"

"You claimed that it was with your second husband that you first reached a climax. I beg to differ."

"I beg your pardon. How insufferably male of you. As if that had anything to do with the matter at hand."

"You did with me. Remember, Mrs. Craigmont?"

"No, I do not," she lied. "Besides, it never happened."

"Oh, it did. The first time, you sat on my lap with my hand under your skirts. I kissed you the whole time to stop you from making any sounds. Afterward you laughed and said something in French about the saints. I was surprised. I thought you'd cry." He gazed at her. "I've never seen you cry until now. I'm sorry."

"So you should be, and I remember none of that. Besides, it was Mr. Craigmont who brought me to climax first during the act itself."

He flushed. "You mean when you and I—"

"No." Good. He looked embarrassed now.

"Ah. Well, not the first time, maybe. I remember it being rather fast. But how about the second?"

"No." She drove her victory home. "Nor the third or fourth. I was merely sore."

"But you—why didn't you say something? I would have—"

"Adam, I was young and foolish, and I wanted to please you because I was in love with you. And it seemed such a matter of great urgency to you that I was sorry for you."

"*Sorry* for me?" His voice rose to a shout. He grabbed the brandy glass, refilled it, and drank the contents in one gulp.

"Yes, indeed." She watched with some satisfaction as he leaped to his feet and turned away from her, resting his arms on the mantelpiece. "May I ask you what else you wrote in that letter? And why you thought you were going to die?"

"Ah, that letter. I hardly know where to begin." He sat down again and stretched his booted legs out, hands in pockets. Now she saw the fatigue on his face, shadows under his eyes and stubble on his jaw. "Yesterday Sanders and I encountered each other. He insulted my daughter most vilely, and I had no choice but to provoke him to challenge me to a duel. We met this morning, and much to our mutual regret, failed to kill each other. You may ask your brother about it—he acted as my second." He shook his head. "I am a dreadful shot, and I thought I should die, but my opponent shook with fear so that his shot went wide. The only creature in danger from my shot was the physician's horse."

Good God, men, she thought. *What on earth was wrong with them all?* "So honor was satisfied?"

"Hardly."

"You English are mad," Fabienne said, "and you, worst of all." She took a gulp of tea, changed her mind, and accepted another glassful of brandy from Adam. "What will happen now between you and Sanders?"

"I don't know. Oh, officially, it is over, this time." He stood and wandered over to the mantelpiece. "You wish to know about the letter. I am still alive, Mrs. Craigmont. I assure you it is of no consequence, now." He stared at her as she held the brandy glass out again. "Do you think so much brandy is wise? All I shall say is that in this instance I trusted you enough to . . ." He rubbed his face with one hand. "Although now, I really wonder whether I was in my right mind."

She stood up, her legs shaking. "You continue to insult me. It is intolerable. Trusted me to *what*? Good morning, Mr. Ashworth."

"Wait, please." He swallowed. "You understand that if I had died today, the consequences for Babs would have been calamitous. I changed my will, leaving one half of my fortune to you and asking that you give her shelter if she left Sanders. The rest of my estate goes to Jon, other than small gifts to my servants, so that Sanders could not get his hands on any of it. In addition I appointed you and your brother Jon's guardians."

She sank back into the chair and stared at him, as tears of a different sort rose to her eyes and fell down her cheeks.

"Fabienne—Mrs. Craigmont—I did not mean to distress you further." He knelt in front of her and took her hands in his. "I said also that I loved you. You know that, I think. I realized that too late, years ago, after you jilted me—"

"I jilted you?" She snatched her hands away from him. "After you seduced and betrayed me, you mean. You have an extremely bad memory, Mr. Ashworth." She found her bonnet and knotted the strings with hands that would not keep steady. Where on earth had her gloves gone?

He handed them to her. "I'll have my carriage called for you. I am sorry you are so angry with me, Fabienne."

"Of course I am angry with you. You have deceived and insulted me at every turn. You kissed me in your library, and now I think it only so I would not see your writing. You tell me you love me when you are safely dead, and besides, you—"

"Fabienne—" He sounded amused.

"I told you not to use my Christian name!"

"I beg your pardon, Mrs. Craigmont. Continue your catalogue of ills against me, if you wish."

"You know what I mean, you bastard. You would not make love to me."

"Oh, that. Well, that is nothing to do with you."

"Nothing to do with me?" She sat down again, not trusting her legs to support her. She waited and watched as he stared at the decanter of brandy, fingers tapping on the mantelpiece. "Adam, for God's sake, what are you trying to tell me?"

"I think you had better leave, Mrs. Craigmont."

"You damned hypocrite." She stood, feeling quite drunk, and sank back down again. "You bloody seducer, you—"

"Excuse me." He crossed the room. Fabienne heard him speak to someone outside as she pulled on her gloves on; buttoning them was quite beyond her. She closed her eyes.

"Mrs. Craigmont?" He was quite close to her, his warmth and scent in her nostrils. He lifted one hand, and then the other, fastening her gloves, and she felt his breath and lips on her wrist. "My carriage is here. Can you stand if I help you?"

"Why wouldn't you make love to me, Adam?" Her voice was breathy and forlorn, but she hardly cared.

"Fabienne, look at me." She opened her eyes with great reluctance, and found herself gazing into his face.

"You need to shave." She ran her hand down his cheek.

He turned his lips briefly to her fingers. "I know."

"Tell me."

He swallowed. "My wife died over ten years ago. I have not lain with a woman since."

She had a brief recollection of his arm around her, helping her outside, the sting of cool morning air and the noise of the street, the scents of leather and horse manure, and no memory at all of the journey home.

Chapter Thirteen

"You have betrayed me, madam."

Elvira shrank from her captor's harsh visage. "Sir, I am bound by a sacred oath to another. I can say no more. My heart shall never be yours."

"You must choose, madam, ere break of dawn. Either you shall be mine, or the cloister cell and a lifetime of silence await."

—The Ruined Tower by Mrs. Ravenwood.

"My dear sir, I am most dreadfully sorry," Greenmore said when they met in the Eglintons' drawing room. He wrung Adam's hand. "I do hope you appreciate what a truly awkward position it was for me. I regret that Sanders behaved in such an ungentlemanly way."

"Do not concern yourself," Adam said. "It is over. I understand that you had little choice."

"Very true, brother," Greenmore gripped Adam's branded forearm. "Have no fear. He has wronged you, he is no gentleman, and we do not tolerate those who injure our brothers. You need worry no more."

"What do you mean?"

Greenmore clapped him on the shoulder. "Believe me, you have nothing to worry about now." His attention was caught by a new arrival. "Ah, the fair Mrs. Craigmont is here. She ages remarkably well, although her first bloom is long gone. I always think there is an advantage to having a mistress of somewhat advanced years—she knows what she is about between the sheets, and is less likely to embarrass one with a bastard."

"Indeed. She is also less likely to risk her own health and life, sir, in producing that embarrassment." Tension crackled between the two men as a horrible thought struck Adam. "Is she your mistress?"

Greenmore laughed. "Thankfully, no. In my opinion, she is trouble. More than adequate in bed, I'd wager, but not inclined to know her place, and too demanding. Besides, she has lost her luster. She was ravishing when she was first in London, merely acceptable now. Is she yours? I beg your pardon for my bluntness. I should not like you to commit yourself to two duels in as many days."

"No, she is not my mistress, but I have always considered her one of the most beautiful women I know." He watched Fabienne, whom he had last seen as a tearful, drunken wretch, railing at him, her face red and blotchy, and scarcely able to walk. Tonight she was beautiful and desirable, her moss green gown revealing most of her bosom, and emeralds sparkling at her ears and neck. He stared at her with regret and longing. Not his mistress. Not yet, and possibly not ever.

"How does Mrs. Sanders do?" Greenmore asked, with one of his disconcerting shifts from cynicism to sympathy. "I trust there were no repercussions between her and the captain after this morning's business."

"She will not receive me." Adam bowed and moved away. Despite Greenmore's cordiality he did not trust the man enough to confide further in him. He watched Elaine move to Fabienne's side and whisper something in her ear. Fabienne's expressive face broke into a smile, and she kissed Elaine on both cheeks, then drew her away, her arm around her daughter's waist. Luke joined them, and Fabienne took his hand, her face alight with happiness. He could tell from their expressions that good news had been shared, and he could guess what it was.

"Uncle Adam!" His niece Mary appeared in front of

him, curtsied, and then burst into giggles and threw her arms around him. "I am so glad you are come. I have a great secret to tell you."

"If it's a secret, Mary, you shouldn't tell anyone," he said. "Are we to see the portrait unveiled tonight?"

"Yes, indeed. Miss Twyford says she will return to add a few details in a day or so, after the paint has dried. I have hated sitting still all this time. It was dreadfully tedious and I do so long to see it. But that's not my secret."

"So are you engaged? Or Sylvia?"

"Oh, Uncle Adam, you are so silly. Not me. It's—" She broke off as her mother approached.

"Adam, you look quite respectable." Prissy tweaked his neckcloth to a position of her liking and frowned at him. "You do look rather tired. I trust you have not been leading a debauched life?"

"Of course not, sister." He tried his best not to assume the innocent look that had never in their lives fooled her.

"I have some very pleasant women for you to meet tonight. I expect to hear happy news about you soon, Adam."

"Certainly. My valet is in complete agreement with you. Maybe you could join in the bets that he and the other servants have placed."

"Shame on you. You are far too lax with your servants. Margaret was forever complaining to me about it, and it must be even worse now." She tapped him with her fan. "Adam?"

"I beg your pardon." He dragged his gaze away from Fabienne, who was in animated conversation with Eglinton and Luke at the other side of the room.

His sister frowned and turned her attention to Adam. "I suppose Mrs. Craigmont is your mistress? You should be more discreet."

"I have no connection with Mrs. Craigmont, and I'll thank you to mind your own affairs, sister." His response came out more sharply than he intended, and Prissy stepped back, her brow furrowed.

"I beg your pardon, but I have my own family to protect. I wish for my daughters to make good matches, and I cannot afford scandal. I regret that I have had to break off connections with Barbara, but you know why." She gave a quiet sniff and wiped a finger quickly under one eye, trying to smile. "Do not make me cry. I will look a fright."

"It's regrettable indeed, Priss." He gave his sister's hand a squeeze, hoping that his gesture would express sympathy even if his words did not.

She smiled, took his arm, and led him off to meet other women, who seemed insipid, plain, and empty-headed. The only woman he was interested in did not even attempt to catch his eye. She was busy with a cluster of attentive gentlemen, ranging from a nervous lad a little older than Jon to a tottering white-haired octogenarian, who leered into her bosom and whose tremulous hand hovered frequently around her waist.

How many of them have been in your bed, Fabienne?

"Uncle?" Luke interrupted his thoughts as they went into dine. "Sir, I have some great news. At least, I believe it to be so, and I trust that you will agree. I—"

"I know. I guessed. My congratulations," he added and clapped Luke on the shoulder.

The dinner was long and tedious. At the other end of the table, Fabienne flirted and laughed. Adam watched her capture the ancient rake's hand and place it on the table with a stern yet mischievous smile and a tap of her fan. He wondered how long the wandering hand had been beneath the table and what liberties she'd allowed.

He was becoming insane with jealousy and lust, a modern-day Othello, suspecting her with any man able to walk, or even lie flat on his back. It would not do.

Adam did not linger with the other men around the table after the women had left, but muttered an excuse to Eglinton and made his way to the drawing room. Elaine's portrait, draped in black velvet, stood in a prominent position in the room, ready for its unveiling later in the evening, and Adam's other niece, Sylvia, played the pianoforte for the guests.

A few women looked up with curiosity as he entered

and made his way to Fabienne's side. "I need to speak with you," he murmured.

She nodded but did not look away from Sylvia's performance on the pianoforte.

"You look very well," Adam said.

"As do you."

He shifted in the chair and folded his arms. "I expected something from you today, Mrs. Craigmont. I did not receive it."

"You did, sir? What could that be?"

"You know damned well, Fabienne. The letters."

She unfurled her fan and examined its painted surface. "Ah yes, the letters from 'Mrs. Ravenwood.' Well, I hardly see what interest they could hold. She does not exist."

"Don't be obtuse, Fabienne. They are in my hand. I should be obliged if you send them back to me."

"No, I shall not."

"What now, Mrs. Craigmont? Explain, if you will, why not."

"I think I will keep your letters a little longer. They have sentimental associations for me." She sighed and looked up at him through her lashes.

"Blackmail is an ugly occupation, madam."

Sylvia ended her piece on the pianoforte to scattered, polite applause.

Fabienne laid her fan in her lap and leaned toward him. "There is no need to glower at me, Adam. What use do you think the letters would be to me, or what damage do you think they could do to yourself?"

Forcing himself not to peer into her bosom, he said, "Must I spell it out? You provoke me deliberately, madam. Very well. Writing is thought by many to be an effete occupation, and to do so from behind a woman's skirts even more unnatural. It is not only an unmanly occupation, but an ungentlemanly one since I have made a fortune from my work, and you know a gentleman does not make money by the sweat of his brow. I suppose the novels are well-crafted enough, but they are beneath my learning, and frankly they do not encourage women to think and act as rational beings. Or men either, for that matter."

"They bring great pleasure to many," Fabienne said. "I truly think, which you obviously do not, that women at least have the sense to perceive what is fantasy and what is reality, without losing their enjoyment in your work."

He stared at her for a long moment, then kissed her hand. "Thank you. I believe that is one of the highest compliments I, or Mrs. Ravenwood, could ever receive. Then I take it you have no objection to returning the letters to me?"

"I will not return them, sir. It is my prerogative, if you like. I am the wronged party here, not you." She ran her fingertips down the handle of her fan, looking up at him through her eyelashes.

"Hell and damnation, Fabienne! You may not wish to blackmail me, but I have fewer scruples than you." He looked across the room to where Elaine sat, deep in conversation with his two nieces. "Return the letters to me within the week or I'll tell Elaine of her parentage."

Fabienne's quick, sharp breath told him he had hit his mark. "What? Surely you jest."

"Now she is engaged she should know her origins. And you admit yourself you should have told her months ago."

"Yes, but—it is nothing to do with you, sir. Nothing. You have no right—"

He whispered with barely controlled anger, "Nothing to do with me? She is three months older than Babs. It computes exactly. She looks like me. She favors my family. You would deny me my child, and I'll not lose another daughter."

"You claim you love me," she spluttered. "Yet you threaten me so? You, who claimed I was a woman of honor? And you trusted your children to me?"

"So I did," he said. "Had I died this morning, of course Mrs. Ravenwood's true identity would have been revealed. I should not be alive to suffer the taunts of society. And as for declaring my love, let us say that imminent death adversely affected my judgment."

She raised one gloved hand to her mouth, while the other tightened on her fan.

He stood and bowed. "I'll bid you good evening, Mrs. Craigmont. I trust one week from tonight will suffice."

To his great satisfaction, the fan she clutched so tightly snapped with an audible crack.

Chapter Fourteen

Serena clutched the thin silk of her nightgown to her bosom as the light of her candle cast a lurid glow over the moss-bedecked walls of the secret passage. In an alcove, a shrouded corpse lay.

A veiled figure stepped forward to block her way and lifted the winding sheet. "You must look upon the face."

Serena gave a horrid shriek and swooned.

—The Spectre of the Abbey by Mrs. Ravenwood.

"**D**ear Luke said the painting was my finest yet." Elaine crumbled a piece of toast on her plate. "And Lord and Lady Eglinton said they liked it above all things, and will have it framed and hung on the wall of the drawing room. Fabienne, did you see the children's faces when the velvet was cast aside to reveal it to everyone? I thought Lady Mary would weep. Do you think I should go over there now to finish it? Or is too early after the party last night? I am so happy. Oh no, I cannot go over today, for Luke says he wants to take me out in his curricle—it is new, you know, a gift from his godfather, and just the thing, he says. He has a matched team of bays, with white slashes on their faces, which Mr. Ashworth also bought him, and I do so long to see them. And Luke too of course." She paused for breath.

"Do try and eat something," Fabienne said. Her own breakfast lay untouched on her plate.

"Oh, I must write to my mother and father to tell them. I shall do that directly."

"Why, I've never seen you giddy before," Ippolite commented. He picked up Elaine's hand and kissed it. "I wish you all happiness, my dear. Luke's a good man."

"Thank you, Lord Argonac. May I be excused, Fabienne? I have much to do." Elaine gave up her pretense of eating breakfast.

"Of course." Fabienne breathed a sigh of relief as Elaine ran out of the room.

"It is curious to see our little Puritan become a giggling chit now she's engaged," Ippolite said. "I must admit I'm rather relieved that she is a normal woman after all. And I imagine that jangle of the doorbell can only signal the arrival of her beloved."

Fabienne's footman showed Luke into the room.

"I apologize for my early arrival," Luke said. "I wish . . . that is, if it's convenient, to see Elaine."

"Of course. I know she'll be glad to see you." She directed her footman to show Luke into the drawing room.

"Unchaperoned?" Ippolite murmured as Luke left.

"They are engaged." She doubted that anything improper would occur, but decided, after a few more minutes, that maybe she should join them. Twenty years ago, if she had been alone with Adam, God knows what they would have done by now. Besides, there were wedding plans to make.

As she entered the drawing room, Elaine and Luke sprang apart on the sofa, both of them red-faced and flustered.

"I beg your pardon, Mrs. Craigmont. I intend to take Elaine for a ride in my curricle this morning. Would you care to join us?" Luke asked.

"No, thank you." Fabienne shook her head. "You are engaged now, so it is quite proper for you to drive together."

"Fabienne, we shall not have to take Reuben with us, I hope?" Elaine asked.

"He'd reduce a curricle to splinters. I can't imagine

him perched on the back like a huge ape. No, I think Luke can look after you, in the Park and in broad daylight."

"Oh, good. I don't like Reuben. He is so strange-looking and says so little."

"I did not hire him for his conversational abilities. He is big and threatening in appearance, and that is what you need to keep you safe. He cannot help his looks. I believe he was a pugilist, which is why his face is so scarred. But shall we all go to the theater tonight? I should so like to go out with you both, and I have not been to the theater in a long while."

"Oh, yes!" Elaine clapped her hands and looked at Luke. "If you are not engaged elsewhere."

"I should be delighted. I believe my godparents, Lord and Lady Eglinton, that is, plan to attend tonight also. They are very pleased about the engagement. They have come to appreciate Elaine." He smiled at his betrothed.

"Good. Go out and enjoy yourselves," Fabienne said.

I can't do it, she thought after they had left. *Not while she is so giddy and happy. Certainly not before tonight. Tomorrow. I must do it tomorrow. Maybe after we have been to the dressmakers for the wedding dress—oh, there is no appropriate time for this, and before I know it, time will have run out. And then she will hate me even more for my silence.*

Fabienne was grateful that Luke and Elaine were so absorbed in each other that neither of them noticed her dour mood that evening. The play seemed to please everyone except her; she found the plot vapid and foolish, the painted scenery ridiculous, and the posturing and declarations onstage absurd. She really should have stayed at home.

She gathered her wrap and fan. "I've had enough. I think I shall leave."

Luke and Elaine turned to her, surprise on their faces. Of course, no one else in the entire universe could feel anything other than bubbly elation.

"I insist I escort you home," Luke said.

"Oh, Fabienne, do you have a headache?"

They fluttered and fussed around her. Luke offered to fetch a glass of wine, and Elaine gazed at her with sorrowful eyes and patted her hand. Fabienne wanted to scream.

"No, no," she said. "I am tired, that is all, and I shall ask Ippolite to take me home—or even better, I shall send for Reuben." She gestured into the pit, where Reuben's bald head and hefty shoulders loomed amongst the crowd.

She had no intention of seeking out either. Ippolite was probably backstage in the ladies' tiring room, flirting or worse, and Reuben was needed to look after Elaine. She forced herself to smile and deflect Luke's and Elaine's concern—it was borne of guilt, she was sure, for their total absorption in each other and neglect of her. Perhaps she should encourage the idea of a special license and get the pair of lovestruck cuckoos out of her nest.

She pushed away the uncharitable thought, and assured them that she was merely fatigued. Finally she escaped into the relatively quiet passage outside the boxes, and took a deep breath.

As she turned the corner toward the staircase, she ran straight into a large, familiar male body. His hand gripped her arm.

Adam released her as her gown brushed against him— it was some flimsy fabric that barely covered her breasts. He looked away and cleared his throat. "Good evening, Mrs. Craigmont."

She curtsied. "Good evening, Mr. Ashworth. I trust you will enjoy the play."

"You're leaving? Alone?"

"Yes. Luke and Elaine are driving me mad." A flash of sadness passed over her face.

"Indeed. Why is that?"

"I don't know. She is so happy, but she irritates me beyond belief, and then I feel ashamed of my lack of forbearance."

"Yes, I remember you said once as much in one of your letters."

She flushed. "Pray do not quote my words back to me."

"I beg your pardon." He bowed.

"Good night, Mr. Ashworth."

He sought a safe subject to delay her departure. "So how is the play?"

"Dreadful."

She took a step forward to walk past him and he stepped into her path, as though meeting her in a fencing bout.

"Fabienne, listen to me. You must return those letters to me. I will . . ." Exactly what was he about to say? What, if anything, could he have, or say, that might appease her?

She laughed. "Are you offering me your body, Mr. Ashworth?"

He stared back at her as the air between them came alight with sensuality. "That was not quite what I had in mind, Mrs. Craigmont, but it is a very interesting proposition. Is it an offer you would accept?" His fingers slid down her bare arm and over her kidskin glove to circle her wrist. She stilled, but did not move away.

"I should be hesitant to storm the fortress of your carefully guarded celibacy." Her breasts brushed against his chest as she tilted back her head to gaze into his eyes.

"Carefully guarded?" He gave a short laugh. "More like grief that became a habit, and then that strengthened by lack of opportunity. Everyone in the country knows one another's business, and I don't tumble milkmaids in haystacks."

"But . . . I cannot imagine the man I knew to take such a turn."

"I'm not that man. I was an arrogant, randy, young ram, and a selfish one, as you reminded me."

"Adam." She laid her palms against his chest. "You may offer me all the pleasure in the world, but I'll keep those letters."

"So I've led you to the top of the high mountain, and

you refuse me?" He laughed and she smiled back. "I must admit I'm rather relieved."

"Indeed? You injure me, sir." She feigned hauteur, tossing her head back and gazing at him with disdain.

"Ten years is a long time," he said. "I'm no longer young. I—"

She laughed and flicked open a button on his coat.

He froze at her touch.

"You won't have forgotten. It is like riding a horse. You know how to do it always—"

"What an obscene analogy. Please stop that." He took a step backward.

She moved forward, trapping him against the wall, just as he'd trapped her against his bookcases. "I should be very gentle with you, Adam. You have nothing to fear." She undid the next button, lifted one foot and caressed his calf.

"Stop that." He couldn't hide his arousal with her pressed against him. "What, madam, do you intend to have me here against the wall, where anyone could come upon us?"

"Yes," she said, a breathy moan, and rubbed against him. Her eyes were dark, her lips wet and parted.

"For Christ's sake," he said through gritted teeth, grabbing her by the bottom, and lifting her against him. Her legs wrapped around his waist. "This is a very bad idea, Fabienne."

"Yes," she said against his neck, biting softly under his ear. She smelled wonderful, a hint of cinnamon, a touch of salt, the scent of burgundy, rich and potent.

"Please control yourself, Mrs. Craigmont," he said with an effort and reached for one of her legs, attempting to unwind her.

She moaned and slid down his body, a delicious friction that he suspected she made last as long as possible.

"Very well," she said. "You are right, of course. This would be most unwise. I shall bother you no more, since you find me so undesirable."

"I mistrust you when you act the innocent, Fabienne." He was probably safe as long as he kept his tight hold on her, her body pressed to his. At least she could not reach into his breeches or do some other indecently pleasurable thing to him. His cock gave a rude twitch against her at the thought. "Come, give me those letters back. You're a reasonable woman."

"No. I cannot." She gave a deep, heartfelt sigh. "You must think very poorly of me."

"No, indeed, I do not. I—" He gulped as her breasts, forced by her stays, the expansion of her rib cage, and the constriction of his arms around her, popped from the top of her low-cut gown like a cork from a bottle. He released her, horrified but unable to tear his gaze away.

"Oh, dear! Oh, Mr. Ashworth, do forgive me!" She giggled, and began to fuss with her gown, taking what he thought was an extraordinarily long time to put herself to rights. "What a shocking, dreadful thing indeed. Mr. Ashworth, do you think you could only—"

He pushed her away. "For God's sake, madam, you drive me mad! I will not yield to you, by God. What do you think you are, to torment me so? I am not made of stone—I burn like any other man. If you think it easy for me, you are mistaken. I work hard to sublimate my desires, and if I must I take care of the business as best I can—" Furious, he waved a clenched fist in the air in demonstration. "And may I suggest, madam, that you practice the female equivalent and save yourself much time and trouble and, above all, leave me alone—"

He stopped, trembling.

Her mouth dropped open and she stared at him.

He was appalled, both at his own crudeness and at the dramatic effect it had on her.

She opened her mouth and let out a huge gasp.

Alarmed, he wondered whether he should call for help.

And then she slumped against the wall and laughed, her whole body shaking. He had never seen a woman guffaw that way, holding her sides, helpless with mirth. It was infectious; his lips curved up in a smile, and he began to laugh too.

Someone behind him gave a small, polite cough. He whirled around to see Argonac, standing only a few feet away, eyes narrowed. At Argonac's shoulder stood that human mountain of a manservant they'd hired to look after Elaine.

The manservant stepped forward, one huge fist clenched, and muttered something to Argonac, who waved him back.

"Good evening, sir," Argonac said. "Is my sister well?"

"I believe so." Adam wondered how long her brother had stood there while his sister behaved like a she-cat in heat and he railed like a Calvinist minister who'd been caught with his breeches down. They both looked at the woman who held her sides, helpless with laughter.

"It is rather late," Argonac said. "I think Mrs. Craigmont needs to go home."

"Of course. I do apologize. Good night." He bowed to Fabienne, whose laughter had subsided to hiccuping giggles and gasps. He and Ippolite bowed to each other with cool formality.

Adam made his way to the Eglintons' box grinning from ear to ear. He had low expectations of the play; what could possibly match up to Fabienne's peerless performance?

"Mr. Ashworth?" A man wearing the Eglinton livery approached him. "Sir, his lordship wishes you to meet him in his carriage outside. He needs you to help him on some urgent business."

"Very well. Pray make my apologies to Lady Eglinton." He hurried downstairs.

Eglinton's jovial face was grave when Adam joined him. "This is a bad business, Ashworth." He tapped on the roof of the carriage, signaling the driver to move forward.

"My daughter—" For one dreadful moment he thought he would stop breathing.

"No, no, she's . . . well, this will affect her, of course. Have you seen her recently?"

"No. She will not receive me. For God's sake, man, tell me what the matter is."

"I regret George Sanders has been murdered."

"Murdered?"

"I am afraid so. The news was brought to me this evening, and so I have sent your sister and nieces on to the play, hoping I should find you there."

Adam's first reaction was of relief, then shame and shock. The carriage rocked and slowed as they turned from a main thoroughfare onto a rougher and more crowded street.

"What happened?" he asked Eglinton.

"I believe it to be a robbery. His money and most of his clothing have gone. He was found in a low part of town, dead from a blow to the head, and much beaten. Such crimes are all too common, I fear. Hs body lies in a house nearby."

Adam nodded. "I'll take him to my house."

"I heard an extraordinary rumor that he'd been in a duel recently, with you of all men."

"Indeed. I thought you paid no great heed to gossip, Eglinton."

"The law has to consider all possibilities in the murder of a *gentleman*." There was a slight, contemptuous inflexion to Eglinton's voice. "I am almost wholly convinced it to be a robbery that turned into a murder."

"Indeed. I cannot say I am sorry. My daughter will finally be free of him." Adam paid little attention to Eglinton until his brother-in-law's next words caught his attention.

". . . but there's one odd thing. Someone took a knife to his arm, here." Eglinton gestured to his own forearm. "The limb is much slashed and cross-hatched, as though the assailant wished to hide a mark. What do you think of that, Ashworth?"

"An odd thing indeed."

With a shiver of unease, Adam recalled Greenmore's words. *Have no fear. He has wronged you, he is no gentleman, and we do not tolerate those who turn against their brothers. You need worry no more.*

*   *   *

"How do you feel, my dear?"

"Much better, Papa." Barbara managed a wan smile from the sofa where she lay.

Adam had broken the news of Sanders' death to her late the previous night, after his formal identification of the corpse. Her lodgings were mean and damp, and he suspected she and the children had had little to eat recently. To his relief she had agreed to return to his house.

"The children are doing well this morning, although Will has a cough."

"Yes, we have not been well." She sat up. "Will you tell me now what happened to George?"

"He was robbed, we think, and killed." He added, "I'm sorry, my dear. I brought his body here to the house."

He hoped she would not want to see the corpse. The woman who had laid Sanders out had done her best to minimize the damage, but there was no denying the man had met an ugly end.

"I want to see him." Her voice was cold and remote. She stood, clutching her shawl about herself.

"Are you sure?"

"Yes, sir." As he moved to take her arm, she added, "Alone, if you please."

He stepped back, and summoned a footman to escort her.

After a while she returned, leaning on the servant's arm, her face blotchy and her eyes red. She sank onto the sofa and twisted a handkerchief in her hands. "I know what you think," she said. "You think I am a fool."

"I did not say that."

"You did not have to."

Her gaze moved to the tea that Adam had ordered in her absence. She lifted the heavy silver teapot, biting her lip.

"Let me call Robert back. He can pour. You are still weak and distressed—"

"No, thank you, sir. I am sure your footman has more important things to attend to." She broke off, put the teapot down, and rubbed at her skirts where tea had splashed. When she handed Adam a cup he saw how her hands shook.

"Babs," Adam said. "It's all right. You are free of him now. It's over."

She pressed her lips together and did not reply. He saw her take a deep breath. Her fair, fine complexion, inherited from her mother, was washed over with crimson. "You think it can be dismissed so easily? That I married the wrong man, and suffered for it, and now he is dead, so everything is well?"

"I did not say that—"

"He is the father of my children. Once I loved him. Or had you forgotten that?"

"Babs—"

"I am most grateful, sir, for your protection of myself and my children." She twisted her hands together and swallowed.

He could tell she was trying not to cry and pitied her. He wished fervently her mother was alive. *Why did you leave me, Mags?* He controlled his anger with an effort. "Let me call your maid; you must be distressed. You will make yourself ill again if you continue in this way."

She stood up and hurled her teacup across the room. "It has always been this way, always. You condescend to me, and never once consider my feelings. You think you can laugh and pat me on the head and all will be well. I saw you do the same to Mama, and to Luke—"

"Pardon me, miss," he said, furious and hurt. "I have done my best for you, always, and you reward me with reckless and foolish behavior."

"Indeed. Do you know, sir, I have known the identity of Mrs. Ravenwood for some five years, and never breathed a word to a soul? You never realized I knew, and certainly would never have given me credit for my discretion. I hate you!" She dropped back into her chair and stared at him, a horrified expression on her face. "Papa, I did not mean it. I swear, I did not."

"Then you should not have said it." He walked away from her across the room, which seemed acres wide. His butler approached and asked him something, to which he muttered a noncommittal reply. Then he continued on to his study, where he shut the door and sat at his desk. He dropped his head onto his arms.

"Grandpapa, Grandpapa, wake up."

"What?" He raised his head and rubbed the back of his neck.

"Grandpapa, may I keep him?" Will stood in front of him, a kitten dangling from his arms and mewing feebly. Will tightened his grip under the little animal's forelegs as its hind legs kicked and dangled.

"I don't think he likes to be held that way, Will."

"He's mine. I want to keep him."

"Where did you find him?"

"In the kitchen."

The kitten mewed again.

"Maybe you should ask your mama," Adam said. "Let him go, now. I think he cannot breathe."

Will nodded and dropped the cat. It landed with a thud on the floor and fled. Will's mouth turned down. "He was mine. He was my friend."

"You can see him again." Adam put his arms out for Will to climb onto his lap.

"Why were you asleep, Grandpapa?"

"I wasn't asleep."

"You were."

"Maybe I was." Adam sighed and rested his cheek against the top of his grandson's head.

Will squirmed on his lap. "May I write with your pen, Grandpapa?"

"Surely. I will cut it for you, and you must be careful not to make a mess."

Will watched him with obvious envy as he cut a nib. "When can I use your knife?"

"When you are bigger. Your mama would be angry if you cut yourself."

He sat with Will on his lap and watched his grandson work his way through several clean sheets of paper to create an inky, sand-strewn chaos of his desk, until the little boy tired and slipped to the ground.

"Maybe there is cake now. Come with me, Grandpapa."

"No, boy. Go to your mother on your own."

"I don't know how to get there. I don't like this house. A servant said there is a dead man here."

Adam wondered how much Will knew, or need know. "There is," he said. "But he can't harm you. Tomorrow he'll be put in the ground. Remember when our old dog died and we buried her? It will be like that."

"Was the man as old as you?" Will looked worried.

"How old do you think I am?"

"One hundred."

"One hundred? Do I look like someone who is one hundred years old?"

"You are my grandpapa. In stories, the grandpapa is always old."

"I suppose so. Come then, let's find some cake. And your mama and sister." He stood up and held out his hand to Will.

"And the other lady, the lady who rode on tigers." Will swung on his arm.

"Who?"

"The other lady. I like her."

He had a nasty suspicion who the other lady might be. Fabienne was perfectly capable of riding a tiger. What the hell was she doing here?

"He told me it was my fault, all of it, that I made him beat me. And I believed it. I tried so hard to please him so he would love me again. I beg your pardon. I run on and on," Barbara said, and gulped. "I cannot believe him dead. I expect him to walk into the room and tell me that he has made a great deal at cards and that we should celebrate. I think he will be all smiles and goodwill, as he could be."

Julia, on her mother's lap, plucked at the front of Barbara's dress. Barbara smiled at her daughter as the baby grasped her breast and sucked vigorously, one curious eye fixed on Fabienne. "I should wean her. I was ill recently and lost my milk, but I have a little now. George said I was a milk cow."

Fabienne took Barbara's hand. "I am sorry. So sorry."

Barbara managed a weak smile. "I have thought very often of the day we spent together at Papa's house, even though George followed behind. I even thought that Papa—but never mind."

"I am glad you have your father to look after you. He has told me how much he loves you."

Barbara nodded as more tears leaked from her eyes. "He has never told me that. I suppose it is his way, but he . . ." She refastened her dress as Julia slid from her lap and prepared to crawl across the drawing room. "He is not an easy man to live with."

"Why did he not remarry?" Fabienne asked. "Most men would want a wife to bring up their children."

"I don't know. I wish he had. Many girls would not want a stepmother, but I longed for one. I think Papa will cast me out now. I have said terrible things to him, and perhaps this time he will not forgive me." She bowed her head.

"My dear—" Fabienne squeezed her hand. "Do you have no other relatives you can go to?"

"I don't know. I cannot stay in London."

A scuffle at the door caught Fabienne's attention. Adam knelt on the floor, spat on his handkerchief, and scrubbed at his grandson's face. "Damnation," he said. "You are all over ink, boy."

Will screwed his face up and twisted his head aside. "Damnation," he echoed.

Barbara gave a hiss of annoyance. "Come here, Will," she said. "And do not repeat bad words your grandpapa says."

"Very well done, Babs," her father said. "He knows what it is now. Mrs. Craigmont, you have a knack of turning up at interesting times for my family."

"I beg your pardon, sir. Your butler told me you were receiving callers."

"Hmm." He planted himself in front of the fireplace, hands behind his back, and glared at the two women. "I regret we cannot invite you to dine, Mrs. Craigmont."

"It is no matter, sir. Your daughter invited me some time ago, but I have declined. My brother will be here shortly to take me home. I do not wish to tire Barbara when she is not well."

"Mrs. Craigmont came to see me and the children, sir, not you," Barbara said, to Fabienne's dismay.

"Pray remember whose house you are in, miss, and behave accordingly."

Fabienne stood and drew on her gloves. "I shall wait for my brother in the hall. Good-bye, Barbara, Mr. Ashworth. Barbara, please rest and get well. Good afternoon." She bent to kiss Barbara and, as she straightened, saw her brother enter the room. *Thank God,* she thought, and smiled at him.

"Barbara, this is my dear brother, the Count of Argonac."

Barbara stood, straight and graceful, and held out her hand. "Sir, I am pleased to meet you. I am Barbara Sanders."

Ippolite stood transfixed for a moment, then moved forward to take her hand. "Mrs. Sanders, I am indeed sorry for your loss."

"Thank you." She smiled at him, and for the first time Fabienne saw in her some of her father's charm, despite her reddened eyes and pallor. "Fabienne has told me much of you."

Ippolite blushed, still with Barbara's hand in his.

Fabienne could not resist a glance at Adam to see how he reacted to this exchange. He looked simply furious.

"Argonac," he barked by way of greeting, gave the briefest of bows, and stalked out of the room before Ippolite could respond. The door slammed behind him.

Chapter Fifteen

"My mother! My father! No, it cannot be!" Tearing herself from Percy's embrace, Madeleine ran to the castle battlements. Below, a thousand horrid rocks pierced the air, and a lone corpse dangled from the gibbet, its features ravaged by the ravens' feast.
—*The Castle Perilous* by Mrs. Ravenwood.

"*I* must speak with you," Fabienne said.

Elaine looked up from fastening her pelisse. "Now? I am about to leave for the Eglintons' house. I really must get the details finished on the portrait."

"No. No, I am sorry. It cannot wait."

"What is wrong? You do not look well." Elaine undid her pelisse. "Is something wrong?"

"No. Not exactly wrong. Please, come up to my room. We shall be undisturbed there." Fabienne led the way upstairs, telling herself that what she was about to do was right. This was it. No going back, now. She had put this moment off for too long, for years. Adam's ultimatum, if high-handed, was only a reminder of where her duty lay.

She led the way into her room and bolted the door.

"Fabienne? Are you sure you are well?" Elaine's voice interrupted her thoughts.

"Yes. Please sit down. This will not take long."

Elaine sat, blushing dark red. "It's all right. I know."

Oh, thank God. But how? "You know?"

"Indeed, yes. My mother told me."

"Your mother?" But Mrs. Twyford had promised never to tell. And if that were so, why had Elaine chosen to keep silent also?

"Oh, yes, indeed. She said it was something every mother should tell her daughter." Elaine looked shyly at Fabienne. "And now, with Luke, I begin to understand it, for my first reaction, I must admit, was why anyone should want to do such a thing. But now . . ." She leaned forward. "Is it not strange, Fabienne, that all men have a similar member hidden inside their trousers? And that once you become aware of one man's, you notice—"

"Elaine, please." Good Lord, what had Elaine and Luke been up to? Thank God they were to marry. "I am relieved indeed that you are prepared for the intimacies of the marriage bed, but that was not why I intended to speak with you."

"Oh." Elaine blushed again and twisted her hands in her lap. "I beg your pardon."

"It is this," Fabienne said, and could not continue. Gesturing to Elaine to stay seated, Fabienne crossed the room to her desk and opened the drawer where she kept her jewelry. "There is something I should like you to have."

"Oh, Fabienne, you have given me so much already. I . . ." Elaine took the pendant in her hand. "This is very pretty. I have never seen you wear it. Is it a diamond?"

"Yes. It is the last one left of a necklace that belonged to my mother. If circumstances had been different, that necklace would have been passed on to me. I had to sell the other stones, and then I had this one set in gold."

"Fabienne, I cannot take this. It is your mother's, and yours." Elaine looked troubled.

Fabienne sat beside her and dropped the chain over Elaine's head. "No, it is rightly yours. From mother to daughter."

Elaine's hand rose to clasp the stone. "You—you mean . . . ?" She took a deep breath. "You mean, you are my mother?"

"Yes. No, that is, Mrs. Twyford is your true mother. But yes, you were mine. I gave birth to you. I . . . I am sorry." Her words sounded inadequate and clumsy. "I should have told you before. I should have . . . Forgive me. It has been difficult for me to do so."

"Or perhaps you should not have told me at all," Elaine muttered, not looking at Fabienne.

"I considered that, also."

"I always knew I was a bastard." The inflection in Elaine's voice made Fabienne wince. "What else could I think? But until now, I was content with what I had, and what I knew."

"I am sorry," Fabienne said. "I have longed for you for years. The day you agreed to come to my house in London was the happiest day of my life. I wished to make amends to you, for bringing you into the world and then leaving you. The more time passed, the more difficult it became to tell you the truth."

Elaine shrugged.

My God, she shrugs like me. Did she learn it from these years in my house, or has she always shrugged so?

"My mother told me I was not her child and she was my wet nurse. She said my true mother had gone away."

"So I had," Fabienne said, "until I came back from India to find my lost child. Mrs. Twyford is truly your mother, not me. She has been since you were less than a day old and they bound my breasts and took you from me. I saw you one time after that, when you were but a few weeks old. I think you smiled at me."

"You are my mother," Elaine said, as though she had taken a strange fruit into her mouth and tested its flavor.

"Yes."

"I don't look like you." Elaine glanced in the mirror. "Do I—do I look like my father?"

"You look like yourself," Fabienne said. "You are beautiful, and you were beautiful when you were born, all red and covered with wax, and your head lumpy. I kept your shape in my arms for years, longing for you."

"But you gave me away." Elaine's hand tightened over the diamond at her throat.

"I had to," Fabienne said.

"Who is my father?"

"I cannot tell you."

"Who is he?" Elaine's voice was cold and hard.

Fabienne hesitated. She could take the easy way out; she could tell Elaine what Adam expected her to say. Or she could tell the truth, or as much of the truth as she could. She repeated, "I cannot tell you. Anything else you wish to know of me, I will tell you, but I cannot tell you who your father is."

"You— Why? Do you not know?"

Fabienne said nothing.

"You mean, you had—you . . ." Elaine glanced away, her cheeks staining red. She stood and curtsied. "I am most grateful for what you have done, madam. I know you meant well and you have taken great pains with me. But you must surely see I cannot stay here. This is not my station in life, and although I prayed much before I left my family, I fear now I was tempted by pride and vanity. If you wish me to pay you back for any money you have spent on me—"

"I wanted to spend money on you. Do not deny me that." Fabienne's voice roughened and she struggled to keep her composure. "Please, Elaine, forgive me."

Elaine stared at her. "It is all vanity, Mrs. Craigmont. I should not have come to London with you. My painting too is vanity. It does not glorify God."

"First you judge me, and now you presume to know the mind of the Almighty." Fabienne tried to keep her voice light. "Elaine, consider—"

"No!" Elaine backed away from her. "You are a-a-an unclean woman."

"And you are an ignorant, arrogant child. Insult me and you insult yourself." Fabienne was torn between wanting to embrace Elaine and slap her, and her eyes stung with tears.

"I will go." Elaine's voice was small and sad. "There is nothing you can do or say to stop me. I will pray for you." She turned away, and added in a low voice, "I shall never forget you."

"Where will you go?"

"Home. But first I shall go to the Eglintons' house as

I intended and finish the painting. Good-bye, Mrs. Craigmont."

"You are breaking my heart." Fabienne began to weep in humiliation, not caring that Elaine saw. Nothing mattered, now.

Elaine turned, and Fabienne started toward her, arms held out. She shrank back at the coldness on her daughter's face.

"Madam, I regret I cannot accept this gift." Elaine plucked the diamond pendant from her throat and dropped it into Fabienne's outstretched hand. She walked over to the door without looking back, opened it, and was gone.

"So now Babs is respectably widowed," Adam said, "I trust you'll receive her, sister."

"You are dreadful." Prissy stabbed her needle into her embroidery. "I am not totally without feelings. Does she need to borrow more gowns from us?"

"Thank you, no. She had the dressmaker visit this morning for her mourning clothes, and then she retired to bed with a silly novel for the rest of the day."

"Oh, what does she read?" Adam's niece Sylvia asked. "I am reading *The Ruined Tower* but Mary takes it from me all the time."

"I began it first. If you take it from me again, I—"

"Girls," their mother interrupted, "I'll have no quarrels about books in this house. I am sure Mrs. Ravenwood will publish another one soon."

"I have heard that she will not write another," Adam said, and regretted it as three horrified faces turned toward him. "I could be wrong," he added.

"Yes, Mrs. Ravenwood is indeed a creature shrouded in mystery," Adam's sister murmured.

Adam gave her a quick glance. Did she know? But his sister's head was bent over her embroidery again, her expression serene.

"Cousin Sylvia, did you know they put my papa in the ground?" Will asked.

Prissy frowned at her brother. "What exactly did you

tell him, Adam? Will, your grandpapa meant that Papa is with the angels now."

"The angels live in the ground too?"

Prissy threw Adam an exasperated look. "Are you sure this child should be out of bed? He has a bad cough. I shall give you some liniment for his chest. And, yes, I should like to call on Barbara when she has recovered her strength. Even better, Eglinton's sister Maria intends to visit Brighton soon, and I know she would be delighted if Barbara and the children accompany her."

"Maria?" Adam asked. "I can't recall which one she is."

"She is widowed and extremely respectable. I am sure that would be agreeable and I'm sure this young man would enjoy the sea." She smiled at Will.

"Thank you, Prissy. That's very generous, and I think it would be an excellent plan."

"I can sleep in Mama's bed now that Papa is not here," Will said. "But when Papa comes back, I will have to sleep in a little bed on my own, or he will be angry with me." His lip quivered.

"It's all right, Will," Adam said. "Your papa will not come back."

Will climbed onto his grandfather's lap and stuck a thumb in his mouth.

"You're too big a boy to suck your thumb," Prissy said.

"Let him alone," Adam said. "I think we'd best go home."

"Adam." His sister laid a hesitant hand on his sleeve. "Do not be angry with me."

"I try not to be, Prissy." He dropped a kiss on his sister's cheek. "Is the portrait finished yet?"

"As a matter of fact, I believe Miss Twyford is here now, putting the finishing touches on it."

"Is she? I'll visit her, if I may." Maybe he would find out if Fabienne had broken the news to her. "Will, would you like to see the lady artist?"

Will removed his thumb from his mouth. "I want to play with my cousins."

"Very well." He deposited Will on Sylvia's lap, and left for the bright and sunny morning room, where Elaine worked.

When he entered, she dropped him a curtsy and turned her attention back to the canvas. After a while, she stepped back and gazed at her work.

"It's finished," she said in a quiet voice. She dipped her brush into a jar of clear liquid, and then rubbed it dry on a scrap of cloth.

"May I see it?"

She nodded, and stood aside.

"It's very good," he said. "You have caught their expressions and air exactly. Congratulations, Miss Twyford."

"Thank you, Mr. Ashworth." She removed the smock she wore, and folded it. A large canvas bag lay nearby on the floor.

"May I help you pack up your paints and brushes?"

"No, thank you. I don't need them anymore. I may as well leave them here."

"You don't—Miss Twyford, I hope you do not succumb to some nonsense of Luke's, that a viscountess should not paint." He had mentioned the issue once to Luke, who had given his usual open, frank smile and claimed that Elaine would have little time for painting once she was absorbed with keeping his house and breeding.

"I am no longer engaged. I wrote to him today."

"What? Miss Twyford, what on earth has happened?"

She sat on a chair, raised the folded smock to her face, and burst into tears.

He offered her his handkerchief, suspecting her unhappiness resulted from more than a broken engagement. "Please, tell me what has caused you such distress."

She lifted the smock from her face, red-eyed, and blew her nose loudly on his handkerchief. "You know I was born out of wedlock, Mr. Ashworth."

"I guessed as much."

"Today, Fabienne—Mrs. Craigmont—told me of my origins."

"Ah. She did?" He waited for her to fling herself into his arms and address him as "Papa."

"She is my mother."

"Yes, I know that. You're very alike." *And . . .* he prompted her silently.

"We are?" She looked at him, surprise on her face. "She told me also . . ." She began to cry again. "She told me that she did not know who my father is."

"She said *what*?" What was Fabienne thinking?

"Yes. I thought . . . I thought she was a decent woman. I am so ashamed."

He was torn between wanting to kill Fabienne and defending her. "Come, girl," he said. "You expect her to live like a nun for your sake? What right do you have?"

"Oh." She snorted into his handkerchief again.

"What did she say, exactly?" *Who was it, Fabienne? How many others did you rut with then?*

"She said she could not tell me."

"Well," he said, trying to convince himself as well as her, "that does not necessarily mean what you think. She might have been trying to protect someone." *Or injure him.*

"So," Elaine continued, "I wrote to tell Luke I cannot marry him. This is a wicked place, and I must return to my family and my true station in life."

"You mean you're not Luke's equal? I would say you're far above him, except in this instant you act like a fool, Miss Twyford. I would have thought better of Fabienne Craigmont's daughter."

There was a long silence. "I should say good-bye, sir."

Adam took the handkerchief and cleaned up a smear of paint that had transferred from the smock to her cheek. "I think you and I had better talk. I suspect you are running off to save your soul?"

"I have nothing more to say to you." She folded her smock again and stuffed it into the bag.

"For God's sake, girl," Adam said, "it is never as easy as that. I know you are determined to go, but will you listen to me first?"

She sighed. "If I must, sir."

"So you disapprove of Mrs. Craigmont's behavior. It is the way of the world, Miss Twyford. When two people esteem and desire each other, it is what happens."

"You talk about it as though it were nothing, like shaking hands," Elaine said.

"It's as simple and natural. And it is a mystery beyond imagining, that quickening of the flesh. If you do not know now, one day you will; you'll be seized by madness too, and your world will be turned upside down by desire."

She stared at her hands and muttered, "I do not believe decent women behave that way."

"Elaine—Miss Twyford—it is how women are. And men. It is how God, if you will, made us."

"Luke said you were like this," she said. "He said you would make anyone argue themselves into a corner. I am not clever, sir. I wish only to be good. And I thought Mrs. Craigmont was."

"She is." He held out his hand. "Come with me, Miss Twyford."

"Why?"

"You'll see. Leave your things here."

"But I am going—"

"Never mind that." He grasped her hand tightly with his and pulled her along with him. "Through this doorway, here, and up the stairs."

"But this is the way to the countess' private rooms—"

"Hush." Pushing her into Prissy's bedroom, he pointed at a portrait on the wall. "I knew it. The first time I met you, remember, in London? I was devilishly rude to you, when I thought you set to ensnare Luke. At my house, I have a copy of this portrait, and something, a thought, set in my mind soon after. Look at her, Elaine."

"Who is she?" She clutched his arm.

"My mother."

She touched her forefinger to her forehead and eyebrows, tracing her features and the spring of her hair as though she looked in a mirror. "You—you are my father?"

"Yes, I was Fabienne's lover when we were both quite

young. I guessed the truth some time ago, and am glad to tell you of it."

"Why did you not marry?"

"There was some misunderstanding, and I did not know of your existence until very recently. I thought Fabienne, since you are close to her, should tell you first."

"Why would Fabienne not tell me about you?"

"I don't know." Adam did not want to reveal how Fabienne's reticence troubled him too.

Elaine continued to stare at the portrait.

He took her elbow, concerned that she might be about to faint, or fall into a trance like one of his heroines. "Do nothing rash, please. Would you like to come back to my house and meet Babs and the children? We can give you a bed for the night, or for as long as you need one."

"Thank you, no. I must leave. I said terrible things to Mrs. Craigmont, and I fear she will not forgive me."

He took her by the shoulders and gave her an affectionate shake. "Babs has said some terrible things to me, and I to her, and we tolerate each other. One day I expect we shall apologize and laugh together again. And so it will be with Mrs. Craigmont and you."

"I don't know. I need to think." She shook her head. "I have not seen my mother and father for some time, and I miss my brothers and sisters. I must pray too."

"Very well," Adam said. "Do you have money enough for your journey? I'd accompany you, but I have my daughter—my other daughter—to look after."

"Reuben will escort me."

"And what of Luke? He loves you."

"Then he will wait for me," she announced with a self-righteousness that made him wince.

"I should not count on it," Adam said. "He'll smart from your rejection, and he's a good catch. He could be snapped up by some ambitious miss within days."

"Oh." She looked uncertain for a moment. Then she raised her face to his—she was the same height as Babs and did not have to stretch far—and kissed his cheek. "I am sorry, Mr. Ashworth. I truly am. Good-bye."

Chapter Sixteen

"I am bound to you by chains of love and honor, stronger than life, stronger than death itself."

The veiled woman gestured to him to kneel at her feet.

"Madam, command me. I am yours, heart, soul, body."

—*The Curse of the Molftains* by Mrs. Ravenwood.

After Elaine had left, Fabienne huddled on the sofa and abandoned herself to grief. Sometime that day, Susan touched her shoulder. "Ma'am, will you not eat something? I'll send to the kitchen—"

"No. Leave me. I have a headache."

Later she heard movement in the room, and the door click closed as someone settled on the sofa next to her. "Go away," she said, hoping it was not her brother.

"Sweetheart." He touched her hair.

"Adam?" She turned over, swiping her hand across her face. "What are you doing here?"

He held out his arms to her. "It's all right," he said. "Elaine's safe. Cry if you must."

She leaned on his shoulder and cried all over his shirt and waistcoat. He was a warm and comforting presence, his strong arms wrapped around her, holding her close, but then she remembered he was also the cause of her misery, and she pulled away. "Why are you here? This is all your fault. You were the one who insisted I tell her."

He drew away from her. "Possibly, yes, but you are

the one who botched telling her. I should have done it myself, and I attempted to undo some of the damage."

She sat up and wiped her face with her hands. "I hate you for this."

"I can hardly blame you."

"I don't want your comfort or pity. I don't want you here. Where is Elaine? Is she safe? Tell me, and you may go."

"She left for her home. Reuben is with her. I saw her onto the stagecoach."

"What?" She sprang to her feet in fury. "How could you do that? How could you let her go away?"

He stood too and gripped her elbow. "Listen, Fabienne. She wanted to go. You and I turned her world upside down today, and she suffers the consequences of it. She needs time to think, and she needs time away from both of us. It's for the best."

"I cannot believe you. She's gone," Fabienne wailed, no longer caring about dignity, and collapsed against his chest in a heap of misery.

He sighed and stroked her hair. "I braved your cook for your sake. I thought he would murder me with his cleaver. He is most upset that you don't want dinner."

"I'm not hungry."

"Here, you must eat something." He gestured to a small table. "I have bread and butter with honey for you. And coffee. Your cook said you preferred it to tea. Come, one bite," he wheedled, as though she were a child.

"Very well." She allowed herself to sink into the comfort of being fussed over, his arm around her, crumbs falling over both of them.

"Better? Good." He took her hand and licked honey from her fingers, a gesture that made her draw breath sharply.

She took a sip of coffee. "I suppose you told her she is your daughter. What did she say?"

"Very little. She was confused by what you told her."

"Indeed." She moved away from him. "You had no right to tell her anything."

"On the contrary, I had every right." He looked angry now. "I defended you, Fabienne. She thought you had bedded every man who crossed your path—"

"She said that?"

"Not in so many words." He shrugged. "It matters not. Give her time. She'll come back."

"It's so easy for you, isn't it, Adam? Everything is so clear-cut, like a mathematical problem. There is only one answer, and it's always yours, and it's always right."

"In this case, madam, I am right."

"So you think she is your daughter?"

He stood up, uncertainty on his face. "Of course she is. There is a portrait of my mother at her age; it might be of Elaine. You must have noticed yourself how similar she and Babs are in height and build. Why are you silent?"

"What do you remember of our time together, Adam?"

He walked away from her and rested one hand against the mantelpiece, staring into the flames. "That last night, I was drunk. Drunk on wine, and with you. I had not had enough wine that I didn't burn for you, because I always burned for you, and you flirted and teased and drove me wild. You had no idea then, I think, what power you had over me. So I took you, that final step we had both danced around, very fast and with little tenderness. I wish it had been better for us both."

"And afterward?"

"You jilted me." He rested his arms on the mantelpiece, his head bent. He straightened up. "For God's sake, what are you trying to tell me?"

"I jilted you?" She stared at him in disbelief. "What do you mean?"

"Fabienne, you sent me a charming letter telling me you did not intend to see me again, and that our affair was over. I left London that same night."

"I never sent such a letter." An immense weariness settled over her like an overthick quilt, making words difficult to find and form.

"Someone did. I was mightily offended. But what was I to think?" He knelt beside her and took her hands. "You're cold." He rubbed her fingers between his. "Fabienne, what are you telling me?"

"I was seventeen, Adam," she said. "I was young, I loved you madly, and I trusted you. I too received a letter that day, signed by you, asking to meet me that night."

"I did not send you a letter."

"I went there," she said, her eyes closed. "I made some excuse to my mother to go out alone. The woman who owned the house—I know now it must have been a brothel—showed me into a room with a bed, and said you would be there soon. Finally the door opened and two men came in."

"Who—"

"They were masked." She opened her eyes with an effort, fighting weariness and an oppressive heaviness. "One was about your age, I think, and the other a few years younger. His voice sounded barely broken when he made a comment about how I was a pretty whore. They mocked me, and told me they'd written the letter under your name. Then they locked the door.

"I never saw their faces, and they barely said enough, and that in low whispers, for me to recognize their voices again. They raped me, Adam. They took it in turns, one holding me down while the other took me. I begged them for mercy, I promised I would not tell, and they laughed. They each carried the brand of the Sons on their forearm, and that is all I know of them. And you think Elaine is your daughter."

He stared at her, his face gray and strained. "I did not know." His voice cracked. "Oh, Christ, I did not know." He sat beside her and dropped his face into his hands.

Fabienne slumped back on the sofa, eyes closed. "I have never told a soul of this. My brother thinks I am going mad because I dream of this almost every night, and wake screaming, ever since I found Elaine and brought her back to London. Sometimes I think I am going mad too. I told you in one of my letters that all I wanted to do was find peace. That is why I asked you to break your vows for me."

"Who the devil could it have been, to plan so?" Adam shook his head. "The whole Brotherhood knew of our liaison. After all, we were not particularly discreet, and besides, they could have just asked you. Many of the women associated with the Brotherhood were as adventurous in sensual matters as the men."

Fabienne sat bolt upright. "You think I—you are disgusting and depraved! Besides, how do I know you tell the truth?"

"You can't. All you can do is trust the man I am now, and believe that I have changed."

"But you claim you don't know who those men were."

"Fabienne." Adam's hand gripped hers. "I swear on my honor I do not know, and I should avenge you now if I did. I may have been a randy young fool, but I would never have abandoned you to rape. When I received your letter, I was distraught and angry. I thought your mother had persuaded you to accept someone else. I loved you."

She came wide-awake. "You loved me! You liar!" She launched herself at him, slapping and scratching, while he gripped her arms and tried to restrain her. "I was seventeen. I was an innocent straight out of a convent school. You seduced me, and you would have abandoned me in some equally cruel and callous way when you tired of me. Don't deny it. I may have been a silly little fool at seventeen, but I am not a fool now." She sobbed with anger and tried to catch her breath. "I have hated you for this. I hate you for making me fall in love with you when I thought you were Mrs. Ravenwood. I hate you for driving Elaine away. I want to kill you!" Her voice rose to a hysterical pitch.

"Fabienne, calm down. Please. I swear I will do everything in my power to find them and avenge you. The issue is, whether you can trust me to do so."

She gulped and rested her face against his chest. "At

first I too thought of revenge. And then . . . I realized
it was not enough."

"What do you mean?"

"It's difficult to explain. I want to talk to them face-
to-face, to ask them how they could do that, treat me as
a—a thing to slake their lust on. I wonder if they thought
about it again, or even if they managed to justify it to
themselves somehow." She raised her face to his. "Why
did they do it?"

"I don't know." He looked uneasy. "Maybe all men
have that propensity. I seduced you. I may have been
more gentle, but one could argue the intent was the
same. I used you." He rubbed at the back of his neck. "I
suppose there is nothing more of them you remember."

She shook her head. "I dream of it every night, but
can tell you no more. And there is another matter too."

"And what is that?"

She touched his face, her fingers trailing across his jaw.
"You and I, Adam. You say you aren't the man you
were, but I need you to prove yourself to me."

"Ah. Can you trust a man who'd break his vows for
you?"

"You are my only hope."

"I trust I am—or could be—something more than that,
Fabienne. You know my heart." He kissed her hand. "I
regret my harshness to you, that I forced your hand with
Elaine. Above all, I regret that I treated you as I did
when I was a young fool."

"And as a female fool, Mrs. Ravenwood."

He gave a shrug of awkward laughter, and put his arm
around her, a shy, clumsy gesture that surprised her for
its tenderness. "So. Command me."

"Very well."

His eyes were serious. A slight movement of his fingers
on the arm of the sofa revealed his tension.

She took a deep breath. "Everything has changed,
Adam."

"What do you mean?"

"Yesterday I was a different person. I thought I knew

how the world would continue. It is like waking and finding the sky a different color." She leaned her head against his shoulder. "I need to find myself again. I need to find the Fabienne Craigmont who could wake from her nightmares and face the world, not the wretch who spent all day on her sofa in tears."

"My grandson described you as the lady who rode tigers. He spoke the truth. Let me help you find the way, Fabienne."

"Very well." She straightened to look at him, to gaze into those stormy blue eyes. A pulse beat in her belly, her hands tingled, her thigh pressed warm against his. "Stay with me tonight. You will do anything I say."

The reformed rake blushed, to her great amusement. He stood and bowed. "Madam, command me."

When Adam entered her bedchamber, Fabienne, wearing her nightgown, sat at the dressing table. The window was open to receive the sounds of the London night and the heady scent of a honeysuckle plant that coiled onto the windowsill. It reminded him of home.

"Why do you sigh?" She picked up her hairbrush and pushed back the hair that curled onto her shoulders.

"I was thinking of my pigs."

"Indeed." She raised her eyebrows.

He cursed himself for his clumsiness. It was a long time since he had entered a woman's boudoir, and as far as he could remember, it was not customary to hold a conversation about farmyard animals. He took the brush and she made a quiet, contented sound in her throat as he drew it through her hair.

Her eyes were closed, a smile of pleasure on her face as he plied the hairbrush. "You do that well."

"I used to brush my wife's hair often. She had very lovely hair. You do too," he added hastily. Worse and worse. Maybe he should direct the conversation back to the pigs.

"Ah. You loved her greatly, I think."

"Yes, I did." He ran her hair, dark brown silk, through his fingers, and inhaled its scent. "I'm afraid quite often

I talk to her still. She lectures me, tells me when I'm being a fool."

Fabienne smiled. She raised a hand to push back one of the shorter, curling tendrils at her temple, and he stared in the mirror at the slick of hair beneath her arm, the dark shadows of her nipples under the thin cotton garment.

"You are very aroused. I intended only to sleep. . . ."

"As you wish. Whatever you want."

She stood and kissed him briefly on the mouth. "Thank you."

As she climbed onto the bed, she said, "Lie down with me and hold me."

He flung off waistcoat and boots, and lay beside her on the bed. With an arm wrapped around her, and his nose buried against the back of her neck, he tried to steady his breathing. Did she really only wish to sleep? Although his arousal was inconvenient and painful, he felt at peace, happy to hold her, to be alone with her in this quiet room.

Her breathing slowed.

·This was pleasant enough to lie curled up to someone sweet-smelling, warm, and trusting. It was like being one of a litter of piglets or puppies, a blend of coziness, innocence, and comfort. He could fall asleep . . . possibly. "Fabienne," he whispered. "Are you awake?"

"Mmmm." A drowsy murmur.

"Do you remember the stories you used to tell me about the girls at the convent?"

"What stories?"

"You know. You remember, Fabienne."

She turned toward him, her lips brushing his neck. "No, I don't."

She did. He could tell by the slight tension in her body, a glimmer of interest. "You used to tell me of such things. I'd become greatly aroused. Don't you remember?"

"No. You'll have to remind me."

Oh, she was definitely interested now. She turned onto her back, stretching against him, one hand falling carelessly against his groin.

"You'd share a bed, like this. Then you could whisper to each other after the lamps were blown out. You'd giggle together about the handsome young priest who came to take your confession. You liked to engage him in conversations about impure thoughts and make him blush and stammer."

She gave a breath of laughter. "I remember a little. We were such naughty girls. Go on."

"Who was your particular bedmate? Was it Veronique?"

"Oh, yes. She was so pretty."

He skimmed his hand over her stiffened nipples. "And after a while, you'd talk about what the priest would do if you kissed him." He propped himself up one elbow and traced a finger over her lips, following it with his tongue. "What would it feel like? Like this, maybe?"

"It would be very wicked," Fabienne murmured.

"Indeed, yes. And then he'd probably want to touch your breasts." He pulled the ribbon at the neck of her nightgown. "Such lovely breasts. See how they've hardened at the tips? They're so round, like little apples."

"I think he'd kiss them. Very slowly. Very gently."

He cupped her breasts in his hand, and fastened his mouth to each nipple in turn, swirling his tongue over the hardened dark flesh. "Like that?"

"Oh, yes. *C'est très méchant.*" She moaned and moved against him, her fingers in his hair.

"Very wicked indeed."

He raised his head to look at her breasts again, and rolled her nipples between his fingers. "So. Something shameful is happening to you elsewhere, is it not?"

She moaned. "I am so wet. There. You know where. And it is like an itch, a pain."

"Where? I cannot imagine. Tell me."

"Oh. I cannot tell you, but I must. It is my . . ." She whispered the blunt, crude word in his ear, breath warm against his skin.

He slid one hand down her body, and rested his hand on her mound, feeling the crinkle of hair beneath the nightgown. "It is indeed a shocking thing." He tried not to grin like an idiot. "Maybe the sensation will disperse on its own."

"I think not. Oh, what shall I do? It is so dreadful."

"I had best help you." He pulled her nightgown up. "How distressing. It is indeed wet, and here, where I push my fingers in, it clasps me."

She groaned and raised her hips. He stroked stiffening wet flesh, and tongued her lips, her nipples. "Yes," he said, as her breathing quickened, and he slowed his movement to a feather, a breath. "Oh, yes, Fabienne."

She convulsed against him, her body shaking, and released a sobbing cry of completion before sagging back into his arms. Then she laughed and sat up, pulling her nightgown to rights. "That was extraordinarily depraved behavior for a simple country gentleman. I am quite shocked."

"Did you really do such things, Fabienne?"

She hesitated. "Not really. I am afraid it was based on a certain erotic memoir which was passed around at the convent with much giggling." She laughed. "You look so disappointed." She pleated her nightgown between her fingers. "I wanted to please you, and in telling you those stories, I could delay our consummation. I knew what a risk I took."

"Clever girl," he murmured.

"No." She shook her head. "Silly, desperate girl."

He raised her hand to his lips and kissed her knuckles. "I must admit I wondered if that was why you were attracted so to Mrs. Ravenwood."

"Nonsense." She ran her hand over his jaw. "I fell in love with an imaginary person, an ideal. Not a real person, and one whose gender was immaterial."

"Of course. Not a real person." Fighting back a vague sense of disappointment, he rolled onto his back, arms over his head, offering himself in surrender to her will and desire. *Here I am. Do what you will with me.*

"Ah," she said. "In a moment."

He heard her move around the room, felt the shift of the bed as she lowered herself onto the end, and some movement at his stockinged feet.

"What are you about?" He looked down. She was busy with her stockings, tying them around his ankles, and thence to the bedposts. Dreadful knots. He could break them in an instant, but he wouldn't. Certainly not.

"Am I your prisoner, madam?"

"Apparently so." She finished tying his wrist with one garter, and leaned over him to restrain the other arm, her nightgown gaping open. "There."

"I am at your mercy," he said, trying not to sound too pleased about it. He shifted his hips toward her as she knelt over him.

"So you are." She tugged at his shirt, pulling it from his trousers, and examined him. "You have more hair here now." She ran a fingernail down his chest.

He squirmed at her touch and groaned as her finger stopped at his waist.

"Please." He discovered that her inept knots were not so bad after all.

"You are still beautiful," she said.

Damnation. Should he have told her that too? He'd forgotten entirely. "You too."

"Oh, no. Childbirth has done some damage." She pulled her nightgown up and placed one hand on her stomach. "See, these marks here, down my belly." She raised one knee, giving him a casual view of her sex.

He groaned again.

"And my breasts." She pulled the nightgown over her head. "They are rounder now, and the nipples larger." She brushed them over his face in illustration.

"Witch," he said, with somewhat more affection in his voice than he'd intended.

"And now, as for you . . . I remember the first time I felt your cock against me. I thought you must have a cucumber on your person." She trailed the nightgown over his face, releasing a whiff of female musk and sweat.

She kissed his lips, drawing away as he tried to slide his tongue into her mouth, then kissed his chest, moving downward with agonizing slowness. He flinched as she licked his nipples, something he had tolerated before with other women, but now found to be extraordinarily arousing. Again she stopped at his trousers, and stroked her hand along his erection.

"Please, Fabienne." Oh God, he was almost begging. *Almost?*

She unbuttoned him and released his aching cock. "Ah, you are truly in need."

She slid one hand around him, and gripped his shaft tightly at the base as his hips bucked up. "Wait," she whispered. "Wait. I'll give you something even better."

Sweat trickled down his forehead and he whimpered, helpless in her grasp. She bent her head to lick a gleaming drop from the tip, still restraining him. Her tongue flicked over him, teasing him unbearably, and he strained against his bonds.

"Wait," she whispered again, and took him into the warm sweetness of her mouth, her tongue swirling. It lasted for a brief moment until she lifted her head and smiled at him. "Would you rather have this or your letters, Adam?"

"This." An aching surge of white-hot sweetness rose, gathered, and coursed through him. "This, please, now, oh, Fabienne. *Fabienne.*"

Chapter Seventeen

For three days they drove at full gallop past towering crags, by thunderous waterfalls, and through valleys ripe with vines and pleasant greenery, stopping only to change horses. Serena could not elicit from the swarthy and savage brigands what their final destination might be, nor who was responsible for her terrible ordeal, but noted how they shrank from her in fear.
—*The Spectre of the Abbey* by Mrs. Ravenwood.

*S*he could tell he wasn't used to sharing a bed. The only time he remained still was after he had climaxed, when he lay limp and panting while she untied him and hauled trousers and shirt from his inert body.

"That was . . . that was . . . magnificent," he said and fell asleep.

She awoke after a brief half hour to find his head between her thighs, her whole being balanced on the splinter of pleasure that was his flickering tongue. He didn't let her go, but held her still and took her to the lightning flash again and again, until she wept for mercy, begged him to stop. He laughed, apologized, kissed her hard and wet, and moved between her thighs, murmuring her name.

"May I?" His erection nudged against her, hard and strong.

"And what would you do if I said no?" she asked.

"I should suffer extreme disappointment. But I hope

you'll say yes." He bent his head to her breast, touching his tongue to one nipple, and small spasms ran through her belly.

"Let me consider it." She could not resist teasing him, and herself too, as desire licked once more up her thighs, flamed in her belly and breasts.

She reached to stroke his belly and he made a small sound of satisfaction as his erection rested in her hand.

"I think . . . I think my answer is . . . yes."

"Excellent. You are quite certain?"

"I believe so."

"If you need a little more time to consider—possibly you should like to consult with your maid, or anyone else in the house, first. . . ."

She wriggled beneath him, lifting her hips to his. "Well, of course, I do not wish to be rash about this."

"Of course not."

He nudged against her, and then he was inside her, filling her—and stopped, as though suddenly frozen.

She moved tentatively beneath him. "Adam, my love?"

"You are so sweet," he murmured, and began to move, with slow, deep thrusts. "Let me get used to you. But I don't want to get used to you. I never will. I want it always to be like this for us, my love."

His slow, careful strokes woke her body again, while she struggled to savor the rasp of his chest hair on her breasts, his tongue at her neck and mouth, the powerful flex of his shoulders and arms as he moved above her. The sheet beneath her back, the scent of the honey-suckle, the brush of his lips, the creak of the bed, and the salty tang of his sweat were precious sensations, strung together like jewels.

"Stay with me," he said with some urgency.

She knew he fought for control, wanted to let go while she lingered in the bewildering richness of the senses they created together.

Trust him. Let him take you. Trust him.

And she did, flinging herself into the place where taste

and touch, hearing and sight, melted into a swirl of blinding heat, and he answered her with his own cry and spasm.

"I love you. Stay with me," she said, when they were finally quiet and at peace, sweat and breath blending, and sleep beckoned them.

"Always. I love you."

"Adam?"

"Hmm?"

"Adam, I didn't dream."

"You hardly slept."

"I did, a little. But I didn't dream."

"Good." He stretched. "I'd better leave although I dread returning home. I'm too old to creep into my house at dawn. The servants will find it exceedingly entertaining. By the way, for whom did Reuben work before you hired him?"

"I can't remember. He had excellent references. Why?"

"I don't know. He seems familiar, although I only saw him the once and he's so ugly he'd be easy to forget." He sprang out of bed and retrieved his clothes.

"What's the matter?"

"Nothing." He looked embarrassed. "I have to write. I had come to a certain point in the book, and now things have resolved themselves in my mind and . . . well, I must write. So I should go."

"Very well." She lay back against the pillows, received a perfunctory farewell kiss from him, and heard him greet Susan on the stairs, and the front door open and close. *What have I got myself into?*

Not another knock at his study door.

Adam pushed his half-written page under a sheet of paper. "Come in."

"Sir?" His daughter entered the room, Will at her side and Julia in her arms. "I am sorry to interrupt, but we leave for Brighton now."

He stared at her, his mind numb. Brighton? Yes,

Brighton, with that sister of Eglinton's who looked like a horse. And Barbara was angry with him. He remembered that now.

"Are you well, sir? You look tired."

"I'm perfectly well, thank you." Wonderfully well, after a few minutes of sleep snatched between amorous acts . . .

"Why are you smiling, Grandpapa?"

He bent to grasp Will's shoulder. "I'm thinking of what a fine time you'll have."

"I wish to thank you for your hospitality, sir."

"Oh, Babs. Write to me often, my dear." He grabbed her and kissed her cheek. She stood rigid in his arms, then stepped back and curtsied.

"Good-bye, Will." He hugged his grandson. "Be a good boy, and look after your mother. You're the man of the family, now."

"Yes, Grandpapa."

He kissed Julia, who gave him a wet and smacky kiss in return, and ushered them out, eager to return to work again.

"Mr. Ashworth." Another timid knock at the door.

"Pay them and tell them to go away," he said, waving a sheet of paper in the air to dry it. "When I said I was not to be disturbed, I meant it."

"It's a lady to see you. She—"

"Out of my way, if you please." The door opened and Fabienne burst into the room.

"Fabienne, sweetheart." He pushed his sheet of paper away from her gaze.

"Oh, for God's sake, I do not wish to see the silly drivel you claim to write. Reuben is—"

"I never said exactly it was silly drivel. I said that—"

She gave a dismissive wave of her arm. "It is no matter. Reuben has not come back, and I am at my wit's end."

He pulled out a chair for her. "Calm yourself. Possibly the Twyford family find him beautiful and charming and wish to adopt him."

She glared at him. "That is not amusing, sir. We must travel there ourselves."

"Wait," he said. "Let's do nothing rash. I'll see if I can find the coachman who drove the coach north, and we'll know then if they arrived at their destination. Then we'll decide what to do. What time is it?"

"Near three o'clock. Adam, please hurry."

"First I'll escort you home, and then—"

"No. I am coming with you. Bring your razor or whatever else you need."

"Why?"

"Just in case." She stamped her foot at him. "Do not look at me as though I am a madwoman! Send for your manservant, and get him to pack a bag for you."

"Fabienne." He took her hands. "Please, calm yourself. I'll do as you wish. Have you eaten today?"

"No, I could not, for fretting and worrying." She gave a nervous sob. "I know you think I am foolish, but I fear something has happened."

"It will be all right," he said, hoping it would be. He gave orders to servants to pack food and an overnight bag, and they set off in his carriage to the inn from which northward-bound coaches departed.

After several inquiries, they were directed to a stout, red-faced man who sat in a corner of the taproom, methodically working his way through a tankard of ale and a large pie.

"Please, don't get up, sir," Adam said. "Would you care for some more to drink?" Fabienne blew her breath out in a gust of impatience at his elbow.

"Thank'ee, sir. I'll have a hot water and brandy," the man replied. "Will you and the lady join me?"

They sat at the table while the man finished his pie, brushed crumbs from his chest, and wiped his mouth with his napkin.

"I believe you drove the coach to Lichfield yesterday," Adam said. "I daresay you don't remember me, but I saw off a young lady who traveled with her manservant."

The man took a large mouthful of his drink. "Oh yes, sir. I do remember the poor young lady." He shook his head. "I hope she is better now."

"Better? What happened?" Fabienne interrupted.

"Why, ma'am, she was taken ill at the Swan in Stevenage, but a few hours from here, when we stopped there. She swooned, and her brother—"

"He is not her brother," Fabienne said. She reached across the table and clutched the man's sleeve. "What happened?"

"Well, ma'am, he said he was her brother, though I did wonder, with him being so big and ugly and she such a pretty, slender young thing. He said they had relatives in the neighborhood and would stop at their house until she was better. So we left them behind."

Fabienne gave a gasp of horror. "We must go, Adam." She stood and kissed the coachman, French style, on both cheeks. As he spluttered in embarrassment, she said, "Thank you, thank you."

Adam handed the man a guinea. "Thank you, sir. We're much obliged."

Fabienne was silent as they drove north, her lips pressed tight, strain on her face. "I knew it," she muttered. "You should not have let her go."

"I had no way of knowing anything of the sort would happen," Adam said. "I believed I acted for the best. I thought that if I let her go she would return willingly."

She threw him a look of contempt. "It is all your fault."

He couldn't argue with that. "I believe you're right. Forgive me."

"I don't know whether I can." The passionate, demanding lover of the previous night was gone, a stern and tense creature in her place. She stared out of the window and would not look at him.

"I wonder who Reuben acts for," Adam said, after a few miles. "Did you ever have any idea of who was following her?"

"None. I should have taken better care of her." Fabienne's voice shook and she clutched the leather strap that hung inside the carriage as it swayed. "Can the horses not go faster?"

"They're going as fast as they can." He took her hand and it lay limp in his before she drew away. "Please, do not reproach yourself. If she really is taken ill, then maybe we'll find her this evening."

"And maybe we will not."

They both fell silent as the coach jolted along the road and the minutes and hours ticked away into a long summer twilight. Rain began to fall.

It was almost dark when they arrived at their destination, and Adam and Fabienne made their way through the bustling courtyard into the inn, an old, dark-timbered place with uneven floors and smoke-stained walls.

As they both feared, Elaine was no longer there.

"Why, yes, I remember the young lady," the landlord said. He puffed reflectively at his pipe. "She came into the inn with that big, ugly fellow, and he ordered her some tea. She swooned soon after and we could not wake her. So the coach went on its way without them. I was much alarmed, and was glad when her uncle arrived to take her home."

"Her uncle?" Adam said.

"Oh yes, sir. A gentleman of around your age, although somewhat sickly looking."

"What sort of carriage did he have?"

"A fine team of horses, bays, although looking as though they had been driven hard. I think he must have come some distance. And, yes, he must have been of the nobility, for there was a coat of arms on the door."

Fabienne clutched Adam's arm. "Greenmore. It was Greenmore. His house is near here, I know." She began to cry. "We must go there now."

"In the morning," Adam said. "You have a room for us, sir? Excellent. Come, Fabienne."

"No. We must go, now. He will . . ."

"Listen," he said. "I'm not taking my horses on a country road in the dark, and it's pouring with rain. You're exhausted, and whatever he intended . . . well, it is regretful, but we will arrive too late—"

Fabienne pushed his arm away. "You are a monster. How can you talk of my child so?"

The landlord poked a twig into his pipe, and coughed. "Will you take the room or not, sir?"

"We will," Adam said. "And send us up some dinner, if you please."

She could not bear that he was so authoritative, so cool, and clearly in charge. *Because he's a man,* she thought. She knew that had she tackled the coachman alone, or even the landlord, they would not have been so free with their information. She hated hanging on his arm like an appendage, the obedient wife. It was tempting to think that he cared more for his horses than for Elaine, but she knew he was right—if a horse foundered in the dark, on an unfamiliar road, they would be delayed even further. What he said made perfect sense, and that made it worse.

Meanwhile, her daughter was at the mercy of a dissolute aged rake, whose penchant for young women, any woman, was well known. And Adam was quite right on that point too—Greenmore had probably violated Elaine hours ago.

She swallowed a sob and picked the crust from a slice of bread. Across from her, Adam, equally silent, stared at a chop in a puddle of congealing gravy.

"I saw Reuben before," he said, pushing his plate aside. "I have only just realized it. At the duel he was in Greenmore's livery, and wearing an ill-fitting wig. He looked quite different, though no less repulsive. It was a trivial detail—I noticed such things, thinking I was to die, and everything was sharp and clear. He has been in Greenmore's pay all along."

"But—surely my brother saw him too?"

Adam gave an ironic smile. "Your brother is a count. I know he may have spent his early childhood in reduced circumstances, and is still somewhat down in the world, but does he ever notice servants?"

"That is a very insulting thing to say."

Adam topped up his wineglass. "It's true, though, isn't it?"

"I don't want to sleep with you tonight." It was petty, but the only weapon she had left. If he was even thinking that some sort of reconciliation could take place in the intimacy of the bed that stood just a few feet away, he was in for a rude shock.

"That's a good idea." He didn't seem particularly disturbed by that either. "I think you should try and rest as much as you can. You look very tired. I'll take the settle."

Damn him. She should have demanded that she wanted him to perform for her like a randy young buck, and was then appalled that she should think of such a thing now.

He looked at her as though expecting a reply, and she realized she had missed his last statement entirely. "I beg your pardon."

"Nothing. I only asked if you would like some more wine, and I, um, said, that, ah, I love you."

"Oh." She looked at him, dumbfounded. "I think I want to get ready for bed, now."

"Very well." He rose and bowed.

Once in bed she turned her face into the pillow and shed the tears she had kept at bay all day. She cried for a trusting innocent, terrified and violated. Herself and her child, whom she had failed to protect.

Adam spent a pleasant enough hour downstairs in the taproom. At least it would have been enjoyable if he was not embarked on a journey to rescue a child past saving. He tried not to let his mind dwell on the consequences. He would have to challenge Greenmore and hope he survived—not only the duel itself, but any attempt the enraged earl might make to dispatch him afterward. And then there was Elaine—the specters of disease and death in childbed haunted his mind. Even if she was spared, would Luke, or any man, marry her after?

Maybe they should have continued on their way, but Fabienne's exhaustion worried him. He hoped she would rest; he'd half hoped that she'd invite him to bed. He could imagine, all too easily, holding her in a comfortable embrace as if they had been married for years. Nothing more. It would be inappropriate. A kiss, maybe.

He made his way up the uneven staircase and lifted the latch to their room. A candle burned on the table. The dinner things had been cleared away, and Fabienne appeared to be asleep. He walked toward her as quietly as the creaking floor would allow, and saw the traces of tears on her face. She slept curled up, one hand resting under her cheek, eyelashes damp. Careful not to wake her, he bent and kissed her forehead. She didn't move.

He sighed and plucked a pillow from the bed. He did not dare risk her displeasure; he had offered to sleep on the settle, and so he would.

Exhaustion had done what laudanum failed to do. She slept deeply and well, despite her worry and rage, and half hoped, when she turned in bed, to find the warm comfort of Adam there.

To her disappointment, he was not; and to her annoyance, he seemed to be perfectly comfortable on the hard, narrow settle, fast asleep in trousers and shirtsleeves.

She sprang out of bed. Elaine, they had to find Elaine. Her heart pounded with anxiety.

"Adam, wake up!" She shook him.

He grunted and opened his eyes. "Good morning. I'll get the team harnessed immediately. Order us some breakfast."

"I can't eat."

He looked up from pulling on his boots. "I can and shall, and you should try." Boots on, he stood up and pulled on his waistcoat and coat. "Get dressed, Mrs. Craigmont."

She felt an odd pang. He was back to addressing her formally, as though they had never been lovers, or whatever they had been. She splashed water over her face, dressed, and twisted her hair back and up. So maybe this was the end of it, their curiosity sated, bodies explored enough. Maybe she should have been kinder to him yesterday. And maybe he should have been kinder to her, she reminded herself with a frown as she laced her boots.

After a hurried breakfast they set out, the horses

rested and fresh. Despite the rain the roads were not too
bad, and the driver was adept at finding the least muddy
path while maintaining speed.

"Two hours, so they told me at the inn, to Greenmore's," Adam said.

She nodded, queasy and tense. "Do you—are you
armed?"

He reached into one boot and withdrew a wicked,
razor-sharp blade. "Italian," he said. "I hope I shall not
need it." He replaced the weapon and looked out of the
window. "The corn is doing well here."

He wants to return to the country, she thought. *He
wouldn't be happy in the city, even if he wanted to stay
with me. I expect he found someone in the inn to talk to
about pigs last night.*

She recognized the approach to Greenmore's house,
the long avenue of lime trees, now in full bloom, and a
lake with swans floating on its glassy surface. They
rounded a corner and the full glory of the house, glowing
golden stone and mullioned windows, came into view.

"What now?" she said as they alighted from the
carriage.

"We're paying a call," Adam said. "It's a little early—
about ten in the morning, I believe—but Greenmore and
I are old friends." He led her up the steps and pounded
the knocker on the imposing steel-studded front door.

She loosened her tight grip on his arm, not wanting
him to see how frightened she was, and he turned to her,
laid his hand over hers, and smiled briefly. "Courage,"
he whispered.

The door opened and Adam led her inside, stripping
off gloves and hat with superb confidence, and tossing
them to a manservant who opened his mouth to protest.
This was the Adam of two decades ago, cocky and
arrogant.

"Tell his lordship Ashworth and Mrs. Craigmont are
here," he said.

"His lordship is not receiving visitors, sir. If you—"

"In the morning room, I think. Thank you." He tugged
Fabienne's arm and whispered, "I haven't been in this

house for twenty years. I remember it as a rabbit warren. Guide us through, if you please."

The manservant followed them. "Sir, if I may, I'll announce you."

"No matter. His lordship and I don't stand on ceremony."

Fabienne tugged Adam to a stop and he released her arm and flung the door open.

Greenmore, clad in an embroidered dressing gown, sat at the table, the remains of breakfast in front of him. He looked up, and his haggard face broke into a smile.

Chapter Eighteen

By the light of the flaring torch, the hooded figure drew a casket of rich ebony and ivory from its robes, and uttered in sepulchral tones: "Here, sir, is my legacy. Examine this and all will be revealed, all understood."

It could not be, it was impossible, but Ferdinand saw with a thrill of horror that there was no visage inside the hood, merely the darkness of the grave.

—*The Curse of the Molfitains* by Mrs. Ravenwood.

"Why, Ashworth and Mrs. Craigmont. What a delightful surprise."

"Greenmore," Adam drawled. "Forgive us for this early intrusion."

Before his mind could keep track of his body's actions, he had drawn the knife from his boot and was at Greenmore's side, the blade against the earl's throat. "Where is she?"

"I'm here, Mr. Ashworth." Elaine appeared at the far doorway and ran into Fabienne's arms. "I'm so sorry. Please, please, let us leave."

"What did you do to her?" Adam asked Greenmore. Just one small movement would be all it needed to dispatch him, as easily as slitting a pig's throat. It was a curiously intimate moment, the scent of Greenmore's hair pomade in Adam's nostrils, the throb of Greenmore's pulse against his hand.

"Sir, take that knife from my throat," Greenmore said, his voice quite calm. "Will you have some coffee?"

"Damn you! I'll cut your throat like the cur you are. I don't care if you're my brother. Whatever vows I've sworn, if you've harmed a hair of my daughter's head—" Adam stopped and lowered the blade. *I have betrayed the Brotherhood.*

"So. You break one vow here and now, sir." Greenmore smiled. "Well, you always were an impulsive fool. We tolerated him, Mrs. Craigmont. He was a pretty enough boy, as you may remember."

Adam turned his back on Greenmore and strode toward Fabienne and Elaine.

"Did he dishonor you?" His voice was a furious bark.

Elaine shrank back. "I want to go home, please. I—I was frightened. He says—he thinks—"

"Did you?" Adam turned back toward Greenmore.

"What do you think? Continue, sir. It makes no difference. I am a dying man."

Adam's knife whistled across the room and landed in a shower of splinters in the wood paneling next to Greenmore's head.

"Dying?"

"Aye, so my physician says." Greenmore began to sob, shoulders heaving. "Do not deny me my child, I beg of you."

"Your child?" Adam stepped forward.

Greenmore buried his face in his hands. "Mine. My only child."

"You're a madman. She's mine. Look at her."

"Ashworth, she is an artist, as were many of the women on my mother's side of the family. She is my daughter, I tell you."

A minute ago he had wanted to kill Greenmore. Now he wanted to shake some sense into him. "So you acknowledge your child by frightening her half to death and stealing her away? What were you thinking, sir?"

"How else could I make myself known to her? You know my reputation."

Fabienne spoke, her voice clear and calm. "It was you, then."

"Yes, Mrs. Craigmont. It was easy enough to divert Ashworth with a letter supposedly from you. Of course he would have tired of you soon enough. We merely hastened nature."

"You whoreson!" Adam lunged toward Greenmore.

"Stop." Fabienne held out a hand. "Adam, I wish to speak with Lord Greenmore alone. Please take Elaine into the garden."

"No. Fabienne, let me—"

"Go."

"Mr. Ashworth, please," Elaine whispered. She took his hand and tugged at it. "Oh, please, let us go outside. I prayed for him, and for you and Fabienne last night, that you would come to save me. This is a dreadful place, and he wishes me to live here until he dies."

"You'll do no such thing, girl." He let Elaine lead him outside into the garden, where bees buzzed around flowers and birds sang—a normal, pretty world.

Adam took a deep breath and sank onto a stone bench, his legs shaking.

"Sir, would you have killed him?"

"Probably. I could not when he told me he is dying."

"It is true," Elaine said. "His physician told him he has maybe one month to live."

"What happened, Elaine? They said you were taken ill at the inn."

"I had some tea, and I think Reuben—he is Greenmore's man—put a drug in it. I fell asleep and woke up here with a dreadful headache. Lord Greenmore kept calling me 'daughter' and saying I was heir to his fortune. I am not his daughter, am I?"

"I don't know whose daughter you are. I was Fabienne's first lover, and Greenmore and one other man raped her." He hadn't meant to blurt it all out to her so crudely, but maybe there was no other way.

Elaine began to cry, holding his hand.

He sat in dappled sunlight among sweetly scented roses, and let the child who might be his daughter grieve for the loss of her innocence.

* * *

Greenmore rang a small bell that stood at his elbow, and a footman brought china and cutlery for Fabienne. The scene was so entirely civilized and normal that before she knew it she accepted a cup of coffee, but her hand shook so badly she could not raise it to her lips.

"Do you believe in hell, Mrs. Craigmont?"

His question surprised her. "I don't know. Do you?"

"Now I do. I have lived in hell these past four years, when my physicians first told me of my condition."

"Why? Why did you do it?"

He looked at her, an ironic smile on his face. "Because that is what I am, what many men are. Ashworth is not so. He played at being the rake the way he plays at mathematics and his novels—ah, you know of them, I see. I was most moved when he dedicated *The Ruined Tower* to me, a friend he had not seen for two decades."

"You knew about Mrs. Ravenwood?"

"Oh, yes." He leaned forward. "I knew him. I heard his voice in every page. I loved him. Do not be naive, Mrs. Craigmont. I assure you Ashworth has few, if any, tendencies that way, but what I did . . . If I could not have him, I would have what was nearest to him."

She took a sharp breath. "Neither he nor I were yours for the taking. What choice did I have?"

"True, Mrs. Craigmont."

"Who was the other man?"

"I'll tell you, but you must promise not to reveal his identity to Ashworth."

"Why?" Her hands clenched in fury. "Why should I make bargains with you?"

"Because the other man was George Sanders. He was little more than a boy then, as you may remember."

"Oh, God." She pressed her knuckles to her mouth.

"Ashworth probably suspects I had him killed, but I do not think he knows why. I could not bear to think that any man other than Ashworth might claim Elaine as his own."

"That's entirely dubious, sir. The only sure thing is that she is mine."

"I beg you do not tell him. If you need another name,

say it was Henry Foster. He's been dead some fifteen years." He clutched her hand. "For his sake. For the love, however unnatural, I bear him. And I think you love him too."

"Very well." She took her hand from his. "I suppose you do not seek forgiveness."

"Would you grant it?"

"Yes. I have to go on living, sir."

"You're a courageous woman, Mrs. Craigmont."

There was nothing else to say. Fabienne stood and walked away, through the open glass doors into the garden.

She was released.

She should feel . . . She didn't know how she should feel. In some ways she felt much the same, she was the same person. There were no blinding revelations, no visitations from angels, hardly any sense of a new beginning in her life from what she had learned.

She knew the worst, and it left her feeling relieved and, in a way, empty. With nothing left to be revealed, things would go on much as they always had, and she would continue to deal with loneliness and love and all the petty fragments that made up her life. She also had a new burden, which she hoped she would have the strength to carry. Her arm did not carry a brand, but she was bound by a vow as strong as Adam's.

Adam sat with his arm around Elaine. At a distance, they looked alike, with the same graceful angularity, the same set to their heads.

She'd never know.

They both stood when she approached, and Elaine glanced at Adam. He frowned and nudged Elaine forward.

"Fabienne, I am so sorry. I know . . . I know what happened. Please forgive me."

"You're forgiven. From the depths of my heart." Fabienne kissed her. "Will you come back to London with us?"

"Yes, but if you do not mind, I should like to visit my

family as I intended." Elaine gave her a pleading look. "But I will come back, I promise."

"Very well." Fabienne took her hand. "I need to speak with Mr. Ashworth for a little."

Elaine smiled, her face illuminated. "Of course. I shall go back into the house and work on the drawing."

"Drawing?" Adam said. "What drawing?"

"I am drawing Lord Greenmore."

"Certainly not. I don't want you going anywhere near that poxed-up madman. Fabienne, you tell her she should not."

"Mr. Ashworth, he is an old, ill man. He will do me no harm. You should pity him and pray for him as I do," Elaine said with her usual certainty, and walked back toward the house.

Adam watched her leave with astonishment. "Maybe she is his daughter," he muttered. "She's mad too. And 'old'? He's two years older than me. Fabienne, are you all right?"

"I don't know."

She took his arm. He was warm and solid, and he gazed at her with worry and concern in his eyes. She wrapped her arms around his waist.

"Fabienne?" He tipped up her chin with one finger.

"You haven't asked me what he said."

"It's your choice to tell me or not. If you wish to, tell me. Tell me anything you want to."

She stood on her toes to kiss the side of his mouth. "I love you for saying that."

"Oh. Good." He stared at her.

"The other man was Henry Foster."

"No, it wasn't. I suppose he told you to say that. It was Sanders. Why else would he have him killed?"

His matter-of-fact tone took her breath away. "But . . . Adam, he said the truth would destroy you."

Adam frowned. "It makes my flesh crawl, that Sanders abused two women I love. It's not pleasant, but I have a tougher skin than Greenmore thinks."

"He loves you. I think he wished to protect you."

Adam shrugged. "He knew long ago I would not, nor could not, give him what he wanted. When he chooses, he's a sentimental fool with a taste for the dramatic, and he cannot resist a last attempt at mischief or intrigue."

"No wonder he likes your novels."

He laughed, then touched her cheek with his finger. "Would you truly have kept silent to spare my feelings?"

"Yes."

"I'm honored, Fabienne, but I wish there to be no more secrets we keep from each other. Were all your questions answered?"

She sighed. "I think so. I believe Elaine is safe with him. And she is now an heiress. It is strange, the whole business. I do not feel I have become wiser from it."

"You are wiser than I." He brushed her lips with his. "I have broken my vows for you, as I said I would. And the strange thing is that I don't care. You are all that matters, now."

"Enough." She placed her finger on his lips. "Let us fetch Elaine and leave this place."

Adam was silent on the long ride home to London, and both she and Elaine were tired. Fabienne fell asleep, and woke only once to overhear a brief conversation between Elaine and Adam.

"Is Luke very angry, sir?"

"I saw him later in the day after you had left, when he'd received your letter. He cried. You injured him, Miss Twyford."

"I'm sorry," Elaine murmured.

"You'd best tell that to him. If, of course, you have the opportunity."

Dimmock made it very clear his employer had offended him again.

"You shouldn't go alone on such trips, sir," he said in mild rebuke as he inspected Adam's unpolished boots. "You need a manservant with you. It's not respectable."

"There was little about this trip that was respectable," Adam told him.

"Ah. And the lady . . . ?"

"Never you mind about the lady." Adam turned away to unbutton his trousers. He had assumed, in a gentlemanly sort of way, that Fabienne would be too tired by the events of the day for lovemaking. He, apparently, was not, although the rest of his body was bone weary.

"I have my money on Mrs. Craigmont," Dimmock said with a familiarity that would have appalled Adam's sister. "Though Miss Branwell is also a front runner, according to the butler."

"Who the devil is she? By the way, I'm supposed to sack any servants who bet openly."

"Then you'd have to sack us all, sir. Miss Branwell is a lady you met at Lady Eglinton's house, very respectable and with a handsome fortune."

Adam tried to remember Miss Branwell and failed. "I trust I won't cause you any financial embarrassment. You may go to bed, Dimmock. Good night."

"Thank you, sir. Good night." Dimmock gathered up his master's discarded linen and rumpled, travel-stained clothes and left.

Adam lay in bed, hands linked behind his head, and contemplated marriage to Fabienne. Of course, it was not his decision alone. She had no need to marry. She'd said she loved him, and he'd said he loved her, but there were practical considerations. Where would they live? Would she agree to come to the country? He certainly couldn't spend too much time in town; even now, anticipating the next night with her, he was itching to get back to the country. In a month or so it would be harvesttime; he wanted to see how high the corn stood and admire the young fruit on his trees and grapevines, and of course, there were the pigs.

He wanted to make sure Luke was well—poor Luke, who had wept in pain and bewilderment at his broken engagement. There were so many complications, not the least of which was that Fabienne might refuse him.

And then what would he do?

Chapter Nineteen

Alas, neither maiden nor bride, and shamed and con-
demned in the eyes of the world, so the legend has it,
she met an untimely end at this very spot. It is said,
even now, her shade walks, wringing her ringless
hands, her gown spattered with gore, as she seeks that
which she has lost for eternity.
    —*The Curse of the Molfitains* by Mrs. Ravenwood.

"**W**e are alone in the house," Fabienne said with
a wicked smile when Adam arrived.

"Indeed. Shall we dine in a state of nature?" He
started on his neckcloth.

"Certainly not." She poured wine and offered him delicious, faintly foreign food—pigeons flavored with a hint
of nutmeg, fresh peas with mint, a salad dressed in oil
and lemon, and fruit and cheese to follow.

He watched her mouth, the small deft movements of
her hands, and almost forgot to eat, dizzy with her near-
ness. "I love you," he said.

She touched her tongue delicately to a ripe strawberry,
reminding him of how she'd tongued that part of him
which was much the same color and shape. He stiffened immediately.

"I have strawberry beds," he offered. "Orchards too."

She took a delicate bite. "At home, in Normandy, we
had apple trees. We made cider and a sort of brandy
from them. I remember the blossoms, like snowdrifts, in
the spring. Sometimes we would break off a branch in

the winter to bring into the house. It would bloom in the warmth, and scent the air."

That was something he had not anticipated, her possible return to France. As if reading his mind, she added, "My brother says he intends to return if we are ever at peace. I doubt whether he will. Possibly he will have to buy back his estates, and he will not accept my money."

Her money. That was another consideration.

"What are you thinking about?" She reached for another strawberry. He watched the juice spill over her lips and trickle onto her chin.

"You."

"Ah."

"I want to kiss you."

She stood and came round to his side of the table, hoisting her skirts so she sat astride him. Her eyes widened. "You're hard."

"It seems to be the way I usually am around you. It astonishes me. You astonish me." He put his lips to her neck and touched his tongue to the hollow above her collarbone.

"Do you think this chair could hold our weight if we, oh, became more active?"

"Let's find out."

They moved from the chair to the sofa and finally to her bed, leaving a trail of abandoned clothes on the floor. He was ardent and masterful, bending her into a variety of colorful positions, whispering deliciously wicked suggestions into her ears. Finally they lay exhausted and sweaty on her bed, his head on her breast.

"I have something to tell you," he announced. "I'm going away tomorrow."

"Where?" She tried to keep her voice neutral. She wanted him in her bed every night, and every morning when she awoke. If he returned to his house, she anticipated the exchange of intimate notes, running their servants ragged across London.

"Portsmouth. I received word today that Jon's ship is expected within the next fortnight. I have not seen him for eighteen months, since he set sail. He'll have maybe a week ashore."

"Well, of course. How wonderful. Will you see Barbara too?"

"Possibly." He rolled his head off her and lay next to her, then clasped her hand in his. "And I should spend some time at my house, just to see that all is well with things there."

"I shall miss you." Of course she didn't expect him to ask her to accompany him; he could hardly introduce his son to his mistress.

His mistress.

She was his mistress.

She'd not realized it, but the signs were all there. She had spent most of the day planning the menu with the cook, deciding what to wear, and bathing and adorning herself. She, the independent, sophisticated Fabienne Craigmont, who had no need for a husband, and was at no man's beck and call, had become Adam's mistress. And she wanted to burst into bitter, disappointed tears because he planned a trip away from her to see his children.

"I expect you'll keep busy," he said to her annoyance.

"I'm sure I shall."

He circled her nipple with one finger. To her annoyance it stiffened and tingled.

"Adam?" She pushed him away.

"Mmm?" He lowered his head to her breast.

"Listen to me."

"May I listen and do this?"

"No."

He sighed and propped his head on one hand. "Continue."

"There is the matter of Mrs. Ravenwood. Do you expect me to keep silent about her identity?"

"What harm will it do? I daresay public taste will move on to something else soon enough." He lowered his mouth to her ear. "Let me tell you a story. A very wicked story."

"Adam . . ." She squirmed against him.

"There has been a shipwreck, and you are cast ashore and enslaved in the sultan's harem."

"Oh, Adam, that is so dreadfully old-fashioned."

"And I am the chief eunuch who is to guard you and wake your desires in preparation for the sultan's pleasure."

She snorted with laughter.

"But . . . but I am not what I seem. Under my very baggy pantaloons I am miraculously intact."

"So you are." She pushed him on his back and knelt over him, dipping her breasts within reach of his mouth. "It is a miracle indeed. And you say the sultan himself is thus endowed?"

"His is not nearly so big." He grinned like a wicked schoolboy. "Allow me to show you what his excellency will require of you."

Fabienne shuddered with pleasure as his mouth closed on her nipple. She didn't want to think about what a rational woman should do. She should refuse him, pleading a headache, or fatigue, or just lack of interest.

She couldn't.

He wanted to escape awkward questions and issues, and any well-trained mistress would help her lover distract himself.

A summer storm slashed rain against the windows and turned the London street into a misery of mud and liquid filth. Inside, the women of Fabienne's household leaked and seeped blood and irritability. Fabienne discovered her female staff, huddled by the fireside sipping brews of tea, gin, and licorice, and bewailing their female lot.

Her cook growled and hacked beef bones with a cleaver. Doubtless he was depressed by the atmosphere of feminine gloom, and enraged by the presence of the first batch of menstrual rags blatantly hung out to dry in front of the fire.

Fabienne made tea herself and lifted the tray to take it upstairs. Her breasts were tender and her lower belly ached and cramped. She should have bled over two weeks ago; she felt tired and bloated. She was furious that her body had refused to take this opportunity to plunge her into the menstrual misery of the household. It must be Adam's fault. Everything was his fault. Her unaccountable sadness, the bad weather, his reticence about when he would return to London, the relentless cheerfulness of his letters. Everything.

In the past month he had written her letters she tried hard to enjoy, about how much Jon had grown, and with details of their activities and outings. She had replied in equally positive terms about her salon, trips to the theater, and parties she had attended, while raging at him between the lines.

Elaine had returned, shy and deferential for about two hours. Thereafter she alternated between her normal, opinionated self and a new Elaine—a nervous, weepy wreck who was afraid she had lost Luke forever.

As Fabienne went upstairs, tears rose to her eyes again at the thought of her unhappy daughter.

"I am sorry," muttered Elaine, a miserable bundle on the sofa, arms wrapped around her abdomen.

"It's all right. You can't help it." Fabienne sat beside her and stroked her head. "Can you take some tea?"

"I've been drinking tea all day. I should work."

She made no move to sit up, for which Fabienne was grateful. If Elaine was serious about working, Fabienne would have to rouse the servants to light lamps and re-arrange furniture. Elaine had taken on, in addition to her portraiture, the creation of some murals for a wealthy client, and worked on preliminary watercolors at home.

"Sweetheart, does it hurt very much? Maybe we should try some laudanum."

"Why won't Luke call? He is in London, I know."

"You hurt him. He's probably afraid you will reject him again."

Elaine sat up. "Perhaps I should refuse him. Maybe it would be for the best."

"I don't know." Fabienne poured them both tea. "Do what you think best. If you have the chance at happiness and you choose to throw it away, that is your choice."

She stopped, appalled at the bitterness in her voice and the hurt in Elaine's eyes.

"What shall I do?"

"Wait."

Elaine nodded, hands around her teacup. "I miss Luke so."

"I'd like to see him too," Fabienne said.

"And Mr. Ashworth. Are you in love with him?"

To Fabienne's relief the front-door bell rang.

Her footman entered the room. "Viscount Tillotson and Mr. Ashworth, ma'am. I told them you were indisposed, but they insist on seeing you."

Elaine leaped to her feet, pushed her disordered hair into place, smoothed her gown, and wailed, "Oh, I look a fright!"

Not as much of a fright as I. Fabienne remembered the last time she had looked in the mirror, and shuddered at her dull hair and shadowed eyes. She drew herself up as the two men entered the room.

Adam looked the picture of health, his face tanned by the sun. He pushed at Luke's arm, urging him forward.

"Luke, how very pleasant to see you." Fabienne kissed him on both cheeks. "I have missed you. If you'll excuse me, I have some business to see to elsewhere in the house."

Elaine looked at her in terror.

Adam bowed. "Ah, may I accompany you, Mrs. Craigmont?"

"If you wish. I'm going to the kitchen." As they left the room, she said, "And how were your children?"

"Very well, as I told you in my letters." He sounded surprised. "You did read my letters, I hope. Jon is a head taller, and quite broad in the shoulders, and burned darker than I by the sun. He's becoming a man; his voice is breaking."

"So you did. I remember."

"Could your kitchen business wait a few minutes?"

"Very well." She stopped in the hall.

"Are you angry with me?" He looked at her with such concern and longing that tears rose to her eyes.

"No, Adam. I—I am out of sorts, that is all."

"I would rather not say what I have to say here, in the passage. Could we not—" He glanced upstairs.

"No. We had the chimney sweep today and it is all over soot. Susan is cleaning upstairs."

"You're being very contrary, Fabienne. Well, if I must . . ." He cleared his throat.

"I won't be your mistress anymore." Fabienne was appalled at her words.

"Good. I came here to ask if you'd be my wife."

She stared at him in amazement.

He continued. "I have thought about it for some time, and see it is the only course open to me. I have, as you know, certain responsibilities toward my children. I should like to acknowledge Elaine as my child. Regarding practical considerations, I know you are a woman of some fortune, but I should not want to concern myself in your financial affairs. I hope you would consent to live in the country. We could come to town whenever you wish. I should not wish to intrude on your artistic pursuits. I"—he stopped and drew in a deep breath—"I beg your pardon. I am botching this entirely."

"You are." *Say you love me, Adam. Say it, for God's sake. You'll say it when you're in my bed, or about to get me into it. Why not now?*

He hesitated and dropped to one knee. "You know, of course, that I harbor the tenderest regards for you—"

The door to the kitchen opened and Susan emerged, giving a shriek of surprise as she nearly bowled Adam down. "Ooh, good afternoon, Mr. Ashworth."

"Good afternoon, Susan." He straightened up and looked at her clean apron and cap. "I trust cleaning up after the chimney sweep is not too arduous a task."

"Cleaning up after—why, no, sir, I have been separating eggs and have come to find Mrs. Craigmont."

"I'll be down in an instant, Susan," Fabienne said, mortified. She pushed Susan back through the door and closed it. "And what of Mrs. Ravenwood?"

"What of her?"

"You said there were to be no more secrets between us. Do you remember, Adam? Do you think marriage will buy my silence?"

"But, Fabienne, is it so great a matter?"

"Yes," she said. "Yes, I think it is." She waited, silently begging him to speak.

"I regret . . . the identity of Mrs. Ravenwood must remain a secret."

"Very well. Excuse me, Mr. Ashworth. There is something I must fetch from upstairs." Her hands were cold, and she pressed them against her skirts to stop them from shaking.

In her room she fumbled with the catch to the secret drawer on her desk, her fingers clumsy, the mechanism unyielding as though reluctant to reveal its contents. As she took the package of letters out, she could swear they held his scent. She descended the stairs and handed them to him without a word.

"So." Adam turned the packet of letters over in his hands. "This is how it ends?"

She nodded her head, not knowing what to say and not trusting her voice to reply.

He looked bewildered and hurt and she ached to take him in her arms one last time. "Fabienne, what is wrong?"

She hesitated, knowing the damage she did to him, to both of them, before she spoke. "I will not marry someone who proposes to me because his duty to his family demands it, and tells me it is his only recourse. I certainly will not marry to give my child a name. Are you aware she is being offered the same by Tillotson even as we speak? I will not lie for you about Mrs. Ravenwood or anything else, and above all, I cannot marry a coward." She added, "I'm sorry," before she pushed past him, opened the door to the kitchen, and hurried down the stairs before she could change her mind.

The heat, humidity, and mingled odors of the kitchen

struck her like a dizzying blow to the face. Monseer bellowed orders at Susan and Polly, who chopped vegetables at the table, while he beat a bowl of egg yolks.

"Voilà, madam," he said, nodding his head toward a large pot on the fire.

Fabienne picked up a spoon and a cloth and lifted the lid. She dipped the spoon into the broth and raised it to her lips. *Adam has gone. I've lost him. He's too proud to come back.*

Small, shiny globules of fat and a gray-green sliver of bay leaf floated in the translucent brown liquid, and a fragment of bone protruded, jagged and pale.

"More wine in it, you think, madam?"

Why couldn't I just have told him I loved him? Why? The spoon fell from her hand, splashing into the pot and spattering her with boiling liquid.

"Ma'am!"

Susan ran forward and grasped Fabienne by the waist and arm as the kitchen began to fade from her vision. Her last coherent thought was that in the eyes of the world refusing an offer of marriage might have been an even more serious mistake than she had first realized.

Elaine and Luke were driving Fabienne mad. Five weeks before—the same day she had refused Adam, but she didn't want to think about that—Elaine had agreed to become engaged again. Now it seemed they were continually underfoot, a pair of besotted lovebirds in her house. They insisted Fabienne accompany them to parties and plays when all she really wanted to do was stay home to sleep and cry.

"Ma'am?" Fabienne came awake to find Susan standing over her. She must have fallen asleep on her sofa in the middle of the afternoon again. "Miss Elaine wants to know if the viscount can stay to dine."

"I suppose so." Fabienne swung her feet to the floor. "Are they in the drawing room?"

"Yes, ma'am, and his lordship is home too." Susan reached into her pocket and placed a small parcel on the dressing table. "Here are the stockings you asked me to buy, and a few other things."

Downstairs, Fabienne listened to Ippolite's account of his day and then asked Elaine how her most recent work progressed.

Elaine blushed and glanced at Luke. "I took a holiday today. Luke and I went for a drive, and then—"

Fabienne interrupted her. "Elaine, you have work to do. You signed contracts before you became engaged and you should honor them. You and Luke will see plenty of each other once you are married, and begin to tire of each other."

Elaine flushed bright red. "But I am well ahead of my work, madam. I have finished the murals and—"

"Do not argue with me!"

Fabienne saw Ippolite shake his head at Elaine, and his gesture enraged her further. "For God's sake!" she shrieked. "I have made mistakes in my life and tried to make amends, and you repay me with your slatternly ways. I am tired to death of you all!" Fabienne saw their shocked faces and blundered out of the room.

"Ah, don't fret, *ma chère*," Fabienne heard Ippolite say as she left. "She's just jealous. If she had a man herself, she'd be a lot sweeter."

She ran back into the room, enraged. "You whoreson!" She swung her hand, slapped his face, and had the satisfaction of seeing him stagger back and fall.

"What are you doing?"

Fabienne's brother stood in her bedroom doorway.

"Nothing," she said. "Please leave me. I am sorry I hit you, Ippolite."

He walked over to her and took the bottle from her hand. " 'Mrs. Culver's Remedy for Gentlewomen,' " he read aloud. " 'Cures all female complaints, including irregularities of the menses, et cetera, et cetera.' " He put the bottle back on her dressing table. "So you seek to rid yourself of Ashworth's child?"

"Do not play the moralist with me," she said. "You are not the one who may die in childbirth."

"If this stuff does not kill you first. Where did you get it?"

"Susan brought it to me. I did not ask her to. She knew, of course." His grim expression alarmed her. Despite her reluctance to take this irrevocable step, she tried to reassure him, or possibly herself. "Do not look at me like that. They say it is no great matter. I shall be up and about in no time. There may be some discomfort, but—"

"Does your condition addle your wits?" He frowned.

"For God's sake!" She burst into tears. After a moment he put his arm around her. "I don't want to do this, Ippolite. I don't know what to do."

"You are absolutely sure of your condition?" His voice was quiet.

"Yes. I have not bled in weeks, and I cry all the time."

"Yes, your breasts are bigger too," Ippolite said. "It is quite unmistakeable."

"Oh, for God's sake, you revolt me. I am your sister. You should not even notice such things, let alone mention them to me."

"I am not blind, and I am not without honor. Ashworth must marry you."

"No." She wanted to howl with misery. "No. I don't want him, Ippolite. I don't want to marry him. I would rather marry anyone except him."

"Well, then," Ippolite said. "I must find you a husband. But for God's sake, Fabienne, other women have children and find them a home elsewhere. Surely, that is an alternative—"

"Absolutely not. You forget I have done that and it near broke my heart." Fabienne put out her hand for the bottle.

"This is not right. Please, do not—"

"Do you think there is one matron in London who has not used a remedy of this sort?" Fabienne asked. "And what of all your mistresses? Have you ever wondered why you don't have a fine crop of bastards? Practice celibacy, sir, and then you can preach at me all you want."

"You go too far!" Ippolite grabbed for the bottle, his face contorted with anger, and dashed it to the floor. "Damn you, Fabienne. Ashworth has dishonored our name, and he'll pay for it, I swear it!"

Chapter Twenty

> "It is damnable," Ludovico cried, "that he should cast
> such dishonor upon those I hold dear! I will pursue
> him and he shall not live to injure another innocent—
> I swear it—or I die in the attempt."
>   "Sir!" The veiled woman fell to her knees, clutching
> his naked blade in her hands. "Sir, I beg you. Have
> pity on him. He is my father!"
>   —*The Ruined Tower* by Mrs. Ravenwood.

Jilted again, and by the same woman, twenty years
later.

It was embarrassing and humiliating, and he really
didn't understand it. She had changed in those few
weeks, looking tired and older—that had been a shock
to him—and only that convinced him that she had not
taken another lover in his absence. She lacked that satisfied glow, the glint in her eyes, that characterized her
after she'd had her way with him.

Of course he'd botched the proposal. He'd only proposed once before, and that was a mere formality after
an inquisition by his future father-in-law. He could see
now how he should have proceeded with Fabienne, but
demons of doubt whispered in his ear that it would not
have made any difference. She did not want him. She
had refused his name, his protection, his property. Above
all her refusal meant that she did not believe he loved
her.

She honestly thought if he'd reveal himself as Mrs.

Ravenwood that would make everything well again. Of course he didn't expect her to lie for him—or did he? Mrs. Ravenwood was one part of his life he kept distinct from the rest.

And she'd called him a coward.

Sweat trickled into his eyes, and down his spine under his linen shirt, and the blisters on his hand stung. He stepped forward, and swung the scythe. Wheat toppled aside, gold speckled with the scarlet of poppies and the blue of cornflowers. The harvesttime was something he usually enjoyed. He liked the exertion, the balance and heft of the scythe, the exchange of jokes and gossip with his tenants, and even the hot sun, sweat, and blisters.

This year he longed for it to be over so he could skulk in his library once more, writing letters to Fabienne and throwing them away. Even that pleasure was denied him—he had accepted the invitation of the Viscount and Viscountess Tillotson to attend a ball at their London house, their first public appearance after the wedding. Much to Adam's relief Luke and Elaine had taken a special license to marry. He wondered if the quietness of the event was to prevent the embarrassment of a meeting between Fabienne and himself.

He stepped aside and lifted a stone bottle that lay in a shady patch next to the hedgerow.

"What shall I do, Mags?" He took a swig of sour, cool cider.

Don't be daft, Adam.

"That's easy enough for you to say. She called me a coward," he mumbled, wiping his mouth on his shirt-sleeve.

So you are, you great ninny. Go to her, Adam, and stop feeling sorry for yourself. And put your hat back on. You'll burn.

Something—a branch of hawthorn, a flying insect—brushed his cheek.

Good-bye, my love.

He stood silent for a moment, then laid the bottle back among the cool green of the hedge, and grasped his scythe once more.

Mags had gone, and now he had to find his way.
But not without Fabienne.

"They are very charming," Prissy commented. "It is so unusual to see a couple of the *ton* who will express affection in public. Although, perhaps, it will make them objects of amusement. Do you think we should warn Luke, Adam?"

He shook his head. "No. As you say, it's a rare thing. Let them alone, Prissy."

She nodded. "You look around the room as if you expect to see someone."

"Is Mrs. Craigmont here?"

"I don't believe so. Her brother, the count, is here; I saw him in the crush a little while ago. I heard she was ill, and she gives her last salon this week. All the *ton* plan to go. Her mother, you know, died of consumption. I hope she does not have it too."

Adam sought to change the subject. "Elaine looks well. I should go and talk to them when this dance ends."

He walked across the ballroom when the dance finished. Elaine gave a squeal of delight and flung her arms around him.

"Mr. Ashworth, we have missed you so! And you are quite sunburned."

"Yes, I had two harvests to gather this year since my neighbor was on his honeymoon. You look very well, my dear. You too, Luke."

"Thank you, sir." Luke and Elaine stood close together, their hands clasped.

"How is Mrs. Craigmont? I gather she is not here tonight."

Luke and Elaine exchanged glances, and he braced himself for an inept lie.

"She is indisposed," Elaine said.

"And has unexpected visitors." That was Luke's simultaneous contribution.

"But not very indisposed." Elaine amended her statement. "She only wanted to stay at home."

"To be with her visitors," Luke added.

"Thank you, Luke. Thank you, Elaine. If your husband will allow, and if he can spare you, I should like to claim a dance with you."

"Of course. The one after next, I think—oh, good evening, Lord Argonac."

"Lady Tillotson." Argonac, his face tense and serious, bowed to her and turned to Adam. "Ashworth, I need to speak to you."

"Certainly."

"You have dishonored my sister, sir."

"Indeed." Adam was aware of a stir of interest around them, a whispered comment here and there. "You should know I made her an offer and she refused it."

"All I know, sir, is that she carries your child."

Adam stared as he took in Argonac's words. Fabienne was pregnant. Pregnant with his child, and he wanted to shout for joy. His elation faded as he realized she had almost certainly known of her condition when he proposed, and rejected him. Did she plan to hide another of his children away, deny him his right to give them both his love and protection?

"Sir," Adam said, "this is possibly more complicated than you realize. Let us—"

Argonac let out his breath in a hiss. "My family's name is dishonored." He stepped forward and struck Adam on the face. "I demand satisfaction."

Luke stepped forward, horror on his face. "I'll act for Mr. Ashworth, my lord."

"Very well." Argonac bowed and left as a buzz of voices rose around them.

"Uncle, why did you choose rapiers?"

Adam paused in stretching his hamstrings, hands flat against a tree trunk, one leg extended, the other bent. "I'm a dreadful shot. At least this way I stand a chance. I've fought with Argonac at his fencing academy. I know something of his style."

"But he was not trying to kill you there."

"He wouldn't have many clients if he did."

Luke did not appear find his comment amusing. "Sir, is it true, what he said?"

Adam changed legs. "I'm afraid so." He stretched a little more, and straightened up. "Luke, don't look so worried. Chances are, he'll scratch me to teach me a lesson, and I'll bleed a little, and that will be the end of it. I'll marry Mrs. Craigmont and all will be well."

"Do you really believe that?"

Adam put his arm around Luke's shoulders. "No, I don't. I think he wants to kill me, and if I were in his position, I'd feel the same. So there's nothing for it, Luke. My affairs are in order."

He made a few practice lunges. The grass was wet and slippery with dew. Mist hung in the air; the sun had yet to rise. The last time he had prepared to meet his death, Argonac was his second, not his opponent. It was a bitter trick of fate.

At least this time he had told Fabienne he loved her, although he would not see their child, or make his peace with Babs. He felt a sudden, painful pang of longing for her and his grandchildren. And it seemed grossly unfair that he would not even get to see his latest book, which was still at the printers. Well, his death would almost certainly guarantee a second and third reprint, a small consolation.

A few yards away Argonac's second, another French émigré Adam had met at the academy, beckoned to Luke, and the two men conferred.

Luke walked back to Adam, his face pale. "Are you ready, sir?"

"Yes." He clapped Luke on the shoulder. "Don't fret." It was a ludicrous thing to say under the circumstances, but he hated to see Luke's face so set and grim—so adult. "Luke, I'm sorry for all the times I've been impatient or sarcastic with you."

Luke's eyes welled with tears. "Uncle, you never have."

"Don't be a ninny." Adam walked forward and raised his rapier in salute to Argonac, who returned the courtesy.

The handkerchief fluttered in Luke's hand and dropped, and Adam and Argonac met.

This was no polite bout in a fencing academy, or a formality between gentlemen. Argonac's glittering rapier point drove Adam back and around and the rising sun blazed into his eyes, blinding him for one vital second. Sudden fire slashed across his forearm, and a warm flow over wrist and hand loosened his grip on the weapon and warned him that he had little time.

"My lord, enough!" Argonac's second shouted.

They both ignored him. Adam took a hideous risk, ducked under Argonac's blade, and kicked him on the knee.

Cursing, Argonac staggered back, recovered, and blinked in the rays of the sun before lunging forward. They met face-to-face, panting, blades locked. Adam's blood spattered them both.

"She does not love you," Argonac snarled.

What?

The moment of broken concentration was all Argonac needed to slam his knee into Adam's groin.

Adam dropped his rapier and fell to the ground, breathless with pain. Black and red splotches, like the poppies in his cornfields, floated behind his closed eyes. He waited for Argonac to deliver a final blow, welcoming the oblivion it would bring. Dimly he heard the sound of people shouting, among them a woman.

Babs?

"You are no gentleman, sir!" There was the sound of a slap, and a male grunt of pain. "How dare you attack a man of my father's advanced age?"

"But—he—I—"

Adam guessed she had hit Argonac again. "Be quiet!"

Adam heard his daughter's footsteps on the grass, and opened his eyes with great care. Blades of grass and the serrated leaves of a dandelion were in his direct line of vision. He attempted to say something. It came out as a strangled croak.

"Papa!" She knelt in front of him. "Papa, speak to me."

"Babs. Don't move. Hurts. Ground shakes."

"Oh, Papa!"

He managed to get his hands into a less indecent position and took a cautious breath.

"And you're bleeding!"

He was? Oh yes, a twinge on his forearm and a general sensation of warm wetness reminded him that he was possibly bleeding to death. With a great effort, and hoping that he would not vomit in her lap, he lurched to his knees and met his daughter's horrified gaze. He gripped his arm to stem the flow. "Don't worry."

She stood. "Pray, sir, avert your eyes," she snapped at Argonac, who lurked at their side, the mark of her hand livid on his face. She lifted her gown, ripped off a length of petticoat, and pressed it against the wound on Adam's arm.

She plucked a letter from her bodice. "I came to London last night, and went to your house. I found *this,* along with some other letters, an hour ago. After I read it, I hid the rest for fear my aunt would receive hers and have the vapors."

Adam groaned. Another embarrassing letter gone astray.

Babs unfolded it and read aloud. " 'I am due to meet Argonac this morning in a conflagration in the Park that I am convinced will be fatal.' Really, Papa. You are so overly dramatic. I have made a hackney carriage drive all over the Park. And you, Luke, you should know better than to be involved in this." She glared at them, and then turned her angry gaze on Argonac, who had moved nearer. "Go away, you whoreson."

Argonac gulped. Luke tugged at his sleeve and they backed away.

"Who taught you that word?" Adam asked.

"You, sir. You use it often enough."

Argonac moved forward. "Mrs. Sanders, may I assist you?"

"In a moment, if you please," Adam said. "Babs, did you have to refer to me as a man of advanced years?"

"I'm sorry."

"No," he said and took her hand. She gave a gasp of dismay as blood flowed again. "It is I who should apologize. I have said some dreadful things to you, and yet all this time you knew who Mrs. Ravenwood was and kept silence. Forgive me."

"Papa." She gave a sob. "Oh, Papa." She glared again at Argonac. "What do you want?"

"To bandage Mr. Ashworth, madam. He bleeds all over you." Argonac squatted beside him. "I apologize, sir." He ripped at Adam's shirtsleeve. "You should have this stitched. May I impose on you for another length of your petticoat, Mrs. Sanders?"

"You are most indelicate and no gentleman, sir." She turned her back on them and ripped at her linen again.

"I wish to marry Mrs. Craigmont with all my heart," Adam said to Argonac. "The problem is she won't have me."

"She is a stubborn and annoying woman," her brother said. He wrapped a fresh length of linen around Adam's arm. "Well, sir, I think that should hold you until you see a surgeon."

"If Papa dies," Barbara said, "I will kill you, Argonac, but first I will kick you as hard as I can in the ballocks. Several times."

All three men winced.

"Babs, please moderate your language," Adam said. "Luke will take you home, my dear. Argonac and I must talk."

Argonac gazed after her as Luke handed her into his carriage. "She is magnificent. Mr. Ashworth, may I have your permission to pay my addresses to Mrs. Sanders?"

"Absolutely not," Adam replied.

Fabienne still had dreams, but now she was in control of them, not dragged into helpless terror.

In her dreams now, the door of the room opened, and the two masked and cloaked figures entered. She approached them, tugged at their robes, and watched them crumble into dust, or they jostled comically in the doorway as she laughed at them.

The most vivid version was when Adam entered and tore off his cloak to reveal his naked body and his rampant desire for her. Sometimes he was young; and sometimes she enjoyed the stamina of his youthful lovemaking with the finesse of an older man. He kept the mask on—it was the sort of game Adam would enjoy—and made love to her, playful, passionate, and very, very real. Too real.

This last night there was yet another version. As the two sinister figures entered the room, a small child darted from her side. She couldn't see its face or tell its sex, as it wore the long dress that all toddlers wore. The child laughed and waved a wooden toy sword, and the intruders disappeared in a puff of smoke. She knew it was her child.

She woke and laid her hand on the slight swell of her belly, where someone stirred and shifted. "You're wide-awake," she murmured. "Such a busy little thing, dreaming with me. Can't I sleep some more?"

She raised her nightgown and watched her skin ripple and subside, before rolling on her side to see if she could go back to sleep. It was very early, only an hour or so past dawn.

She heard the clump of male footsteps coming up the stairs, and a hesitant tap at her door.

"Fabienne? Are you awake?" It was Ippolite, addressing her in French, something he generally only did when he was excited about something.

"Oui, entre," she replied. "Out all night again—oh, my God, you're hurt. What have you done?" She jumped out of bed, ran to him, and tugged at his coat. "Let me see."

Blood was smeared over his shirt and coat. "It's all right. It's not mine."

"What have you done? Whose blood is it?"

"Ashworth's."

"Oh, no. No!" Her knees gave way and Ippolite swore and lowered her to the bed. "Tell me you have not killed him."

"Honor has been satisfied," Ippolite replied.

"He's dead."

"I didn't say that."

"Tell me!" She grabbed him by the ear as she had done when he was small and being particularly provoking. He gave a satisfying yelp of pain. "It's bad enough you should challenge him to a duel, but now, to play tricks on me like this, you should be ashamed."

"Fabienne, let me go, please. He's not dead. I pricked him, and he bled a lot."

"Where?"

"In the park."

She shook him and aimed a slap at him with her free hand. "No! *Where on his person, you imbecile?"*

"His arm."

She released her brother and he backed away, rubbing his reddened ear.

"You're limping. Did he wound you?"

"No, he kicked my knee. I'd best get a compress on it."

"He *kicked* you?" Obviously this duel had been something other than a formality between gentlemen.

"Well, yes, but shortly after, I kneed him in the ballocks."

"That is dreadful!"

"I assure you the damage is not permanent, my dear." He grinned at her. "And Mrs. Sanders arrived unexpectedly. She slapped me twice and called me a whoreson. I am trying to think what that could mean. Do you think she favors me?"

"No, brother. I think she takes you for a complete idiot, as I do. Now leave me. I have a busy day ahead."

"Ah yes. Your last salon." He bent to kiss her forehead. *"Ma chère,* everything will be all right. Just you wait."

And what exactly did he mean by that?

Chapter Twenty-one

Amidst tears and laughter the two lovers plighted their troth. Reader, let us leave them in this state of perfect felicity, the union of two hearts in accord, and imagine the delights that lie ahead.

FINIS

—*The Lost Child* by Mr. Adam Ashworth.

"*B*ut, my dear Mrs. Craigmont, we shall be desolated by your departure from society."

"It is so kind of you to say so, madam," Fabienne replied to Lady Eglinton, who, as far as she could remember, had never once come to her salon before.

"And you say you will leave London?"

"Yes, quite soon. I plan to live very quietly in a cottage in the country."

"Indeed." Lady Eglinton's gaze traveled briefly to Fabienne's belly, concealed in sea green muslin. "You plan to live alone?"

"Oh, I shall not be a recluse, I assure you. I shall always be happy to receive visitors, and hear all the gossip of the town."

Fabienne imagined herself pulling up her gown and displaying her slightly pregnant belly to her extremely interested guests. *Yes, there's a baby in here, your newest niece or nephew, Lady Eglinton. Adam Ashworth's bastard. And now, unless you'd like to admire my enlarged bosom, let's get on with the afternoon.*

She worked her way around the room, fending off polite enquiries about her health and her future plans. She had hired extra servants and rented additional chairs for her guests, and was afraid they would run out of room. This portion of the afternoon, usually devoted to political discussion, had degenerated into gossip and flirting.

"Mrs. Craigmont?" Lady Mary, the Eglintons' elder daughter, curtsied to her. "Mrs. Craigmont, have you heard the rumor that there is to be a new Mrs. Ravenwood novel? They say it will come out any day."

Fabienne nodded, not wanting to think about Adam.

"I am so excited," Mary continued. "And I am so glad Mama decided to bring me here today. Papa was furious. He said it would be full of dangerous radicals and poets, but I have not yet met either."

"You are fortunate, then," Fabienne said, and turned to the greatest poet in the universe who hovered at her elbow. "Sir, this is Lady Mary Anston. Lady Mary, this gentleman is wicked, dangerous, and depraved, both a radical and a poet. And you, sir, should know Lady Mary is a notoriously cruel breaker of hearts."

They both looked thrilled and Fabienne moved away, leaving them to flirt with each other.

Elaine and Luke arrived, charmingly rumpled, as though they had kissed in the carriage the entire way over.

"Come," she said to Elaine, "help me encourage people to sit down, or they'll be here all night."

"Fabienne," Elaine said, "you did not tell me you were with child. I thought you might tell me first. And this will be my brother or sister." She frowned at Fabienne. "Oh, why does not Mr. Ashworth marry you? He truly should."

"And that is precisely why I don't want to marry him," Fabienne said. "You and Luke married for love. I think I have the right to do the same."

"He does love you," Elaine said. "Luke said he was much out of sorts."

Fabienne shrugged. "His pride is hurt. A woman refused him."

"He loves you. I could tell it from the way he looked

at you. Do you remember the first time we all met at
Luke's house? I saw it then, and he has looked at you
the same way ever since."

Tears rose to Fabienne's eyes. She put her hand on
Elaine's arm. "You are my first child. I will always
love you."

"And I you." Elaine sniffed.

"No handkerchief?"

Elaine shook her head and reached into her husband's
pocket. *She doesn't need my handkerchief anymore,* Fabienne thought, with pride and sadness.

With her guests settled, Fabienne introduced the artists
she sponsored. A singer performed some arias to great
applause, and a painfully shy playwright mumbled a
scene from his play.

Fabienne stood, smiling at her guests. "Thank you for
attending this afternoon. I shall miss you all. And now,
if there is anyone else who wishes to read . . ." She
paused, and a movement at the end of the room caught
her eye. Someone arriving late.

Someone very familiar.

Adam Ashworth, his hair streaked blond by the sun,
and his skin burned brown—of course, he would help his
tenants bring in the harvest—lounged against the doorway. He wore one of his country coats, out at one elbow,
and with moth holes she could see even at this distance.

"Madam, if I may?" He bowed.

Fabienne found her voice. "Mr. Ashworth, you . . .
indeed, yes."

He strolled to the front of the room, his gaze on her
as though they were the only two people there. "Mrs.
Craigmont, you look exceedingly well." He kissed her
hand and gave her bosom a glance of deep appreciation.

"I have missed you so much." The words were out
of her mouth, in a desperate whisper, before she could
stop herself.

"And I you, Mrs. Craigmont." He smiled, the lines at
the corners of his eyes crinkling. "May I begin?"

"Oh. Oh, yes, certainly." She sat next to Elaine and
gripped her daughter's hand.

Adam looked at the gathering and raised the book in his hand. "The publishers assure me it will be in the shops as soon as possible—*The Lost Child,* by the writer Mrs. Ravenwood. Or, rather, the former Mrs. Ravenwood."

There was a buzz of excitement in the room.

"You may ask how I come into possession of this book, and why I present it here to you. I regret the printing is somewhat delayed, for the author has written a new dedication, which will explain all."

He produced his spectacles from his waistcoat pocket, polished them on his sleeve, and winked at Fabienne.

" 'This book is dedicated to one who taught me to be fearless and to love again when I believed passion to be a volume forever closed to me. It is also she who persuaded me, through fair means and foul, that I should cast aside the protection of Mrs. Ravenwood's literary petticoats, and reveal my true self to the world. She once paid me the supreme compliment and rebuke combined of telling me my books, as escape from the sense and dull reality of everyday life, gave great pleasure to many and should not be despised for any reason. It is with the greatest of honor, pleasure, and humility that I dedicate *The Lost Child* to the one who has my heart and undying love, Fabienne Craigmont. It is entirely due to her that I can now sign this dedication in my own name, that of Adam Ashworth.' "

There was a startled pause, followed by whispers, and a stir of interest from her guests.

Someone began to clap, others joined in, and the room rang with tumultuous applause as Fabienne stepped forward into the circle of Adam's arms.

About the Author

Janet Mullany was reared in England on a diet of Jane Austen and Georgette Heyer, and now lives near Washington, D.C. She has worked as an archaeologist, waitress, radio announcer, performing arts administrator, bookseller, and proofreader. Visit her Web site at www.janetmullany.com.

Now available from
REGENCY ROMANCE

The Rake and the Redhead and
Lord Dancy's Delight
by Emily Hendrickson

A fiery young lass places herself in a lord's path of
conquest and a lord thrice saves a young woman's life
and now she's returning the favor—with passion.

0-451-21587-7

The Captain's Castaway
by Christine Scheel

When a British Navy captain pulls a beautiful woman
from a death at sea, he vows to help her at any cost, to
earn her trust—and her love.

0-451-21559-1

The Whispering Rocks
by Sandra Heath

Fate has granted once-poor Sarah Jane a fortune. But
scandal has sent her to a far-off land where evil seems
to lurk in every corner—and a handsome local man is
filling her with desire.

0-451-21560-5

Available wherever books are sold or at
www.penguin.com